GOLGOTHA

Published by Odyssey Books in 2021

www.odysseybooks.com.au

A Cataloguing-in-Publication entry is available from the National Library of Australia

ISBN: 978-1922311160 (pbk)

ISBN: 978-1922311177 (ebook)

GOLGOTHA

PHIL HORE

ODYSSEY
BOOKS

CHAPTER ONE

ARMENTIÈRES 1916

A SHELL SCREAMED OVERHEAD AND IMPACTED SOMEWHERE BEHIND the ruined section of the trench Sergeant Hank Ash and the rest of his squad were pinned down in. All sported the cloth patch of the 1st Australian division—a white square surrounded by a blue square. The unit had been gathering a fierce reputation since entering the war. Most of the soldiers also wore two chevrons on the lower sleeves of their jackets, each recording a year served since boot camp. The stripes heralded these were Gallipoli veterans—an accomplishment that had begun taking on hallowed status amongst arriving new recruits.

Across the battlefield, artillery shells tore at the ruined countryside, along with the vulnerable flesh of anyone exposed to this manmade maelstrom. Any organised structure to the Australian attack had long since disintegrated under the German defensive onslaught, and the fighting was dissolving into individuals making sure the men under their immediate control continued to move toward their objective.

'How many grenades we got, Red?' Ash yelled at one of the men behind him.

In Gallipoli, the Australians had proven themselves unique,

as every soldier not only had upcoming battle strategies explained to them, but they were encouraged to show initiative and exploit any opportunity that arose during the chaos of combat. This simple step meant that instead of an attack force grinding to a halt with the death of an officer, each trooper knew what needed to be done and had the ability to get on and do it. This was a skillset the Diggers had brought with them to the Western Front, and though new to the style of trench warfare fought in France, the savvy Australians were catching on fast.

Throughout the shell hole, men patted themselves down and held up fingers to indicate what each was carrying. After a quick count, the South Australian nicknamed 'Red', for his almost-white blond hair, yelled back, 'About thirty, Sarge.'

Lying on his back to keep as low as possible, Ash pulled a small mirror from his breast pocket and angled it so that he could peer over the lip of their makeshift foxhole and examine the obstacle before them.

Called 'Pinchgut' by the Australians stationed nearby after Fort Denison in Sydney Harbour, the enormous concrete bunker sitting on top of a ridge over the village of Pérenchies was their target. The village had been a quiet burg before the war, crowning a small crest with a scenic view of the surrounding countryside and the distant city of Lille. When the war began, this elevation proved beneficial to the invading Germans, and they had fortified the area around the town, which became the key to their defence of the region. Not only did it supply the Germans stationed there a view of the Allied trenches stretching out across the countryside, artillery spotters also used the unobstructed view to direct accurate fire against any enemy movement on the low-lying lands. Worse, recently an electric searchlight had been placed along the stronghold, and this was often turned on the Allied lines at various times at night, making a sortie into no man's land a fatal one.

Allied command was aware of the danger the position presented and kept promising to send wave upon wave of screaming men charging up toward Pérenchies. No attack was ever organised, however, and local Allied troops had taken it upon themselves to try to knock out Pinchgut during a series of night attacks. Each time they were driven out by ferocious German counterattacks.

Then the Australians arrived.

Though no braver than the troops of other nations fighting along the Western Front, what made the Australian men different, and ultimately more dangerous, was their esprit de corps. Where most Allied soldiers were conscripts, forced by their government into a uniform and to carry a gun onto the battlefield, every single Australian was a volunteer. They had not been conscripted and pushed toward the front lines—the men from Down Under had chosen to be there.

Though they had supposedly been sent to the quiet Armentières region to learn how to fight and survive along the Western Front, having their positions shelled and bombed, and their men constantly sniped at had left the Aussies in a serious mood to remove this thorn from their side.

The battle for control of no man's land then intensified as the jovial Australians took on the challenge as though it were a new sport. For some time, the most professional units looked at the territory between both armies as theirs, and they would send out heavy patrols to take control of no man's land once night fell. Here, they would try to capture enemy soldiers to interrogate, ascertain what the enemy was up to in their own lines, and perhaps even lay out a listening microphone and trail its wire back to their own trench. The idea was to take control of the unclaimed region and make it fatal for an enemy unit to try the same tactics against them.

There was also the act of souveniring. The Australians were keen to get their hands on German weapons, uniforms, and equipment to show the folks at home, and this added incentive made them ferocious patrollers into no man's land. This theft became so epidemic that after several months being stationed across from the Aussies, many German units began to complain that something needed to be done after they continually entered their trenches in the morning to find much of their equipment gone.

It was during one such foray that someone in the Australian lines had decided it would be a good idea to secretly head over to the German lines and get rid of the searchlight and destroy Pinchgut for good. This little sortie soon grew into a small attack when the extent of the defences around the position were mapped, and other squads were asked to join in the fun.

Soon, hundreds of Australians had either snuck in to attack Pinchgut or stood ready in their own trenches to help withdraw the attackers if things got too hot. One of those squads was Ash and his men, who had managed to sneak most of the way across no man's land before hell erupted around them.

The German defenders must have had someone manning a listening post somewhere and had sent a warning about the attack, as the Germans suddenly opened fire, but their defence was pretty light and the Australians believed they still had an opportunity to pull off their mission. Confident his men would know what to do when the time was right, Ash worked out a quick plan of action against the stronghold, then asked the nearest troopers in the shell hole what they thought. As he explained his idea, he wiped away the tears streaming from his eyes with a sleeve, caused by a teargas shell that had fallen short and exploded nearby. Everyone had breathed a sigh of relief when they'd discovered the gas wasn't one of the deadlier flavours.

Night had fallen as the men crawled into their current posi- tion, and all were dirty from head to toe, yet the brief flash of bright white teeth from their grins told Ash the squad was ready.

'Okay, boys, let's go.'

With three men tossing grenades before them, the rest of the squad charged one side of Pinchgut, toward a spot Ash noticed the German guns had trouble traversing to cover. As the detonating bombs made the enemy think twice about leaning over the top of their trench, the Australians ran forward. Many swept the enemy line with fire from the Lewis light machine guns they were carrying. Between this hail of bullets and the barrage of bombs, the squad managed to reach the outermost edge of the main trench leading to the back of Pinchgut and slide in.

A few surviving Germans rushed the Diggers, but a volley of Lewis fire and a few well-placed Mills bombs forced them back. The foothold the Australians had created was soon widened as other soldiers, seeing Ash and his men breach the trench, rushed forward. Hundreds of Australians and even a few Canadians from a neighbouring trench began fighting through the German lines, overwhelming the defenders and forcing their way closer and closer to the concrete bunker.

Within the constraining depths of the trench, the battle devolved into a hand-to-hand fight. Like some chivalrous battle of old, the large bulky guns and modern explosives were ignored for fear of killing friend along with foe. Instead, more traditional weapons were used; roughly made clubs and maces were pulled from backpacks, along with knives, bayonets, and knuckledusters. All were put to good use.

Foot by foot, the troopers bludgeoned their way through the defenders and soon made it to the rear of Pinchgut. A few men scrambled up the concrete sides of the bunker, pushing Mills bombs and jam-tin grenades through the gun-slits and shell holes. Inside, muffled explosions and high-pitched screams followed, yet the fight raged on.

Those soldiers closest to the bunker mopped up the few remaining Germans about the area, while the Allied officers who'd survived the assault began organising what troops they had left for the inevitable enemy counterattack.

Overturned Maxim machine guns were repaired and repositioned to cover any path leading toward the bunker from the German rear, while new trenches were dug and holes in the defences filled. Men were sent forward to watch for any German movement, and reinforcements and supplies were called forward from the Allied lines.

If the enemy wanted the position back, they were going to have to fight for it.

* * *

Ash and his unit had been amongst the first to enter the bunker, and the gruesome spectacle of what their attack had achieved greeted them in the form of the broken, shattered, limbless bodies of its former occupants. While checking to see if anybody was still breathing, the Australians rifled pockets and backpacks for anything of value, all the while pushing deeper and deeper into the structure.

The few Germans to survive the attack and determined to fight on were quickly dispatched with hand grenades and pistol fire. The bodies were carefully collected in case of boobytraps and thrown out into no man's land. A small team of men carrying a spool of thick wire between them were ordered back toward their own lines, and carefully they began laying a communication cable to the bunker.

Within an hour, the troopers from the 1st Australian Division were communicating their success firsthand through these field phones, though most of what they said and what was said to them was lost in static and other background noises. They managed to report that the men had pushed further along the edges of the former German lines, rolling up the Kaiser's defences like an old, dirty carpet. The entire town of Pérenchies now lay under their control, and its new defenders awaited orders from headquarters. When these came, they were exactly what the tired, bloody Diggers didn't want to hear.

'We have to hold until relieved,' the newly arrived Colonel Blackburn exclaimed to anyone close enough to hear. A former lawyer from South Australia, he had been unaware of the attack, but was professional enough to rally what men he had to exploit the hole in the German defences. He was also more than aware that the bush telegraph of gossiping soldiers meant all his men would soon hear about the command.

Cursing and bitching in the way all soldiers have since the dawn of time when feeling hard done by, as they moved back to man what defences they could, the Australians took a few minutes to catch their breaths and begin the long, cold wait for a German response.

They didn't have to wait long.

Well behind the German lines, information was flowing in about the attack. Some was comprehensive and useable, some scrambled and full of panic. What the German commanders could tell was that an unknown number of Allied troops were moving from a region called Armentières, their forces reportedly having penetrated a limited number of places. Reserve units were already moving to stop any further intrusions, but this only created further confusion when no such attacks arrived along the rest of the front. Paranoia of the unknown was taking its hold on the German army.

Clear communication became as difficult for the Germans as it was for the Allies when more reports flowed in. Some were accurate, most were not. Some were old and out of date, while others were fresh and precise. This meant it wasn't until morning's first light that there was a clear picture of what had occurred. Almost everywhere the German line had held, except at Pérenchies, the Allies had taken over the entire section. As the sole Allied gain, the next move for the Germans was clear. Every gun, every cannon, and every free soldier was lined up against what remained of the fortress above the enemy-held French village.

The order was then sent to the entirety of the 4th German Corp that, as one of the most dominating features on the Flanders battlefield, Pérenchies was to be retaken at any cost.

CHAPTER TWO

PÉRENCHIES

ASH AND HIS SQUAD HAD JUST FINISHED EXCAVATING A PART OF the former German trench and were looking for water to refill their canteens when the first shell screamed out of the night sky. This smacked into the earth with a deep *whumf*, and though falling some distance away, the sheer size of the explosion rattled the air in the men's lungs. Reacting on sheer instinct, the men dropped into the trench to ride out the bombardment.

The German engineers and artillery units of IV Corps knew the location of every strongpoint and trench in their former defences, and they zeroed in on these positions with deadly accuracy. Hundreds of shells thoroughly pounded the hill, and once they felt nothing more could be achieved there, they moved their guns to the countryside surrounding the village. The hope was to catch any units moving across the open terrain to support what Allied troops had survived the bombardment. This action was so effective that very quickly this approach was known as 'Dead Man's Road' to the Australians.

With the bombardment finally moving away from them, Ash and his men began digging themselves out from the mountain of fresh dirt that had been thrown across the trenches. Many of those who had sheltered in the rough holes cut into Pinchgut would remain buried forever.

In just a few hours, the barrage changed the landscape surrounding the ridge, making it look more like the scarred face of the moon. It had the desired effect, though, as many of the new defensive points were useless after being torn open and exposed by an explosive shell.

Seeing the danger, Ash urged his men into action. 'Move, you bastards. We have to get a new trench dug.'

'But this hole is okay, Sarge,' one voice moaned from the rear.

'Grab a shovel and start digging before I dump you back down there and leave you for good,' Ash threatened, pulling his own spade from his pack.

The handful of soldiers followed suit and retrieved the large shovels that partly led to their nickname 'Diggers' and, mirroring their leader, began flinging dirt high as they worked a new trench. No one was sure if the name originated from the shovel or the Australian habit of wearing the detached tool head in a bag over their groin for protection. Fruitlessly, many British officers had bawled out the Australians when they arrived in Europe for not wearing the shovel and its bag correctly, attaching it to the belt over a buttock cheek. Instead, the Diggers wore it across the groin for the obvious protection a large chunk of steel could provide.

As they dug, the troopers positioned themselves in such a way that they could look out for a German counterattack and ensure they were not exposed to snipers. With the new trench completed, Ash ordered some of his men to reposition a nearby Maxim machine gun, while the rest were sent out to look through the other collapsed trenches for any survivors buried within the mud and clay. While they worked, several runners appeared from their own trenches; some carried messages, other tins of bully beef or boxes of ammunition. The couriers also supplied the latest gossip from across the battlefield, including a rough tally of who'd been 'knocked' from the division and those who'd been wounded. As it always seemed to be these days, the news was depressing as far too many of those killed were Gallipoli veterans. The survivors of the attack in the Dardanelles were becoming a rare breed on the fields of the Western Front.

On hearing about the death of a fellow sergeant he'd been close to, Ash picked up a dirt clog and in frustration threw it at a group of passing German prisoners being escorted to the rear lines. Never intending to really hit anyone, when the clog burst on the head of a short German with a huge handlebar moustache, a soldier guarding the prisoners yelled out:

'Oi! Cut that out.'

Sheepishly, Ash held up a hand in apology. He then turned toward the grinning faces of his men.

'Next time pull the pin, Sarge.' Red laughed, lobbing another as though it was a hand grenade. 'They're no better than a potato otherwise.'

The dirt clog sailed through the air and landed just as a German shell dropped out of the sky and exploded. Ash dived into the trench with his troopers, snatching for his gun as he tumbled in. As shrapnel and debris filled the air, Ash strained his ears, trying to hear above the whistling, concussive booms and screams of injured men for the one thing everyone in the trenches feared above all else. Soon enough he heard what he was listening for.

Starting soft, but growing louder and more intense, the sound of the long-awaited German counterattack grew nearer. Tens of thousands of men with bayonets drawn, streaming across the rubble and cratered French field at the Australian lines, was a cacophony that even an artillery barrage could not hide completely.

At some unseen signal, the salvaged Maxim guns opened

fire, with the stream of death spitting out of the large guns scything through the massed Germans. Gaps began appearing in their ranks, yet still they bravely charged forward, trying to retake their former position.

An artillery shell screamed out of the heavens and hit just in front of the trench Ash and his men were fighting in, sending a tidal wave of dirt rolling over the foxhole. It only took a few minutes for the soldiers to claw themselves out of the loose dirt, but by then the German attack had moved closer.

Looking around to ensure everyone was free and armed, Ash yelled, 'Up and at 'em, boys.' He then aimed over the trench and fired into a large mass of enemy nearby. Next to him, a line of 303s and Lewis guns opened up, adding to the carnage amongst the German troops still moving up the hill.

Loading and firing as fast as possible, the troopers never noticed when the first attack faltered, and they began fighting a second, then a third wave. Time and thinking had ended, now replaced by the simple act of fire, load, and fire again.

Further toward the town, the remaining defenders began to tire, allowing the massed German advance to creep closer and closer. From simple dirt grey figures, individual faces moved into focus, only to be cut down by an Allied bullet. Despite the butchery, in a number of places the Germans managed to enter the Pinchgut trenches, and here brutal hand-to-hand fighting broke out.

Exhausted as they were, the Australians fought on. When their ammunition was gone, they used their bayonets and guns as clubs. When the guns were broken or lost, they used their fists and helmets. Savage, bitter men tore at each other's bodies with whatever tool came to hand. Modern warfare devolved into the tribal warfare of something far older, when strength of arm and ferociousness of the soul was a necessity for survival.

Men covered with so much grime they were unrecognisable to each other fought on and on until a stray bullet hit an unexploded, half-buried artillery shell. The subsequent detonation cleared a large section of the trench and buried Ash and his men.

Pressed hard by the German advance, the surviving Australians began withdrawing into the few surviving strong-points, and though they were still fighting, they were desperately outnumbered and outgunned. Worse, what few messages they sent to their own lines were either ignored or disbelieved. As far as Allied command was concerned, if there was an Allied attack going on in the Armentières region, it was an unofficial one and everyone involved was on their own. They ordered no more supplies or reserves to move forward, leaving the desperate and increasingly outraged Australians to hold until the decision could be reversed.

By the time they'd dug themselves out once more, Ash and his men were now behind the enemy line, which had pushed well into the Pinchgut complex. Creeping through what was left of their trench for a quick inspection, Red slunk his way over to Ash and asked, 'What we gonna do, Sarge?'

Taking a deep breath as though he was about to dive under-water, Ash slid back into the collapsed trench and fished out a Lewis gun and a few of the round-shaped magazines the weapon needed. Since first receiving these hand-held machine guns, the Australians had become highly adept at their use, carrying and firing them from the hip as they charged rather than laying prone and setting them up on their almost useless stand—indeed this was often removed for the sake of weight.

Hefting the large weapon over his shoulder and climbing out of the hole, Ash passed the gun to the men for inspection to ensure it was in working order.

Getting a thumbs-up, Ash winked at his squad. 'I don't know about you boys, but I'm getting back into this fight. I need to ask a very hard question to a German over there.'

The survivors nodded in agreement, grabbed what weapons

they could, then on Ash's signal hauled themselves out of the trench and began duck-walking toward what was left of the fortress.

After two hours of non-stop fighting, the diminishing Australians left in the trenches began backing around the last bend before the base of Pinchgut. The large concrete bunker was now the final section still controlled by the Diggers, who were determined to make it cost the enemy more than it was worth. With their hand grenades gone and their Lewis guns empty, all these men were left with were a few pistols and the odd rifle. The Germans advanced, firing and lobbing the occasional stick grenade as they methodically crept forward.

The Australians were all but done when the Germans suddenly lost focus on their attack. A number turned and began firing back the way they had come.

One overly ambitious Digger popped his head around Pinchgut's ruined wall before slipping back with a huge grin covering his muddy face.

'You lads aren't going to believe this.'

Firing from the hip, Ash laid down a withering barrage of Lewis-gun fire while his squad grabbed German guns and hand grenades from the bodies about them. Though outnumbered, the surprise attack from the direction of their own lines caught the Germans off-guard and a wave of panic rushed through them. A few snapped back wildly inaccurate shots at the charging Australians, while most tried to blindly run back down the hill toward their own distant trenches—right where Ash and his men were holding out.

Not everything was going the way of the Allies. Pockets of Germans held their nerves, and thanks to the orders of experienced officers it looked like they were just about to regain control when help for Ash and his men arrived from the Diggers left in Pinchgut.

Together the remnants of the Allied attack managed to force

the Germans into a retreat, and they re-joined inside the ruined Pinchgut bunker. Before they could make a decision on what to do next, officers blew their recall whistles and the Australians began staggering back to their original trenches. They arrived just as a new barrage dropped from the heavens, ensuring the section could not be taken by the enemy. Anyone caught in the open paid the price, as did those unlucky enough to be in a foxhole that took a direct hit. Australian soldiers were once again buried alive, their irretrievable bodies left to nourish the blood-drenched fields of Western Europe.

* * *

Two days after it began, the battle was over. The Allies moved enough support into the area to take the pressure off Armentières, ensuring the section could not be taken by the enemy. The Germans had a growing list of problems in other regions that required their attention, so could not continue their counterattacks, and so the entire section of the front fell quiet once more.

In a war known for its butchery, the Australian 1st Division had suffered more than its fair share at Pinchgut, and now they were to discover that the unofficial battle was being ignored by High Command. Any personal achievements of the men were being dismissed, though fresh reserves were finally ordered forward to replace the ragged, shattered soldiers who had just achieved the almost impossible.

These men, covered head-to-toe in mud and blood, began staggering back toward the relief area behind the trenches. Ash marched beside his motley army, along with only three survivors from his squad. The rest had either been buried in the shelling or had fallen during the German counterattack.

Due to the unit's catastrophic losses, once they arrived back at headquarters there was talk the entire brigade was likely to be disbanded, but the death stares from the survivors made it clear that was never going to happen. Recruits would be found, the injured would heal and return, and the division would continue on.

Making the long trek back to a staging depot to rearm and scrounge some fresh uniforms, Ash and his men passed lines of fresh-faced soldiers in clean uniforms from various Allied countries, many of whom were looking at the Australians with a mixture of awe and horror. Red grinned and announced, 'Enjoy the game, lads. The Germans are playing rough today.'

The youngest of the survivors was a replacement called Smith, sent to the unit after Gallipoli. His paperwork said eighteen, but most of the men believed he was far younger than that. As the group trudged past a gaggle of soldiers, Smith tapped Ash on the shoulder and asked, 'What the fuck is that, Sarge?'

Bypassed by the columns of men moving to the front, as though he was a leper, was a soldier tied to a wagon wheel. About him stood a growing collection of returned soldiers from the front, their grim faces matching their torn and dirty uniforms.

The man was alert and clearly in pain as his feet only just touched the ground to support his weight. As tired as they were, the sheer absurdness of the situation forced the men to investigate.

'What's all this?' a trooper called Touhy asked the soldier on the wheel.

'You haven't heard?' a voice from the crowd said incredulously. 'Last night a squad went on patrol into no man's land and found one of our boys crucified to a tree.'

'It was a church door, and they used bayonets to pin him in place,' a Canadian soldier explained.

'Jaysus,' Touhy spat.

'Yeah, and now some officer has crucified this Tommy here.'

A British lieutenant heel-and-toed through the corridor

between piles of ammunition boxes and food stores and parted the gathered crowd. He pulled to a halt in front of the man on the wheel and proudly boasted, 'Not crucified. Field Punishment #1, I will have you know. Now, I would ask you to not converse with this man.'

'Punishment? For what?' Red asked the young officer in his ludicrously clean uniform.

'I hadn't cleaned my boots before inspection,' the soldier answered in a thick, Yorkshire accent. "Captain 'arwood ordered I do this for two hours a day for the next week and a half as "penance".'

Touhy looked incredulously at the ruined landscape about them. 'They crucified you for having dirty shoes in this hell hole?'

'It could be worse,' the lieutenant said, about to move on. 'I've seen some of those conscientious objector fellows placed on the wheel for three months.' He then spun about and marched back the way he had come.

Having just faced down what felt like the whole German army, the absurdity of the situation took hold of Ash and, before anyone could stop him, he unsheathed his bayonet and cut the man down from the wheel. Instantly, the soldier slumped forward, moaning as blood painfully rushed back into his extremities. The Diggers caught the prisoner before he fell and lowered him gently to the ground. They began rubbing and slapping his hands and feet to help kick-start the circulation back into his limbs again.

'What the hell do you think you're doing?' the lieutenant cried, running back to the wheel.

Ash stood up and faced the officer, who nervously stepped in, nose to nose, and snarled, 'How dare you? What's your name, man? I'm having you arrested for ...'

'You're not arresting anyone,' Ash said coldly, pushing the younger man away with one hand and leaving a dirty print on the man's pristine uniform. 'Isn't this place bad enough without doing this crap to our own? And on today of all days …'

'No one found a crucified soldier,' the officer said with a condescending smirk. 'The Germans wouldn't be that stupid.'

Something in Ash snapped. Friends he had served alongside for three years now lay rotting in the ruins of a French town, and amid this brutality now he was learning both sides were crucifying each other. He grabbed the officer by his shirt front, spun him in place, and forced him to look at the man crucified to the wagon wheel as an answer to the sorts of brutalities a stupid person could inflect.

The lieutenant did not take kindly to being manhandled in such a way and he clumsily pulled himself free, then threw a right fist at Ash's jaw. A blind man could have seen the punch coming, and Ash managed to twist his head, turning what could have been a disabling blow into a glancing hit. As the lieutenant stepped in to follow up with another punch, Ash lifted his right arm to block the blow, then fired off an uppercut of his own. The punch caught his opponent squarely on the chin and sent him tumbling backward into the dirt.

Blinding rage at the punishment for such a minor infringement welled up inside Ash. Ghostly images of the faces of his lost friends superimposed themselves over the pained expression on the crucified soldier. Though he could never get justice for the friends he had just lost or for the man who had been crucified, right now he could get his hands on the next best thing, the evil bastard who had enforced the punishment of the soldier tied to the wheel.

Ash watched as the lieutenant got up from the ground. Before he could throttle the buffoon, however, a swarm of MPs arrived and threw themselves on the sergeant, tackling him to the ground with the sheer weight of their numbers.

CHAPTER THREE

GENERAL HEADQUARTERS, MONTREUIL-SUR-MER

THE LARGE DINING HALL IN THE CHATEAU, WHICH GENERAL Douglas Haig had taken over as his personal quarters, had become something of a morning meeting room to his staff. Officers from the various war departments would gather there before their commander took his breakfast and pass on any urgent news they had received throughout the night, along with any rumours and titbits they had uncovered. It was not only the common soldiers who suffered from gossip.

Once they were all caught up, Haig would pass on any new orders or questions he had, and the men would head back to their departments to get on with their day. All would then reconvene at GHQ for their afternoon orders and strategy sessions.

This day the dining room was bursting with officers, not only from the British army but several of the other nations fighting alongside them on the Western Front. Though countries like New Zealand, Canada, and Australia had their own general staff, as citizens of the Commonwealth they fell under the authority of the British commander.

All stood to attention when Haig, his moustached face the

very picture of the recruitment posters hanging across most of the British Empire, entered the room.

Sitting at the head of the large table, with his chief of staff by his right and his personal secretary—already taking down notes—on his left, Haig gave a nod and the morning conference began. News of German infiltrations and Allied night raids were first reported, followed by provision numbers and supply issues. Only when every conceivable problem and troop deployment had been passed on did Haig bother to ask about the condition of the half-million men directly under his command.

Instantly a dozen hands shot up, asking permission to speak on the matter. One by one, the officers from the numerous divisions that made up the Allied force gave accounts of the conditions the men they represented were facing. Most began explaining the physical and mental condition of their troops, then the numbers of wounded and killed, then finishing up with any court-martials that had been instigated.

The war seemed to be going well, yet the buoyant mood of the room changed when a colonel from one of the Canadian divisions took a large step away from the table, so he could be seen, and then in a clear voice began his report.

'We are having real trouble with the 15th battalion and the 48th Ontario Highlanders. It would seem a patrol entered no man's land last night and discovered a soldier executed by the Germans near what remained of a small farmhouse.'

'Terrible news, Colonel,' Haig's chief of staff said, 'but sadly nothing newsworthy. Why has this got the men upset?'

'It was the manner in which this man was executed, sir,' the colonel answered. 'The rumour is the Germans nailed him to the barn door with bayonets. They crucified him, sir.'

At the word 'crucified', several officers in the room yet to make their reports began adding their voices to the claim. In a war renowned for its horrors and lack of humanity, it seemed that during the night the Germans had stepped up the psychological element of the conflict by crucifying several soldiers from the various nations opposing them. These bodies were left for the Allies to discover in no man's land.

Many officers reported some units were already refusing to move forward, and others were calling for an immediate attack to take revenge on those who had perpetrated the crime. Soldiers, well used to blood on the battlefield, who had killed in the most brutal and primeval ways imaginable, were seeing this act as something far worse. To them, this was a crime, and they were crying out for justice.

Haig looked at his two closest confidants sitting next to him. The nervous looks they returned told him things could get very ugly if they did not move fast. Was this an underhanded way to dishearten the Allied army, or some sort of trap, perhaps to trigger a massed charge forward by outraged soldiers into the teeth of German guns? If they were not vigilant, then the carefully crafted Allied front, meshing units from nations across the globe, was about to collapse.

How did one stop half a million men from charging forward two hundred feet to take vengeance on those they had now demonised? Worse, how did one stop all those soldiers from unifying behind a single cause, and perhaps bring something of a democracy to the Western Front? What if the men began calling for this matter to be resolved before they would follow any further orders?

Haig and his confidants had been contemplating such possibilities for months as rumours of mutiny and mass sedition began to spread amongst the men. Because of this, they immediately realised this crucified soldier situation could turn into something dangerous if it was not suppressed. As the officers around the table argued amongst themselves about what could be done, Douglas Haig began not for the first time, to contemplate how he was going to save the war.

CHAPTER FOUR

WITH THE DINING HALL CLEARED OF MOST OF THE JUNIOR officers, the British High Command's inner circle sat down to confer on what had been happening within their front lines. Many of the departed officers had been visibly upset at what had been discussed, and it had taken General Haig to stand and glare everyone into submission to complete the earlier meeting.

After sorting through the various reports, it became obvious things were not quite as bad as had been initially argued. Instead of a series of brutal crucifixions, to Haig it seemed there had only been a few, or perhaps even just one. Officers from the Indian, South African, and New Zealand regiments agreed their reports were more about the rumour of soldiers being crucified than any confirmation their troops had physically encountered them.

As the English and Canadians were so enmeshed on the front, it was impossible to determine which nation had made the initial report to allow HQ to trace the source of the rumour. The Canadians had been adamant it was one of their men who'd been murdered and, normally so stoic and dependable, their reaction was a worrying occurrence. They were calling for answers and HQ to do something about the crime.

On top of this, intelligence had arrived that the French army —always one bad word away from mutiny—were already talking about pulling troops out of the line to try to restore discipline. Many junior French officers were as outraged at the crime as their men and were proving to be extremely 'French' about the entire affair. Their report this morning was that, though they wanted revenge for the crucifixion, their men— after facing years of unspeakable horror in the trenches— seemed to have lost their nerve for the fight. It just didn't matter to them if it had been French soldiers who'd been crucified or not, the entire population of France was feeling as though they'd already been nailed onto the cross. The French nation was fatigued and looking shaky, and this latest outrage just seemed to increase their distaste for the war.

And then there were the damn Australians.

Renowned for being the most ill-disciplined soldiers in the Allied lines, it was unclear if the Australians had found one of their own crucified or had just taken umbrage at the fate of an Allied soldier. It wouldn't matter as, either way, they were already calling for blood, and if those troublemakers weren't silenced soon, their own brand of soldiering could very quickly spread to the other troops stationed around them.

It was clear to Haig that this situation had to be dealt with before it got out of hand, and though never one to ask for advice, the general tabled the question to the men before him.

'What do we do?'

'Come down hard on the men,' one of the traditionalists at the table called out. 'Discipline, either earned or imposed, is the only way to end this. Take a man from each of the most muti- nous units and punish them.'

'Shoot a few, especially from the colonial ranks, and the rest will settle down,' another British officer added.

General Albert Mackenzie was the only Australian in the room. He stood up at this proposal and reminded those present of the hard line his government had taken on just such actions.

'You shoot a single Australian over such rubbish and you will most certainly have a mutiny on your hands.' Most of those seated around the table rolled their eyes at this bothersome fact. 'Actually, forget that,' Mackenzie continued. 'You shoot one of our men over this and you won't have a mutiny, you'll have a second front. I'm not sure how many times we have to tell you galahs, but we simply won't be made the scapegoat for your idiocy.' Mackenzie sat back down, then added, 'Again!'

'General Mackenzie,' Haig said with a calm, dangerous tone, 'we are all well aware of your nation's stance, especially as you mention it every time we ask you to do anything.'

'History has taught us what happens when we blindly follow England … sir,' Mackenzie replied, not disguising the contempt he had for what had occurred between the two nations in the past. 'We won't be repeating that mistake, so you'll excuse me if I remind you again since you seem intent on proving you didn't listen the first time!'

The losses the Australians had suffered at Gallipoli, stacked on what had occurred in conflicts such as the Boer War, had left a distinct divide between Empire and subject. Things had not improved once the Australians arrived in Europe, and they had proven themselves an invaluable tool in the Allied effort to defeat Germany.

'If I may?' asked an officer from beyond the orbit of the great table.

As all heads turned, this officer, who had been quietly seated in one of the room's comfortable chairs, stood, straightened his well-pressed uniform, then stepped up to the table.

'I believe we are looking at this the wrong way.'

One of the many staff officers standing about the room leaned in and whispered in Haig's ear, 'Captain Fitzhugh. He's the officer from Military Intelligence I've been warning ... err ... telling you about, sir.'

Haig motioned for the officer to continue. 'You have something to add to all this, Captain Fitzhugh?'

'I do indeed, sir.' If it were not for his uniform, Captain Simon Fitzhugh would have looked as though he was waiting for a train. Calm and casual, his officer's cap sitting at a slight, unregulated angle, his intelligent blue eyes seemed to blaze with a mischievousness that certain university-bred students were renowned for. Not terribly tall, nor that well-built, the captain had the air of a scholarly man rather than a soldier, a look that held him in contempt with the more traditional segments of the senior service. His current rank, however, did not reflect his abilities. He was a good field officer who had suffered demotions due to his manner with his superiors. As fast as he earned promotions, he lost them, leaving Fitzhugh in a strange limbo at the rank of captain. Deserving of more, but incapable of maintaining it.

'I believe we may be going at this the wrong way, sir!' the captain repeated, adding the 'sir' as evidence he could play the game. Almost as an afterthought, he added, 'To suppress a rumour is impossible, especially one as gruesome and nasty as this. All you will do is fire more rumours and likely something even worse.'

'Worse?' Haig asked.

'Yes, sir. Suppression will lead to conspiracy theories amongst soldiers with time on their hands, who now have little to think about but why their commanders suppressed the news of a crucified soldier. Not only will they resent you even more, they will question the motives of everything you ask of them from this point on.'

The looks of the men at the table informed Haig that Fitzhugh's idea had not gone over well.

'The men don't seem to mind being the sacrificial lambs in

this war, sir,' Fitzhugh went on, 'but it's probably best not to remind them too much about the fact that's what they are. They might take exception to the idea.'

General Roberts, a man who lived behind a face that permanently scowled at the world, leaned back from the table and craned his head around to gauge the reaction of the other officers seated with him.

'And do you have a solution, Captain?' The emphasis on that last word was clear to all present that in this room, junior officers should be seen and not heard—and it was far better for them if they were not even seen.

Normally, being noticed by men such as those present was not something a mere captain ever wanted to have happen. Fitzhugh, however, was far from a mere captain.

'Well, sir,' he replied warmly, ignoring the thinly veiled threat, 'I was thinking that rather than suppressing the report, why not investigate it?'

'Do you think we would let such a crime pass without an investigation?' Roberts asked incredulously.

'Not what I meant, sir. Don't just investigate it, publicly investigate it. Bring men in from the most vocal units and have them participate in the inquiry. This will almost instantly quiet the men's fears and give us some much-needed moral high ground. How can the men ever claim again that we don't listen to them when we can point to the time we created a special team from their own ranks to investigate one of their concerns —a team they themselves picked?' Fitzhugh added as an afterthought, 'The troops will see we have taken their fears seriously and not just swept this matter under the rug, as it were.'

'And we are to just let them choose the men to lead this investigation?' asked another general, whom the captain could not quite see from his position.

'Yes, sir, and at all times we must remind them of this,

though we should ask for the men they choose to have certain abilities or backgrounds.'

'Such as?' General Roberts asked.

'Well, a police or investigation background would be a start,' Fitzhugh answered as though off the top of his head. In fact, this had been an idea he'd been working on for some time after he heard a group of soldiers talking about one of their own who'd been shot at dawn for refusing an order to put a damaged helmet on his head. The men of the great Allied army were growing angry at the way their officers treated them, and this was just one way the Intelligence officer had come up with to settle things down.

'And we just let them choose the team?' Haig asked.

'No, sir, I will choose the team. We'll just let the men think they had a choice. They will democratically put forward soldiers who meet our criteria, and from this list I will choose a team from those I believe are the most capable. Everyone wins.'

Those at the table went back to arguing the merits of the plan, while Haig sat and listened, never once taking his eyes off the unusual captain, who seemed most comfortable with treating his seniors as his equals.

'Captain Fitzhugh?' Haig eventually said in a soft voice. Though most at the table likely never heard their commander speak, somehow they all knew to be quiet.

'Sir?'

'Issue the order, though there will be one stipulation I will insist on.'

'And that is, sir?'

'Your idea, Captain, so it's your neck on the line. *You* will be in charge of this operation. Run it as you see fit, but make sure you get results.' He then dismissed Fitzhugh with a 'you may go' semi-salute.

Fitzhugh returned the gesture with as crisp a salute as he'd performed in his life, spun about on a heel, and took a step toward the exit.

'*Positive* results, *Captain!*'

Not even the flippant Fitzhugh could miss that threat.

Sometimes it was indeed wise for a junior officer to be seen and not heard.

CHAPTER FIVE

On what had once been a kitchen table, Fitzhugh pored through the reports and requests on his desk.

By the end of that first day, the rumour of the crucified soldier had been passed along the entirety of the front lines, and in response he had word issued that an investigation team was being pulled together from within the ranks. This would be no headquarters-led investigation; the team was to be elected by the men themselves, tasked with investigating the gruesome murder of one of their own.

It did not take long for a list of proposed names to appear, but most of the men nominated were next to useless. One Scottish unit had put forward a soldier who was perfect in every way: a former police inspector who had even been involved in a military inquiry. It was just a shame he'd been killed six months earlier—a fact Fitzhugh was positive the deceased Scotsman had been frustrated with as well.

Still, there were enough names for at least a few candidates to merit an interview.

'Sergeant Andrews,' he bellowed.

The curtain acting as a door to his quarters swung open and

a short, burly man with a boxer's nose and cauliflower ears stepped inside.

'Sir?'

Without looking up from his reports, Fitzhugh lifted a bundle of papers. 'Be a dear and gather these men for me, would you?'

'Yes, sir,' said the NCO, stepping forward and taking the offered sheets. Reading the first page, the sergeant turned back to the desk. 'Sir, you really want this guy?'

'Yes, Sergeant, thank you, Sergeant, you may continue with your duties, Sergeant,' Fitzhugh replied, still focused on the files in front of him.

'Yes, *sir*,' Andrews said, turning and striding from the room. He then said in a tone similar to Fitzhugh's, 'It's your funeral, *sir*.'

At that last comment, Fitzhugh finally looked up at Andrews' retreating back, smiled, then returned to work.

In the end, it proved easier for Fitzhugh to visit the men than have them brought to him. For a war fought in stagnant trenches, soldiers travelled a surprising amount. Between attacks, guard duty, time off, hospital visits, and the simple acts of eating and relieving oneself, in a day a single soldier could be any of a dozen places … or so Andrews complained when he returned with the news he'd found only two of the men on the list.

Both captain and sergeant left the office and began slogging through the thick, soul-sucking clay that turned the French countryside into a morass when there was even a hint of moisture in the air. Their first stop was with Corporal Malcolm McGavin of the London Fusilier Rifles.

With both sides counterattacking to try to take advantage of the chaos the lines had been thrown into, the Fusiliers had been moved three times in the last week. Fitzhugh eventually found them taking their turn in the trenches, guarding an artillery unit sheltered behind the ruins of a small village.

Following protocol, the two men entered the Fusiliers' forward HQ and presented themselves to the officer in command. The Fusiliers had a long tradition of being tough and well-led, so the fresh-faced teenaged lieutenant sitting behind the desk inside caught both men by surprise.

* * *

Lieutenant Frankie Smith had been in command for precisely four and a half hours, his meteoric rise due more to the shocking loss of senior officers to sniper fire and battle than to any particular talent the young man possessed.

As the senior officer entered his tent, the young lieutenant leaped to his feet, knocking over the small inkpot he had been using to fill his fountain pen. The subsequent spill covered much of the small table before him, and all the papers it contained.

Smith, unsure if he should save his paperwork or salute a superior officer, simply stood frozen, his eyes darting back and forth between the growing mess and the captain standing before him, struggling to hide a grin. The rough-looking sergeant next to the captain had no such intention, and he stood there with a monster smile stretching from ear to ear.

'Sir?' Smith stammered, the spell finally breaking.

'Oh, do mop up that mess before it spills off the table and lands on my boots, will you, Lieutenant?'

With relief, Smith dived at the table, his panicked hands knocking over the small candle that had been illuminating the tent. This toppled into the ink pool with a fizz, and the small room immediately fell dark.

After a few seconds of complete silence (though Smith

would later swear he could hear the sergeant's grin), the exasperated Fitzhugh asked, 'Get us a light, would you, Andrews?'

'Sir,' said the sergeant, who turned, tripped on the lieutenant's rifle on the floor, and plummeted headfirst out of the room. His ungainly exit had the bonus of allowing some light from outside to enter, and Fitzhugh used this to locate a small stool and sit down.

'Thank you, Sergeant,' he called out. As Andrews hauled himself back to his feet and went in search of a light, Fitzhugh gestured for Smith to sit.

'Lieutenant, I'm after one of the soldiers in your command. This man has been chosen for a special task and is to be transferred to my office for temporary assignment.'

'Certainly, sir,' Smith said, dabbing at the ink with an old sack that at one time held potatoes. 'I don't know everyone yet, sir, but I'm certain we can find the man you need ... his name, if I may ask?'

'Corporal Malcolm McGavin.'

The lieutenant stopped cleaning and looked up from his table. 'Him I know, sir. Are you sure it's McGavin you're after?'

'Absolutely certain. Why? Is there a problem? He's not dead, is he? That's been happening a lot lately.'

'No, sir. McGavin is very much alive, or at least he was the last time I saw him ... though with McGavin you never can tell. Someone may have shot him in the last few hours.'

'I see.' Fitzhugh nodded, not actually seeing at all.

'It's not that he's a bad guy, sir,' Smith confided, cleaning his hands on the now thoroughly blue rag. 'In fact, he's quite likeable. The problem is the men believe he's something of a Jonah. Wherever McGavin is, trouble is sure to follow, and though he'll be fine, it's often those with him that aren't so lucky.'

'Ahh,' Fitzhugh said, shaking his head with acknowledgment. 'So, he's likely up for a change of scenery then?' Slapping both knees, the captain hauled himself to his feet and gestured to the tent's flap.

'If you show me the way, I'll take him off your hands.'

The lieutenant, his thigh shining with bright blue ink, stumbled toward the flap just as Andrews returned, cradling a small, lit candle in his cupped hands.

'Thank you, Sergeant, that won't be necessary now,' Fitzhugh said, patting Andrews on the shoulder as he departed behind Smith. Once the candle was placed on the small table inside, Andrews joined them, and the three men set off to find their quarry.

* * *

Corporal Malcolm McGavin proved to be a tall, thin man whose uniform just didn't quite fit. Both the sleeves of his jacket and the legs of his pants rode up way too high, a clear sign he was wearing clothes that weren't of his own choosing. Though only twenty-eight, the harshness of life along the frontlines, along with the lack of a proper diet meant the corporal looked more like forty, though the smile that split his face when he saw the ink-stains on his lieutenant's pants helped reveal his true age.

'McGavin, this is Captain Fitzhugh and Sergeant ... err, sorry, I didn't catch your name?'

Before Andrews could answer, Fitzhugh cut him off. 'His name doesn't matter. So, you're the infamous Malcolm McGavin, are you?'

'Yes, sir,' McGavin said, scrambling to his feet and taking the captain's offered hand.

'*The* McGavin from Scotland Yard?'

The look from his fellow soldiers milling about suggested this little nugget of information was one he'd been keeping to himself. Most of the soldiers filling the trenches were from poorer neighbourhoods, where the constabulary was looked upon somewhat unkindly. To find they not only had a cop in their midst, but one of the hated constables from Scotland Yard, well, that could only increase their level of anxiety at the supposed Jonah in their midst.

'Gee, thanks, sir,' McGavin said, rolling his eyes toward the reaction of his squadmates.

'No trouble at all,' Fitzhugh over-enunciated, continuing the now clearly uncomfortable handshake. 'Well, luckily I seem to have a job for you, so come along and let us have a private chat.'

CHAPTER SIX

LEAVING THE CORPORAL WITH INSTRUCTIONS ON WHERE AND when to meet them, Fitzhugh and Andrews left the trenches, commandeered a staff car, and began the long drive to the French HQ situated between the German army and Paris.

Using Andrews as his interpreter—who was as adept at speaking French as he was at finding candles—Fitzhugh asked to see the head of the Gendarmerie Nationale, the French equivalent of the military police. Forty minutes later, and with a frustrated Andrews ready to deck every Frenchman in the room, a French officer who spoke English walked past and calmed everyone down.

The Englishmen were escorted to the Provost Gendarmerie office, the service that dealt with overseas military policing. Here another hour went by before the large wooden door finally swung open and a little bookish man with round, wire glasses beckoned them inside. Fitzhugh wasn't up on French insignia, but he was sure the five gold bands on the officer's shoulders meant he was at least a colonel.

'And how can I help you today, Captain?'

'You speak English,' Fitzhugh said with relief.

'But of course,' the colonel said in a tone that suggested it was an affront the Englishman didn't return the favour by speaking French, which of course to a Frenchman it was. 'How can I help you, gentlemen?'

'I'm sure you have heard the nasty rumour about a crucified soldier.'

'I have. Though the word "nasty" is, how you say, not strong enough?'

'Indeed. Well, to try to combat the dangerous mood of the men, General Haig has ordered me to conduct an investigation, or more precisely, to build a small multinational unit from within the ranks to look into the rumour and help end the speculations, if you get what I mean,' Fitzhugh said with a questioning nod.

'I do,' the colonel agreed. 'How can my office help?'

'I was hoping for someone with experience in such matters from the French ranks to join us if that's at all possible; one with investigation skills, and who speaks at least some English. The presence of a Frenchman would help smooth the way if we need to talk to any locals.'

'I see, and I concur. A French presence in this investigation on sacred French soil is, of course, a must. Give me just a moment and I will find the man I think will suit your purposes.'

Nodding his thanks, Fitzhugh remained seated as the colonel picked up his telephone's receiver and tapped its cradle a few times to get a line.

Having suffered through a classic English private school education, thus fluent in French, Fitzhugh listened in on the subsequent conversation. A long time ago, the captain had learned that people will brazenly talk about things in front of you, enjoying a feeling almost like voyeurism, if they think you don't understand a word they are saying.

'Maurice, I want you to find Jean Danjou ... I don't care where he is or what jail he's in. Unless he's killed the general, I want him washed down, dressed up, and to report to me at once ... Yes, I'm meeting with them now ... No, they didn't seem to know we are investigating on our own.' The colonel gave Fitzhugh a warm smile as he added, 'That's why I want him. If he cannot screw up their investigation, no one can.'

Throughout the phone call, Fitzhugh returned the Frenchman's smile, as though everything was going well. Not once did he give the impression that he understood what was being said. He just sat in his chair like a happy cow awaiting the butcher's knife.

'Well, my friend, I have just the man for you,' the colonel said in English as he hung up the phone. 'It will take some time to round him up—I believe he is in the middle of another investigation. But rest assured I will have him report to your office first thing in the morning.'

Holding out his hand, Fitzhugh stood up, and the French officer shook the offered appendage vigorously. 'My thanks, Major ...'

'Colonel,' the Frenchman corrected him, pronouncing it *Col-O-Nel*.

'Major Col-O-Nel.' Fitzhugh smiled, continuing the handshake.

'No, my rank is Col-O-Nel.'

'I'm sorry, I could have sworn you were a major. Anyway, thank you, Colonel "Col-O-Nel". Fitzhugh beamed, finally letting go of the Frenchman's hand. 'I look forward to meeting your man tomorrow.'

* * *

As the two English soldiers exited the confines of the French HQ building, a bright-faced man wearing a Canadian uniform jogged over to greet them. Andrews took a non-too-subtle warning step between the man and his commander.

'Captain Fitzhugh?' the man asked.

'I am. And you are?'

'Sergeant-Major Hubert Wolk, 3rd Canadian Division.'

'It seems you are outranked, Andrews,' Fitzhugh said, placing a friendly hand on his sergeant's shoulder as a sign the man could stand down.

'And how can I help you, Hubert Wolk of the 3rd Canadian Division?'

'I'd like to be part of your investigation,' the man said straight out.

'And what investigation would that be, Hubert Wolk of the 3rd Canadian Division?'

The smile that had not wavered began to drain from the Canadian's face. He then leaned in closer to the two Englishmen. 'Sorry, I didn't introduce myself properly. My name is Sergeant-Major ...'

'Yes, we got that part,' Andrews snarled.

Wolk continued as though uninterrupted, '... I should say, former Sergeant-Major Hubert Wolk of the Royal Canadian Mounties. You're investigating the rumours of the crucified soldier—the *Canadian* soldier, I would like to point out—so I would like to offer my services.'

Fitzhugh never broke eye contact with the ex-Mountie. 'Was his name on the list, Sergeant Andrews?'

'No, sir,' Andrews answered, refusing to check the list of names on the papers he was carrying.

'Put his name on the list please, Sergeant Andrews,' Fitzhugh ordered. Though Wolk wasn't one of the Canadians he was going to ask, the fact that the man before him had shown enough gumption and intelligence to work out just who he was, and what mission he was currently working on, spoke volumes on his investigation skills. 'It would seem we have our man.'

Sergeant Andrews watched on, clearly not getting the joke.

CHAPTER SEVEN

JUST ONE MORE TO JOIN OUR HAPPY BAND OF ADVENTURERS, Fitzhugh thought as they entered the Australian lines. They were immediately joined by several large men wearing the quintessential slouch hats the antipodean troopers favoured.

These men referred to themselves as 'six-bob-a-day tourists', referencing their daily wage, and their service meant the Australian government and senior commanders treated them with more respect than other nations treated their own men. The most obvious example was that no Digger could face a firing squad for any offence without the permission of the Australian government, and that permission was never forthcoming, despite the pleas of generals like Douglas Haig.

Soldiers being soldiers, the Australian servicemen took full advantage of this leniency by rarely saluting their officers and hardly ever answering with the proper use of rank. Instead, the Aussies called their commanders by their first name, never wore their uniforms in the 'correct' by-the-book-way, nor took part in much of the silliness that soldiers from other nations had to endure.

Fitzhugh knew full well the reputation of these men, both on and—in this case—importantly off the battlefield.

At one point, the unruly Diggers had found themselves located in the lines near the 10th Royal Fusiliers, and here they became concerned for their fellow soldiers when the Fusiliers commander ordered them to parade every morning. The very English and newly minted colonel had decided he would have his men march a full-dress parade, with spit-and-polish uniforms, during their morning mounting of the guard. This was all done as the unit's brass band played a merry ditty for the Fusiliers to march back and forth under the braying vigilance of Sergeant-Major Thomas Rowbotham. A lifelong military NCO, Rowbotham agreed with his colonel that strict discipline within the ranks was the only way to go.

Amid the mud, carnage, and death on the Western Front, the Diggers watched these parades with growing incredulity. Stationed next to each other, the two units inevitably began mixing and the Aussies eventually had to ask their British comrades if they enjoyed all that marching and dressing up.

'Not on your life!' replied one of the Fusiliers.

Another jumped in. 'We have to do the parade during our downtime. Even at rest, we're busy polishing buttons and boots, all so our bloody officers can feel like they're leading proper soldiers.'

One burly Australian grinned an evil grin at his new friends and, slapping the much smaller man on the back warmly, said, 'Right-o, cobber, we'll fix that for you.'

The next day, Sergeant-Major Rowbotham called his men into parade. The Fusiliers all dutifully filed in and the regimental band lifted their instruments, awaiting the Sergeant-Major's signal. As Rowbotham lifted then dropped his arm to signal them to play, he was greeted by a cacophony of what some would later recount fondly as noise.

Marching up and down behind Rowbotham were the Australians, playing what could be kindly described as instruments. Most were rusty and showed the signs of a hard life, but none of this mattered as the Aussies couldn't play them anyway. Instead, they just blew and banged as hard and loud as they could, to drown out Rowbotham's orders. Each time the makeshift orchestra began to wane, and the Sergeant-Major tried to regain control of the situation, the Australians began playing again with even greater vigour. After nearly half an hour of this, the Sergeant-Major, in utter defeat, finally strode away in a huff and the Fusiliers were never called to parade again. The Australian trench band was always watching and ready to start up their battlefield symphony if they did.

'Can I help you, gentlemen?' one of the Australian soldiers asked.

'No, thank you, just passing through,' Fitzhugh answered as Andrews manoeuvred to place himself between the two men.

'What have we here? It seems the officer is taking his dog out for a walk,' another Aussie said. 'Down there, Fido. *Sit!*'

Another of the soldiers asked, 'Does your dog do any tricks?'

'Sergeant,' Fitzhugh cautioned, as Andrews took a threatening step toward the jokester.

'Nice leash, puppy,' the Australian said, indicating Fitzhugh with a nod of his hat.

'Actually, perhaps you men can help me?' the captain asked, his tone remaining warm.

'What're you after? A German flag? A helmet? We got lots of souvenirs to impress the folks at home. You can even say you collected them yourself, you big brave British soldier you.'

'Even have an officer's uniform. It's still a little bloody from where Barney here gutted the bloke.'

Ignoring the clear threat, and taking the statement as a joke, thus passing the test the Australians had laid out, Fitzhugh replied sincerely, 'No, no, do not offer me any of your baubles. I was hoping for some information. Do any of you men know Sergeant Hank Ash?'

'Now what would a proper British officer like you want with Mr Ash?' the soldier called Barney asked with a heavy Irish accent.

Both Fitzhugh and Andrews caught the sudden change in attitude. All had gone from casual, fun-loving jokesters to rigid and aggressively hard.

'I'm here to try to save his neck!'

* * *

The newly demoted Private Hank Ash sat in his cell, his sleeves sporting discoloured sections where his sergeant chevrons used to be. Two armed English guards stood directly outside his cell, situated in a small outbuilding of the farm that was being used as a temporary prison behind the Australian lines. Outside stood more guards, while the farmhouse itself had been converted into a makeshift barracks.

Through a small field that should have been full of feeding chickens and a garden, but now housed a small latrine on one side and a smouldering fire on the other, Fitzhugh, Andrews, and their Australian retinue marched. Approaching the farmhouse door, Fitzhugh took off his cap and stepped inside, returning the salute of the guards as he did. His retinue moved on to the barn, calling out to their mates inside.

Walking into the prison's makeshift office, Fitzhugh found an English major with a Douglas Fairbanks moustache taking a cup of tea from a brawny NCO.

'No milk in mine, Corporal,' he said, inviting himself to sit down at the major's desk.

The corporal looked from one officer to the other, not sure if he should be turfing the intruder out and hoping for a cue from his commander as to what to do. The major flicked a look at the door and the man left.

'Perhaps a little sugar if you have it, Corporal,' Fitzhugh

called after the departing man, 'and a bikkie.'

'How can I help you, Captain ...?'

'Fitzhugh, Major Preston.'

'It would seem you have me at a disadvantage, Captain Fitzhugh.'

'So it would seem, Major,' Fitzhugh replied, mirroring the senior officer's reference to his rank to let the man know he knew that trick and wasn't about to be cowed by an officer just because he had a little more brass on his shoulders.

'How can I help you?'

'Well, sir, I'm here to take Sergeant Ash off your hands.'

'Very funny, Captain. Now, why are you really here?'

Rather than repeat himself, Fitzhugh removed a letter from his breast pocket, unfolded it, then slowly and deliberately smoothed its creases before handing the paper over. As the officer read the letter, Fitzhugh could tell when he read the name scrawled on the bottom of the page, as his eyes suddenly grew very wide.

'This is signed by Haig.'

'General Haig.' Fitzhugh smiled warmly, continuing their game a little longer.

'Are you sure it's Ash you want?'

'I have been hearing that question a lot recently. Absolutely it is Ash I want.'

'And you know what he did?'

'Let me see, he was wounded at Gallipoli after showing enormous courage, and has been serving very bravely here since ...'

'Since he broke a lieutenant's jaw—'

'From what I heard, the lieutenant deserved a broken jaw.'

'He was still a superior officer,' Preston said.

'*Senior* officer, Major. I'm not too sure how "superior" the man was. Let's not be conjuring facts we have no actual evidence. Personally, I refuse to condemn a man standing

against a practice more in tune with the brutality of the inquisi-
tion. Now, I believe Sergeant Ash is yet to be convicted of this
crime?'

'That's true.'

'May I ask why it's taken so long to court-martial a man who
struck an officer? The official report is frustratingly vague on
why he has missed his last three court appearances. For that
matter, how are you still in charge, having failed to get your
prisoner to his hearing … if I may be so bold as to ask?'

'Very simple.' The major opened his hands, as though
displaying something on the table before them. 'My predecessor
was a total and utter moron.'

Biting off a laugh from the unexpected comment, Fitzhugh
regained control of himself. 'Care to elaborate, sir?'

'The buffoon arrested Ash and placed him in this stockade, a
stockade, I'd like to point out, that is surrounded by the entire
1st Australian Division.'

'Gotcha,' Fitzhugh said, realisation striking.

'Every time we have tried to move 'Private' Ash, those
bloody Australians have intercepted us. It seems they are determined to make sure he never sees the inside of a courtroom,
and their own officers are uninterested in doing anything to
help clear our path.'

'How are they stopping you?'

'Well, you may have noticed the Aussies have men posted
along every route into and out of this place, and they seem to be
ready to move on a moment's notice if they sense we are up to
something. The first time we tried to take Ash to his court
appearance, we found nearly a thousand men choking the road,
doing the finest parade drill I have ever seen. Every time we
tried to cut through them, some unseen voice would order a
platoon to move into our way, and they would begin vigorously
marching.'

No longer interested in hiding his mirth, Fitzhugh asked,

'And the next time?'

'We tried to sneak him out after making sure the time of his hearing was never announced. Somehow, when we went to move him, we suddenly had hundreds of Australian soldiers pushing into the little courtyard out there. They managed to never disobey an order, as the ones who could hear us became hopelessly trapped by the men at the rear continuously pushing forward. It took hours to disentangle everyone, and by then the court had dispersed for the day.'

'So, I assume you next tried to bring the court here?'

'We did, and here's why I really hate those fucking antipodeans.' The major almost spat. 'Clearly, they have either befriended or bribed some of my guards, as no sooner did I have it planned for the court to visit us, the Australians struck again.'

'Struck?'

'Well, of course, I have no proof of this, but I find it suspicious that the horses the court were going to use to get here disappeared, and of course, they refused to walk all the way, and vehicles would never have made the journey through the trenches.'

'The Australians stole the horses?' Fitzhugh asked, grinning.

'They steal everything not tied down, bloody convicts.' Sensing he may have said too much, the warden backpedalled. 'Well, as I said, there's no proof. Though the Aussies did seem to eat well for the next few days. They had themselves a grand barbeque. They even invited us for a meal.'

Fitzhugh gasped and looked toward the heavens. 'Thank God!'

'Captain?' the major asked, a little confused.

'Sorry, sir, I was just thanking the Almighty that they're on our side, because I wouldn't want to be facing the bastards if they ever got really angry at us.'

'I hadn't thought about that,' the warden said. 'Thank God!'

CHAPTER EIGHT

FITZHUGH STRODE ACROSS THE FARM'S COURTYARD UNDER THE watchful glare of a growing number of Australian soldiers. With half a salute to the guards stationed outside, he entered the ancient stone barn and made his way to the only locked door in the building.

'Open the door, please,' he said, not so much ordering the guards inside, but asking politely.

Though the first guard looked at him suspiciously, the second reacted promptly and unlocked the door and pushed it open.

'Thank you.'

Fitzhugh ducked his head as he passed under the small door-frame. Standing just inside to allow his eyes to adjust to the darkness of the cell, when he finally could make out the shadowy silhouette of the room's sole occupant, he moved in and took a seat on the rope bed, the cell's only furniture.

'You don't mind, do you, Sergeant?'

'Not a sergeant anymore, and it all depends on why you're here,' said the tall, burly Australian. As Fitzhugh's eyes became better adjusted to the light, he could see the man had sharp, squinting eyes characteristic of the men from the antipodes. Something to do with the bright sun and the flies of the country, he expected. Ash had not shaved in some time, and a smouldering cigarette hung from his lower lip like a diver thinking twice about jumping from the high-board. Every time he spoke, that diver looked more and more like it was going to plummet to its death, yet somehow it always managed to hang on.

'Well, let's just pretend for a second that the bush telegraph hasn't already informed you, shall we?' Fitzhugh answered, patting the bed next to him. 'I'm here to save your life, Sergeant.'

'You a lawyer or something? The telegraph wasn't all that specific,' Ash asked.

'Not at all. Can't stand the blighters, and I would hang myself if I ever joined the dastardly trade. No, I'm here from Military Intelligence to offer you a job.'

'You have an officer you need thumped?'

'Certainly. Many! But no, that's not the job. I'd like you, my friend, to join an investigation team to help solve a dastardly crime that has been committed against our boys.'

Ash's face seemed to darken as he thought, what could have happened that was so drastic that a British officer would come all this way to spring him? 'The crucified soldier.'

Fitzhugh mentally noted this was a statement more than a question. Figuring that out was a point in the Australian's favour.

'You mean that really happened? I thought it was just soldiers being, well, soldiers.'

'In part, you're on the money,' the captain said, impressed at the intellectual leap. 'Our boys have not reacted well to the rumour, so we—and by "we" I mean you—will be investigating the allegation to see if it has any validation.'

Ash scratched under his stubbly chin in thought. 'Let me see if I have this straight. The crucifixion is only a rumour, but the lads are upset ... The Canucks are threatening to take action, the French are using it as an excuse to bellyache, and my boys are looking for someone to hit?'

'Got it in one, Sergeant,' Fitzhugh agreed, warming to the Digger. 'I knew you'd be the right man for the job.'

'I haven't said yes, Captain.'

'Sure you have. I mean, it's not like you have a lot of choice here. The second you're placed in front of a court-martial, you're done. This way I get you out of here before any sentence can be handed down. Right now, you're just a soldier attached on a short-term appointment to my office. Here, tomorrow, you'll be a condemned man, and that, my friend, is clearly going to be more trouble than it's worth.'

'Good point,' Ash agreed, sticking out his hand and smiling.

Fitzhugh took the hand in his own, and the men shook warmly, introductions over.

Emerging through the barn's low door, Fitzhugh wisely allowed the Australian to go first. Outside, dozens of soldiers crowded the small courtyard, and by the sounds of it there were more on the way.

'Nice to be loved,' Fitzhugh whispered.

'That's him—the Pommy officer who's trying to sneak Hank out of here,' a voice from the back yelled.

'Sneak? What do you mean, sneak? I told you I was here to take him,' Fitzhugh yelled back. Sergeant Andrews began to push his way through the gathered crowd to reach his troubled officer.

'Never trust a toff-officer, they'll shaft you every time!' another voice called out.

'Like to help me out here, Sergeant?' Fitzhugh said over the Australian's broad shoulder.

'You seem to be doing fine, Captain. Trust me, there's nothing the boys like more than a smart mouth, upper crust, British officer looking to hang one of their own.' But instead of moving aside to let the gathered Australians at Fitzhugh, Ash raised his arms, and with a voice only an experienced sergeant could have, called out to the crowd for calm.

'Lads, lads, do you see any guards? Do you see any manacles on me? I'm not under arrest. I've been transferred to the military police. It seems you bastards have scared them so much they've asked me to be a copper and start busting some of your thick noggins together.'

'You really free?' asked one of the soldiers who had accompanied the Englishmen through the Australian camp.

'I'm free.'

Fitzhugh had never been that great a sportsman, and most certainly had never won anything in his life that would warrant what happened next. The Australians cheered loudly, rushed forward, and began carrying him on their shoulders out of the farm's courtyard and back to their own camp.

Fitzhugh only hoped they weren't taking him to a barbeque.

CHAPTER NINE

THE NEXT MORNING, FITZHUGH FOLLOWED ANDREWS THROUGH the curtain and into his office, which suddenly felt even smaller with the three soldiers awaiting him inside. The sergeant had already warned Fitzhugh of who had shown up, and more specifically that the Frenchman hadn't.

Squirming his way through the men, the captain managed to get behind his desk and gestured for the others to sit. This initiated a short game of musical empty ammunition boxes, with Sergeant Andrews missing out and having to stand at the rear of the room.

'You gentleman have been attached to my office for a short-term mission. We are going to investigate the rumour of a soldier, or soldiers, who were possibly crucified out in no man's land. Each of you has some investigation skills in your prior jobs, but at this moment what is far more important is that you're well known within your various units.'

The three NCOs looked at each other, unsure whether to be impressed or suspicious.

'This, my friends, will look something like a publicity stunt to those on the outside. As nasty as the supposed crime was, it's only a drop in the ocean compared to what's going on around us, and let's be honest, it would normally warrant only a brief investigation or a mention in despatches. The problem with this murder is the timing. As you all are aware, the boys along the front lines are a little skittish at the moment, and right now is when we need them concentrating on the job at hand, not running about on suicidal missions of vengeance, and certainly not demonising the enemy to the point we turn them into some mythological bogeyman.'

'Is that really the reason?' McGavin asked.

'No,' Fitzhugh admitted bluntly. 'I intend to try to show Haig that he should care about the welfare of the men under his command, and to do that we need to show that the officers leading this idiotic bloodbath,' Fitzhugh waved his arms about him to encompass everything, 'understand such a crime against our soldiers cannot go unpunished. I hope this experiment will show the men that HQ are aware of their concerns and are willing to act to protect them. In short, we need to show that Haig and his command care …'

'Which they don't,' Ash said coldly.

'Of course, they don't,' the officer agreed, 'but as I said, they need to be seen that they do, otherwise the fools may actually start thinking for themselves and realise they have more in common with the guys in the other trenches than the guys leading them.'

The men laughed half-heartedly at this truth. Fitzhugh was not one of them, and when they settled down, he continued. 'I'm serious, that's a real concern. Imagine if a million soldiers got it into their heads that they didn't want to kill each other anymore. Instead, what if they turned their guns on the guys ordering their deaths? Anarchy, chaos, and communism would be next, which is exactly what we've been hearing about in the Russian lines.'

No one was smiling anymore.

'So, to the job at hand, first thing I need is each of you to return to your own units and ferret out exactly who saw what. Take statements, or better yet, bring any witness back here to be interviewed. We need information, gentlemen, as it's hard to run a murder investigation without an actual body.'

'We need clay to make bricks, as Holmes said,' Wolk offered, warming to the task.

'Indeed. Find me the name of whoever was crucified, and get me anyone who witnessed the crime.'

Fitzhugh waited a beat, and when no one moved, he yelled, 'GO! This is the job for now. Get out there and find me answers.'

As the men moved to leave, Andrews gave a less-than-subtle cough and gestured with his eyes at the table. Fitzhugh followed his sergeant's gaze.

'Oh, and you better wear these.' The captain retrieved several armbands and prepared to toss them to the men. 'We don't have time to be signing orders giving you permission to wander around by yourselves questioning units, but MPs can go just about anywhere, so enjoy them.' Fitzhugh noticed the look of mischief on his men's faces and added, 'But not too much.'

As the men caught their armbands, some of them looked at the strips of cloth with the letters M and P in red stitching as though they were toxic.

'Don't be babies. Put those bloody things on and meet me back here tomorrow morning.'

The men gave the sloppiest salutes in history, then stepped back into the war.

CHAPTER TEN

THE BRIGHT SUNSHINE OF THE PREVIOUS DAY HAD BEEN REPLACED by the heavy, grey clouds and occasional storms of a typical French spring. Men and horses, dragging everything from guns to stores of canned goods, struggled through the increasingly muddy pathways between the few buildings still standing and the piles of rubble that covered the streets.

McGavin looked at the band as being beneath him. To go from a Scotland Yard officer to a simple soldier was bad enough, but since the positions were unrelated, he had consoled himself with this professional back step. But to go from Scotland Yard to an MP felt like a true demotion.

With the orders to move to this new unit, Fitzhugh had not explained if their old ranks were still valid, or if they were all now equals as long as they wore the MP armbands.

'Just put it on,' Wolk said. He was the only one to put his armband on. His fellow Canadians would respect the badge, if not the man wearing it, and would be perfectly happy to deal with him.

'Yeah, you secretly know you want it,' Ash said, pocketing his own armband.

'You're not wearing yours?' McGavin asked.

'Hell no! Do you have any idea what those bastards over there would do to me if I showed up wearing one of these?' he said, gesturing to the Australian lines with his thumb. 'What you need to understand is we are fighting several wars here in France: one against the Germans, the other against the British officers, and the last against the MPs. We hate those bastards ... and to tell the truth, I'm not actually sure why I'm here.'

'Well, I worked for Scotland Yard,' the Englishman admitted.

'I was a Mountie,' Wolk added.

'And I was a train driver,' Ash said. 'So, what the hell do they want with me?'

'To drive a train?' McGavin joked.

'Well, you're a name,' Wolk said thoughtfully, then expounded. 'You're one of the most famous men on the front-lines at the moment. When the boys hear you are part of the investigation, they'll immediately know HQ is making good on their promise that real troopers will be taking part.'

'Plus, I think our friend the captain back there has a hard-on for you,' McGavin said, giving the Australian a wink. The dark look he got back forced him to move on. 'He clearly has no time for our masters, and he knows the value of having someone who, if need be, will steamroll over rank if necessary.'

'Meaning?' Ash asked.

'Meaning, we may need to deal with officers who don't want to deal with us. But if they fear having their lights punched out at the drop of a hat if they get ... *uncivil* with us, well, that could be a useful tool.'

'That's it!' the Canadian exclaimed excitedly. 'You're a tool.' He then ducked a playful swipe from the burly Australian and asked, 'So what do you really think of all this?'

All three stepped out of the way of a message runner sprinting through the street.

'I think we're being set up for a fall,' McGavin mused,

surprising the other two. 'Fitzhugh admitted as much in there, though not in those exact words. Haig needs to be seen as doing something—not "actually" doing something, mind you. He doesn't care if we find the murderer or prove any such crime ever happened. He just wants the men to get back to their jobs, and knowing we are on the case will help him convince them to do just that.'

'You're saying we don't really need to investigate this, we just need to be seen to be investigating this?' Ash asked.

'I am, though that's not exactly what I'm suggesting we do. We know the officers don't care, but I do, and I'm pretty sure you do too. If those morons have given us the tools to examine this crime, I'm more than willing to use them.' The Englishman then placed the armband on and flicked the MP insignia. 'I'm going to find the bastards who did this to one of our lads.'

Looking between both men, Ash rolled his eyes, groaned as though he'd just been kicked between the legs, retrieved his own armband from his pocket, and slipped it on.

'All right, let's do this,' he said, not looking all that happy about his new vocation.

CHAPTER ELEVEN

As the three Allied soldiers left Fitzhugh's office and headed back to their units, a fourth soldier—a French officer to be precise—arrived. Andrews pulled back the curtain and stood to the side. This allowed the officer behind him to step through, stamp both feet before the captain's desk, and fire off a crisp salute. The Frenchman then introduced himself.

'Captain, I am Lieutenant Colonel Jean Danjou. I was told yesterday that I was to be attached to your investigation of the crucified soldier rumour.' Though his English was clear, he had a far heavier accent than the officer Fitzhugh had dealt with earlier. 'I am here to tell you this will not be happening. Despite the ongoing war, this is still sovereign France, and it will be a Frenchman who will discover and persecute the perpetrator of this crime.'

As Fitzhugh opened his mouth to speak, Danjou continued.

'Though I cannot stop you from pursuing your own investigation, I will play no part in it. Have me arrested if you must, but I will be working by myself on this until either manacled or manacling the vile criminal who dared stain the sacred soil of France.'

Firing off a second salute that was the mirror image of the first, Danjou then spun on his heel and marched out of the room.

'Why, come in,' Fitzhugh finally said to the departing man.

CHAPTER TWELVE

McGAVIN REFUSED TO THINK HIS DAY SO FAR HAD BEEN A complete waste of time, though thanks to nearly a year marching about in a British uniform he was feeling relatively fresh. At home, he would never have walked this much; in fact, he'd been issued a driver for the last few years of his career with the Yard.

A few questions had revealed the units most concerned about the crucifixion story, but of these only two had been taking their turn along the trenches at the apparent time of the incident—the rest were out of the line for a rest rotation or other reasons, so could not have seen the crucified soldier. Still, McGavin had begun questioning the units who had been at the front, and what followed was hour after hour filled with rumour and innuendo.

'No, sir, I didn't see it myself, but I know a guy in the 3rd Battalion who did.'

The guy in the 3rd Battalion admitted, 'No, sir, I never seen any such thing, just heard about it.' Although he was pretty sure it had been a corporal in the 8th who'd seen the crucifixion.

With these avenues of inquiry forming little more than a

circle, with rumour and gossip chasing after anecdotes and hearsay, McGavin decided he had no choice. Putting his steel helmet on and picking up an issue of ammunition and his rifle, he began the long, dangerous trek to the most forward posts of the British lines where the incident most likely occurred.

* * *

Ash returned to his unit and was greeted with back slaps and cheers at his unlikely freedom. This warm reception started to cool though when the men of the 1st Australian Division noticed the dreaded MP band on his arm. Many of them had been fighting for three years already, and unlike troopers from the other nations along the Western Front, they never received home leave.

The French and Belgians were fighting on their national soil, and it was a simple trip across the English Channel for the British soldiers for some much-needed home leave. Even some of the Canadians got a brief trip home across the North Atlantic. But for many of the colonial troops, specifically the ANZACs, South Africans, and Indian troops, it was simply impractical to allow these men to spend months travelling to and from their home countries. This meant these men had to find their own way of relieving the stresses of the battlefield.

Their continued service, month after month, year after year, led to some rather explosive downtime behind the lines. Heavy drinking was the norm, and sports and fighting of course soon followed. A real spirit of 'us' and 'them' had grown within the ranks of these soldiers and led to more than a few brawls between the British and the Australians.

This resulted in the Diggers forming a combative relation-ship with the Military Police, or *provosts*, that dated back to the Eureka Stockade and the infamous bushranger Ned Kelly's shoot-out with the police. What often began as an argument between mates would degrade into an all-out riot once the MPs arrived—with the provosts often paying a hefty price for daring to confront the Aussies. These confrontations could involve thousands of soldiers, such as at the Battle of the Wazzir, where unruly ANZACs had destroyed a large section of Cairo in one such fight.

For one of their own, a man considered something of a legend by many, to return from prison wearing an MP armband would be considered nothing less than a betrayal. Ash hadn't been wrong for not wanting to wear the damn thing, but he realised McGavin had also been right. He wasn't there to make friends; he was there to investigate a murder.

Ignoring the dark looks he was receiving, Ash searched for men he knew would have the latest trench news.

'Jack-o,' he called out, entering the dark world of trench living once more. The dirt cave he stepped into—shored up with wooden duckboards put down to allow men to walk through fields of mud—contained a number of secondary alcoves where the men had dug small sleeping nooks for themselves. In one of these, a short man lay on his back, staring as though he could see something far off in the distance.

Mark 'Jack-o' West was a scrounger of the first order. Though deprivations were the norm in the trenches, men like Jack-o had a habit of finding the impossible. Need a birthday candle? Jack-o could get it. Need some cherry schnapps? Well, with money or some rare goods to swap and a few days' notice, the scrounger could procure it for you.

'Hank?' Jack-o beamed, extricating himself from his bedroll and moving over to shake the sergeant's hand. 'Heard you were wearing one of these. Can I ask why?'

'Of course, you've already heard,' Ash said with amazement at just how connected the scrounger was. 'Trust me, these are only temporary. I'm part of a team investigating this crucified soldier malarkey. I was hoping you may have heard something.

Maybe know someone who actually saw it, or if this was some idiot's idea of a practical joke?'

'Well, I'd heard they were going to do something stupid like have real troops investigate it, but you?'

'Apparently, I'm the blunt object the investigation intends to use to make sure officers remain civil while we question them.'

Jack-o gave that a short thought and then grinned. 'Man, who knew HQ could be smart enough to see that?'

'I'm not so sure it was HQ. More like an intelligence officer called Fitzhugh.'

'Captain Fitzhugh? I've heard he's a real odd duck.'

'I've only met him twice, but so far that's bang on my opinion as well.'

'Okay, well, as for the crucifixion thing, I've heard everything you've likely heard. Troops scouting no man's land found a soldier nailed to a door, though I have also heard it was a soldier crucified with barbed wire to a fence.'

'Trench whispers?'

'Most likely. The story changes with the imagination of those retelling it. That alone makes me think it never happened, and it certainly wasn't an Australian who was killed or who found the soldier—that I'm pretty sure I would have heard about.'

'That's why I came to you first,' Ash said, doffing his slouch hat.

'I think it's a waste of time working our boys, though I'll keep my ear out for any information.'

'Well, the investigation is supposed to be only the smallest part of what we're doing.'

'Smallest?'

'We need to be seen investigating to calm the troops down. There's a concern upstairs that we're about to all turn on each other looking for a possible murderer in our midst—or worse, go over the top and take vengeance on the Huns over there.'

'Would that be bad? It might shorten the war if we get a little nasty dealing with those guys.'

'Sure, but then no general can take the credit. They need their plans to be followed, otherwise, what are they good for?'

'I can answer that one right now,' Jack-o said. 'I suggest you look at the Canadians. Of everything I've heard, the majority say it was a Canadian soldier who was killed and a Canadian unit that found him.'

'We have that angle in hand,' Ash said, saying his goodbyes and looking to leave the claustrophobic tunnel as quickly as possible. If this war held any real horror for him, it was the thought of being buried alive in one of those flimsy tunnels after it took a direct hit. He had worked in details ordered to dig out such structures after a battle, and the bodies they found buried inside had died hard, ghastly deaths. The mouths and nostrils of those who had not been lucky enough to be killed immediately in the collapse were always clogged with mud and dirt as they had struggled to breathe ... just the memory gave him the heebies.

* * *

Wolk cut through his fellow countrymen like a knife. Though MPs were never popular, the well-disciplined Canadians were at least willing to talk to the former Mountie, happy about it or not. Like most of the colonials, many of the Canadians fighting the war were from rural communities, making them both tough and disciplined. What it came down to was respect, and so far the North Americans had few reasons to lose respect for the MP badge.

It didn't matter what your rank was, if the men under your command didn't respect you, they were less likely to listen. Many a junior officer was lauded in ways their superiors never were, simply because the soldiers who had personal contact with these men grew to respect them.

Ignoring officers and NCOs, Wolk entered the first of the Canadian messes, took a steel plate, slapped some hot but unidentifiable food on it from the chow line, then sat down. Picking through his meal and eating little, he listened carefully to those talking around him. Though the men at first were wary of an MP sitting nearby, human nature soon took over and they began to talk freely amongst themselves. Between stories and jokes, mostly aimed at someone sitting at their table, the Mountie heard just about every version of the crucifixion rumour circulating.

Much like McGavin was discovering, the majority of the stories were just that—rumour. Some men claimed they had talked to a guy who knew the guy who'd seen the body. Others bragged they had seen it themselves, yet when Wolk began quizzing them, they were very vague with any details.

Though Wolk knew most of this information was useless, he carefully wrote down each detail shared with him between sips of what the cooks called coffee, but what tasted like lukewarm, watered-down mud. He noted names, unit insignias, and locations, and he put a little number next to each. A number 1 was for the least credible; a number 5 was for information he felt might be genuine.

After an hour sitting, listening, and far-too-infrequently interviewing, Wolk had a page full of names, places, and numbers no higher than a two. Still, if nothing else panned out, these would all have to be investigated.

With several similar messes within walking distance, he began legging it down a well-trodden path to his next stop. Inside this tent, he repeated the process as before—jotting down names, units, and locations of any rumour he overheard while sitting in front of a tray of untouched, slowly congealing food. Twice more he repeated the process, though in the last mess something unusual was happening. There was little bragging and open conversing about the crucifixion … indeed anyone who loudly began such a conversation was quickly hushed.

Because everyone was being so careful, the haul of information in this mess was far less than the others, yet what Wolk heard made this information far more credible.

Men concerned about being overheard meant they either had something to hide, or they didn't want to get someone they knew into trouble. In every location he'd been that day, and every conversation he had heard, this location was proving the most likely to know something about the crucifixion.

Wolk spent as much time as he could with that section trolling for news. When some of the men began looking at him suspiciously, he knew it was time to move on before the odd glance could turn into something far more physical. As a Mountie, he had been in similar situations before, be it lumberjack waterholes or tiny, isolated communities where everyone knew everyone else's business but distrusted outsiders to the point of violence. Wolk had a nose for a nasty situation, so he decided it was time to beat a strategic retreat.

He'd be back, however, and next time he'd bring some friends.

CHAPTER THIRTEEN

THE NEXT MORNING BROKE WITH BLUE SKIES AND SUNSHINE SO bright that it almost felt warm to those beneath it. The three MPs, their armbands firmly in place, once again sat before Captain Fitzhugh's desk. All three held steaming cups of coffee, supplied by the industrious Sergeant Andrews, though none had dared drink the liquid after an initial taste revealed it was probably better suited as boot cleaner. Still, the cups helped keep cold hands warm and that was good enough.

'You're telling me you had a whole day and learned nothing?' Fitzhugh asked, disappointed.

'I'm pretty sure there was nothing to know,' Ash said. 'The men who barter such information are now on the case and will hopefully come up with something. Amongst the troopers, all I found was stories, and none were credible enough to follow up.'

'I had pretty much the same problem,' McGavin added. 'All day I followed a trail of rumours that, like the snake eating its own tail, ended up swallowing themselves.'

'The Ouroboros,' Fitzhugh said, nodding sagely.

'No, the hoop snake.' Ash rolled his eyes.

'You have those too?' Wolk asked.

'Anyway,' McGavin said, taking the conversation away from the two colonial yokels, 'I found men claiming they knew someone who'd witnessed the crucifixion; those in turn denied having ever said anything of the sort, but of course knew someone who did know someone who had seen it. I'm pretty sure none of the English units I spent time with yesterday knew anything real about the crime.'

'Exactly,' the Australian sergeant agreed. On his knee sat his beaten, dirty slouch hat. 'Nuffin' but gasbagging. From what I heard I don't think any of our boys were involved either.'

'And you?' Fitzhugh asked Wolk. 'Did you get your man?'

'Aww ... "get your man" ... "Mounties" ... I get it.' Sergeant Andrews guffawed from the rear of the room.

After giving his sergeant a long, cowering stare, Fitzhugh returned his attention to the Canadian.

'I think I have our first evidence that something did indeed occur.'

'You found something?' McGavin asked.

'Nothing specific.'

'Explain,' Fitzhugh said, cutting through the forest of confused grunts and looks from the others.

'As we've all discovered, the rumours about the crucified soldier are legion. I mean, soldiers are worse than washer-women when it comes to gossip. Yet I found one area in the Canadian trenches where no one is talking. There seems to be a complete absence of rumour there, which leads me to think the men know something and are afraid to talk about it—or they don't want people they suspect may have been involved over-hearing them discussing the crime. They seem to be deliberately not talking about it, if that makes sense.'

'There's another possibility,' McGavin mused. 'They may not be joking or telling stories about the crucified soldier because they actually knew who the crucified soldier was.'

'Interesting,' Wolk agreed. 'I hadn't thought of that. It does make far more sense. They don't want to be flippant out of respect for a comrade who had just been killed in such a gruesome manner.'

'So, it's looking like a Canadian soldier was killed, or it was the Canadians who found the man. Either way I think we need to concentrate our efforts along their lines.'

Though Fitzhugh sounded like he was discussing the matter with them, the three MPs soon realised he was thinking out loud. After a few minutes, the captain's focus seemed to return to the room.

'Wolk, I want you to at least look like you're in charge of the investigation over there. The rest of you, Wolk is not in charge, but the appearance of a Canadian leading this team will help smooth things over. People will more likely talk to you if they think you're working for him. I want you to really get into the trenches with these guys, maybe hang out for a while. Don't act like cops and people will forget you're wearing those armbands soon enough. Just be one of the lads. Bitch about the crazy limey officer sending you out on insane missions, maybe fire off bizarre theories about the crime if anyone asks. Give them information or gossip and they're more likely to share. Watch their reactions. Genuine mirth means they think it's equally funny; quiet and interested, then they are … hell, you know what you're doing,' Fitzhugh ended, catching the amused looks from the policemen sitting before him.

'All right, get out of here. We will try to meet here at some time every morning. I won't be upset if you miss a meeting as long as there's a reason. Miss three and I'll assume something has gone wrong and send the cavalry—and what's interesting here is I'm pretty sure I can get my hands on some real cavalry at the moment.'

The three MPs realised it was not going to be hard bitching and complaining about their crazy limey officer.

CHAPTER FOURTEEN

INSTEAD OF STARTING THEIR SEARCH, THE FOLLOWING DAY THE men found themselves fighting for their lives as the Germans tried a sneak attack to wipe out the artillery unit the Canadians were protecting. For two days, a withering barrage landed in and around the forward trenches, softening up the Canadians for a penetration of a new type of German soldier, the Stoßtruppen.

Wearing steel helmets and chest plates and carrying large, medieval-looking shields to help protect the men carrying a new type of terror weapon—a portable flamethrower—these specially trained stormtroopers successfully breached the Allied lines. Reserve forces were rushed in to hold and then push them back out again.

Though frightening, Allied HQ estimated these new soldiers —because of their slowness and inability to hug the terrain thanks to the great weight they carried—had suffered greatly during the attack, with nearly half their number killed during their initial charge.

Some of the Australians who fought these stormtroopers began calling them bushrangers and Ned Kellies, after the 19th

century highwayman who had donned similar armour. Conse-
quently, Kelly's end had been similar to that of many of these
stormtroopers, whose arms and legs were still exposed, and
even their thick armour proved of little benefit against modern,
powerful rifles.

Within a week the fighting had quieted down and most of
the units involved had sorted themselves out, allowing the
investigation to recommence.

The three investigators hadn't been idle during this time.
Between moments of terror as the units fought in the collapsing
lines to help hold the German attack until help arrived,
McGavin, Ash, and Wolk had returned to HQ and pored over
available aerial photos and maps of the region. In these they
located a number of reasonably intact farmhouses, which were
placed in the growing list of locations to be investigated if they
got the chance. Each farmhouse where the crucifixion may have
taken place was then referenced to the soldiers standing the
lines facing these buildings. From this another list was compiled
of the men who'd gone missing in action from these units
during the allotted timeframe. There was every chance the dead
soldier had come from somewhere else—again, if he ever
existed at all—but at least this was a starting point.

Unfortunately, due to the nature of trench warfare and the
length of the front, the list of missing men when compared with
the list of fatalities was incomplete and arguably impractical.
Some serious detective work would be needed to whittle this
list down to just one name.

Fitzhugh was impressed at not only their efforts but the
ability of the three men to think a problem through. For now,
he was feeling good about his decision to invest in his team, and
the spectre of Haig's displeasure seemed a long way off.

* * *

Wolk entered the Canadian lines with his fellow MPs following his lead. From their research they knew the 15th Edmonton Corps had been occupying the trenches opposite the building where the crime most likely occurred. The 15th had also been one of the units most tight-lipped about the crucified soldier.

While the Mountie made their presence known to the 15th's officers, the other two moved through the trenches, supply depots, messes, and even hung about upwind of the latrines for a short time—a place where soldiers were almost religiously happy to chat about anything to get their mind off the filth they found themselves living in. Though the Canadians proved talkative on numerous subjects, including the hatred of Haig and his command, very few said a word about the dead, and those who did speak were clearly trying to deflect the conversation away from the subject. They never came out and directly said they had no faith in the story of the crucified soldier, they just hinted at it in every way they could.

To the experienced McGavin, this made the idea that the soldiers were protecting the identity of a fellow Canadian even more likely. To deliberately offer misleading information to someone who could make your life miserable was an odd stance to take if there was truly nothing to the rumour. He was loath to admit it, but it seemed Wolk had been correct. The Canadians were involved, though just how was yet to be determined.

Wolk found the unit's headquarters situated in the basement of what had been a sixteenth-century church. Unfortunately for the building, its steeple had proven high enough to see well into the German lines, which meant the Germans could also see it— and appreciate its importance. A subsequent bombardment had floored not only the steeple, but the church and most of the surrounding village as well.

But those sixteenth-century masons had built their buildings tough. Though the church itself was rubble, its subterranean chambers had mostly survived. Certainly, some of the rooms were structurally unsound, but they still had quickly become the focal point for the Allied lines in the area as some protection was better than none.

Major Daniel O'Connell was an Irish immigrant who'd only lived in Canada for part of his adult life. While many Irish moved to America, a few decided to remain within the Commonwealth and begin their new life further in the north. Jobs often proved hard to find upon arrival, and O'Connell had joined one of the few industries that relied on those struggling and desperate: the army.

Joining Canada's military, the major added his name to a long list of O'Connells who had fought for foreign nations. One uncle had been a general with Napoleon, while other long-dead relatives had fought for tsars and kaisers. One had even helped rule the colony of Botany Bay years ago, after he married the daughter of the infamous William Bligh.

These O'Connells had generally been fighting for a free Ireland, a subject the major could never be enticed to add his opinion about.

Wolk marched into the major's office, escorted by a prim and proper British captain called Darcy, along with a rough-looking sergeant who could have been pulled from the same mould as Andrews. One would not call Darcy a secretary, as men rarely liked being referenced that way unless as a political appointment. Instead Darcy referred to himself as a 'liaison'.

Haig's office was reluctant to allow international troops to be commanded by their own native officers, but hard stances by governments such as Australia had given them little choice. The High-Command still managed to assert some control, though, by essentially inserting their own spies in those armies not directly under their command. These specialist and liaison officers would report the truth of what they saw within these foreign units, even if that truth was a biased, judgemental British opinion of what was happening within the colonial ranks.

In many cases, it was obvious to the men on the ground just what HQ was up to and they quickly identified and ostracised these officers. A result of this was many colonial troops became suspicious of strangers hanging around and asking a lot of questions. Having to constantly hold your tongue and speak carefully around such officers meant there was always a certain air of anxiety for the soldiers who had to deal with them.

Darcy entered O'Connell's office and snapped him a crisp salute. 'Wolk of the Military Police, sir, on a mission from GHQ, sir.' He then took a stance by the side of the door.

The major looked up from his fried tinned meat on local black bread and acknowledged the salute with a nod. 'And what does Haig want to know now?'

'I'm not really here from Haig, sir. I'm here for the men,' Wolk explained when Darcy gave him a look indicating that question was for him.

Putting down his fork, O'Connell said, 'Intriguing, please do go on.'

'My team and I are here to investigate the rumours of a Canadian soldier being crucified in no man's land. Though there's little actual proof this ever happened, we have been presented some circumstantial evidence indicating if there was a soldier killed in this way, he was likely a Canadian, one stationed somewhere along this part of the lines. GHQ wants us to find out what we can.'

'You mean GHQ wants to be seen to be investigating the crime so that the feral animals we call soldiers do not grow so upset about it that they turn around and bite their master's hands.'

'No, sir,' Wolk said flatly.

'No?'

'I mean, that might be what Haig is after, but that's not why we're here. My team is taking this matter very seriously, sir. If there was such a crime, we want to find evidence of it and ...'

'And what? Bring charges against the perpetrator? See justice done? Are you seriously thinking anyone will ever answer for such a crime?'

'I think what he's trying to say, sir ...'

'If I ever want your opinion about anything, Darcy, I'll give it to you. Now stand there, be quiet, and let me talk to this nice young MP.'

'Yes ... sir,' Darcy answered, snapping back to attention after the rebuke. Clearly the stiffness of his posture was meant to hide his feelings toward the major. It was fooling no one.

'So ... Wolk, is it? Is that what you hope?'

'Sir, I feel the war won't last forever, and yes, once the fields are clear and everyone returns home, we may have enough evidence to bring someone to justice for this crime. But, to answer your question truthfully ...'

'Please do, Sergeant.'

'I don't think it matters one iota if we find the murderer or not. More important at this time is to find the truth of what happened to our boy. This soldier was someone's friend, someone's husband and son. We owe it to him to make sure this crime isn't simply swept under the carpet, sir. At the very least we can say we tried to bring his murderer to justice.'

'And show the men that GHQ truly cares about them, hey?'

Wolk looked into the major's face, searching for any hint this was a trap. Realising his silence was likely that trap, he answered, 'Well, that too, sir. We do have a war to win, and the faster we do that, the sooner we get to go home.'

'Very good answer, Sergeant.' Any sense of victory the ex-Mountie had was soon dashed. 'I grant you no permission to interview my men, and indeed I will be issuing orders that anyone wearing an MP armband found wandering my battalion without my express permission is to be brought to me at once … incapacitated if need be. I am not here to play Haig's little mind games. I am here to get a job done. Please collect your team and leave immediately, Sergeant, or I will have my men turf you out … and I assure you, they won't be saying please.'

'But, sir?' Wolk stammered.

'Darcy, if you would be so kind.'

The captain took one step forward, placing himself in front of Wolk. He then lifted a single finger and pointed toward the stairs behind them. The Mountie looked into the captain's face, who began gesturing with his eyes a possible warning that the MP should leave immediately.

Saluting O'Connell, Wolk spun on his heel and marched away.

Once outside his commander's office, the ice-cool Darcy seemed to warm immediately.

'You handled that well. Any sign of impudence and he would have come down hard. The major rules this place like a despot, and he isn't afraid to hand out his own brand of justice.'

'But how can he …?'

'Get away with it? Simple. Our Major O'Connell in there gets results, and the Canadian command loves him. He doesn't squander his men in fruitless attacks; indeed, he is imaginative, and he's successfully led several attacks on the German lines. Any rumour of brutality is seen as an officer effectively commanding his men, forging them, if you will, into one of the most effective forces along the entire Canadian front.'

'So, what you're telling me is …?' Wolk asked leadingly.

'What I'm telling you is that as long as O'Connell doesn't fall foul of the top brass, he and his command are all but untouchable.'

Suspicious, the Mountie asked, 'And you're telling me this because …?'

'I'm telling you this because I don't like the little shit. I've been liaison to his office now for three weeks and his attitude toward me is getting worse. Truth be told, I am starting to fear for my sanity here.'

'As are we all,' Wolk agreed.

'But rank does have its privileges,' Darcy continued, reaching into his jacket pocket and retrieving a notebook. 'If you are seriously looking to begin your investigation with us,' he said, scribbling something on a blank page, 'then I am assigning you to our divisional runners. You're a Canadian, so you'll be accepted wherever you go, plus runners are free to travel almost everywhere unhindered and their presence is not questioned by other units.'

Darcy tore the order free and passed it on to the MP. 'Hand this to Lieutenant Wilber in our communication tent, and inform him that this is from me directly, and that you're to be assigned to my office as my own personal runner. That way you won't be expected to do any real work, and of course I won't be requiring you to be at my side, so you're free to wander the camp.'

'Thank you, sir, this'll be most helpful.'

'And a word of advice, Sergeant Wolk.'

'Sir?'

'Do not go around asking too many questions—let the men come and gossip with you. O'Connell has everyone so paranoid that a new soldier asking leading questions will come under suspicion.'

'Very good, sir,' Wolk said, taking the note and heading in the direction Darcy had indicated.

'No need for thanks,' Darcy said to the departing MP. 'Honestly, I really haven't done you a favour.'

CHAPTER FIFTEEN

His fellow MPs agreed it was a stroke of genius.

Corporal McGavin was in disguise. He sat at a small desk, buried under an enormous pile of letters. Dropping the name of Captain Fitzhugh, backed by Sergeant Andrews and the power of an MP armband, the Englishman had got himself temporarily reassigned to the Canadian army's censorship office. All letters to and from a soldier had to be read by a division censor and cleared before being posted. While the section had dozens of men reading letters, the office commander, Lieutenant Colonel William Pike, was told that McGavin had been sent to look for a very significant word, phrase, or situation, thus once the office had finished censoring the mail, everything was to then be handed over to him for one last inspection.

Next to the large stack sat a smaller pile of letters containing anything McGavin deemed suspicious, while a list containing the names of men who had died in battle sat by his elbow. This he used as a reference to look for any notes written to the dead men's families from those who served with them. The hope was that these notes might contain a record of how they had died.

An even larger basket by the side of the table contained the letters McGavin considered clean and safe to send. At all times he took care to make sure the letter remained with its envelope. If the two were ever separated, they likely would never be reunited in this room of correspondence.

The concentration required for such a search made it impossible to keep reading for long stretches, and as many of the men's handwriting was what could only be labelled atrocious, McGavin was finding the work mind-numbing.

Though he was not having much luck with the letters themselves, the MP had discovered a real gold mine of information. Each censor had sworn an oath to never reveal what they read to anyone outside the office, but this promise did not seem to include anyone inside the office. Soldiers are gossipmongers after all, and the censors had the freshest, ripest information source on the entire battlefield. They knew who was getting a 'dear Charlie' letter, who was cheating on their wives, and they even got to read the disturbing, disgusting notes some soldiers wrote to their girlfriends, wives, and in one case boyfriend, describing in graphic detail what they intended to do to the other when they got home.

Tea and dinner breaks often devolved into a session of the sickest, most disgusting thing each had read that day, with pride of place going to the man who recounted the worst (or best, depending on your own personal vice) letter.

It was while listening to these accounts that McGavin decided to take a chance and ask if anyone had read anything about strange deaths in the time they'd been working here. Though he had every letter the mailroom had received since his arrival, many letters had been sent from the Canadians before then, and it was likely some of these had mentioned the crucified soldier.

A few of the men retold some gruesome tales, but none were

of a crucifixion. The rest were a little standoffish, but McGavin had his second bright idea: he turned this into something of a sport. He didn't push it, he just mentioned in the lunchtime conversation that he'd read how one soldier reported the death of a German he had killed.

As the hours passed and McGavin's desk was filled with and emptied of letters—too few of which he flagged as suspicious— the true information source soon became the conversation in the office as others joined in his little competition. Though a few felt it disrespectful to be talking about the dead, most of the censors joined in with the most extreme tales of killings they found. Soldiers recounted how they had shot men in the head, the various fluids they saw escape wounds, how they had bayonetted or seen a pal bayoneted, and the faces and the noises the dying made. Once the men were freely talking, they eventually began recounting older stories they had read … and then it happened.

'I did have a letter about that crucified Canadian a few days back,' one censor offered around a mouth full of lukewarm tea and a cheese sandwich. 'Guy said he actually saw the body.'

McGavin hung off the conversation for as long as he dared, hoping others would freely pass on similar accounts or, if he was really lucky, would ask follow-up questions he was dying to have answered. This happened a few times, but when the MP sensed the conversation was about to change topic, he just had to act.

'Did they ever find out the name of the guy who was killed?'

Not even blinking an eye, another censor answered. 'I had one guy write to the sister of the crucified guy. Said his name was Corporal Barth … or maybe it was Garth … I definitely remember he was a corporal though.'

Risking everything, McGavin asked, 'Do you remember who wrote the letter?'

'Some guy in the Highlanders. I remember 'cause I always find it funny that the Canadians are fielding a unit called High-landers.'

And with that the MP unit had their first tangible lead.

CHAPTER SIXTEEN

FITZHUGH WAS NOT LOOKING FORWARD TO HIS UPCOMING meeting about his team's findings—or lack thereof, as the last few soul-sucking, tedious gatherings had proven to be. Though no one could expect his men to have found out much information in such a short time, especially on an active battlefield, that wasn't the way the army worked. In the army, orders were issued and subordinates followed them. Any deviation, no matter for what reason, was frowned upon. Command didn't care why something wasn't done, they just cared that it wasn't done, and who was at fault.

No guesses who would be in Haig's gunsights.

Any excuse to postpone the meeting would have been warmly greeted, and when that excuse marched through his door and saluted, Fitzhugh could have hugged him.

'Sir, I seem to be onto something,' McGavin said, lowering his hand from his temple.

'And what is it you think you have, Corporal?'

'Sir, I thought it wise to spend some time in the censor office,' the Englishman reported, then added quickly, as though an afterthought, 'Before I forget, you might want to expect a reference check on the order you issued to Lieutenant Colonel William Pike to the Canadian censor office.'

'The order *I* issued?'

'Yes, sir. Your sergeant will have the details.'

'I see. So, you were saying?'

'About the censor job? Right. I had the idea that if anyone wrote anything about the crucifixion, the lads there surely had read it, or at least may have knowledge of any units acting suspiciously over the act.'

'But the censors are banned from passing on information they read to anyone outside their direct chain of command without an express order,' the intelligence officer said sternly.

McGavin raised one eyebrow, only to catch the humorous twinkle in the man's eyes. 'Good one, Captain.'

'So, what do you have for me?'

'Well, sir, I think I have the name of the soldier.'

CHAPTER SEVENTEEN

RANK DID INDEED HAVE ITS PRIVILEGES.

Generally, this only came in the form of better food, quarters, longer furlough, as well as slightly more information on what was going on than the lower ranks were privy to. The latter was only partially true these days, though; with the way the trenches worked, soldiers on the ground often received news before their officers were relayed the official information from High Command.

This time, however, Fitzhugh was in possession of information that was strenuously being withheld from the men fighting the war. He watched as McGavin retreated from his office with orders to return to the censor room and continue his investigation. Though he was still to search for information on the crucified soldier, he was now part of the far larger investigation the intelligence officer had been tasked with. Fitzhugh had been ordered to look for the scourge of all armies ... a hidden traitor.

For months, the Germans had been too well-informed on the Allied plans in certain sectors of the front. Of course, this could be due to an especially intelligent officer or a well-placed observation post obtaining and correctly interpreting the information they had gathered, but if the German army was anything like the Allies, that was beyond their capability. No commander could work as effectively as certain units of the German army were proving to be without some sort of help.

Commanders often received the sort of information that could make their unit far more effective, but almost always doubted its accuracy and discarded it. So, for an army to act on the kind of intelligence the Germans had obviously been receiving, it could mean only one thing: there was a well-positioned spy passing on information.

That the German troops who seemed most organised in defending themselves from Allied attacks just happened to be directly opposite the Canadian Highlanders could be a coincidence … but that was highly unlikely.

Something funny was going on along the Canadian lines. For one thing, their ranks were full of officers from other armies, like Captain Darcy. Certainly, the Highlanders were a brave bunch, and the attrition rate for their officers was high as they often led from the front, but there were easily enough Canadian officers to cover these positions.

High Command was aware there might be a spy and had tasked Army Intelligence and the British Secret Service Bureau to investigate. As a field agent, Fitzhugh had been assigned to search for such traitors. The fact that his investigation had now collided with his orders to look for the crucified soldier just made his life a lot more complicated.

It only took one informant listening in to one unwise conversation to reveal an entire plan to a smart agent, so until now he'd kept his main mission to himself and used the investigation into the crucified soldier as a smokescreen.

But this was all about to change because McGavin had come up with a seriously great idea. Fitzhugh decided to include the former Scotland Yard detective in the secret part of his mission. He expanded the parameters of the search the corporal was undertaking in the censor office. McGavin was to look for letters with highly unusual phrasing, as this could indicate a hidden code being used; and he was specifically to keep an eye out for any mail from an officer heading to a number of locations, such as the Peacock Hotel in Leith and its proprietor, Mrs Reimers.

Fitzhugh had not wanted to explain to McGavin why he was being asked to look for these things. In the volatile world of the trenches, even a hint of an officer passing on vital information, and possibly getting his own men killed, was something best kept out of the hands of the foot soldier. He should have remembered the man was from Scotland Yard though, as the corporal caught on immediately.

Thinking about it, Fitzhugh realised this wasn't such a bad thing. He was working near the front, where anything could happen, and if he was ever unlucky enough to be wounded or killed, at least there was now someone else here who knew enough to continue the search.

CHAPTER EIGHTEEN

LIKE A DISTANT SUMMER THUNDERSTORM, THE LIGHTS AND sounds of battle over the horizon masked the sloshing and sucking noise of soldiers moving through a countryside torn into little more than muddy fields.

Faces and weapons had been blackened with charcoal and smoke, yet anyone watching carefully enough would have recognised the men as German, thanks to the Pickelhaube helmets they wore. A mixture of steel and leather, these had small, pointy spears on top to help distinguish German soldiers from the enemy in the confusing battles of the Western Front.

This Strafbattalion had been ordered to investigate no man's land for indications of enemy activity, specifically any preparations for an attack. The signs they were looking for included such things as cut barbed wire, or the placement of field markers for the advancing troops to use as guides to navigate the impossibly confusing, shell-cratered landscape.

Unusually, this seven-man squad was made up from the disposable prison battalion, and the men had been ordered to follow a very specific route—one that apparently bypassed a new minefield their army had placed along a small hill. This rise granted cover to advancing enemy soldiers from the murderous fire of their own Maxim machine guns.

With only the light from a moonless sky to help them, the men duck-walked through the mud and crept past a ruined truck that had become a haven for hundreds of rats, along with flies in the thousands. Advancing soldiers new to the battlefield often sought shelter beside the ruined vehicle as it gave the illusion of cover, but alas it was just that—an illusion. Enemy snipers had long pinpointed the truck for this very reason, and anyone moving near it during the day was going to be shot within feet of its supposed protection. The vermin were legion around the vehicle, assured they were always going to be supplied a meal.

Giving the ruined vehicle an especially wide berth, the squad never noticed the Lewis gun, nor the half-dozen .303 rifles tracking their movement from within the darkest shadow by the hill. With unnatural patience, the weapons tracked the creeping figures, waiting for the Germans to fully expose themselves.

The lead German soldier held up his hand, and his squad slowly lowered themselves, hiding their silhouettes from any unseen danger. Unfortunately, on this night, the enemy already knew exactly where they were.

After a painfully long period, the scout gave the all-clear, and the stationary soldiers rose and moved forward again. Immediately, the ambush was sprung by a long, deadly burst of machine-gun fire. The gunner swung the weapon from the rearmost soldier to the leading scout, and by the time the round cylinder magazine on top of the Lewis gun was half empty, each figure had been struck by at least one bullet. This fire was backed by those soldiers with rifles, ensuring the ambush was a complete success.

It took less than a minute for the fight to be over, and the Highlanders crept out of their hiding spot and ran up to the dead and dying Germans. Practiced fingers snaked through pockets in the dark, retrieving anything of value from the enemy. Only secondarily did the Canadians search for papers and letters for the information officers to investigate.

Corpses pilfered, an almost unheard whistle recalled the men to begin the long trek back toward their lines. The last shadow, a soldier who had been covering the Highlanders in case they had missed anyone or were themselves ambushed, detached himself from his hiding spot to follow the rest. Almost invisibly, he dropped and grabbed a foot of one dead German and deposited a small note between boot and leg. He made sure to force it deep, so that it could not accidently fall out or be easily found, then completed the pre-arranged signal by crossing the dead soldier's arms over his chest. The Highlander then stood and followed his squad back to their lines.

Once the Canadians had cleared the field, a second squad of Germans moved into the area around the truck. They inspected all the bodies of their comrades, and when they found the one with his arms crossed, they searched the man's boots and retrieved the deposited note. They then silently departed before they too fell afoul of some unseen danger.

Before they had even walked a dozen feet, the last soldier in the line recognised the sound of rats running across the field to feed.

CHAPTER NINETEEN

WHEN ASH LEFT THE MORNING MEETING AND LEARNED ABOUT McGavin's plan, he suddenly figured out exactly who he wanted to talk to. The problem was he now had to get to him.

The confusing landscape of the Western Front had created opportunities for those brazen enough to grasp them. Most of the Commonwealth units were formed in small country towns and villages across the empire, and these had entered the war containing mates, brothers, entire school classes, and even in a few instances, fathers and sons. After just a few short months in this meat-grinder of a war, the manhood of so many of these communities had been butchered, so it was impossible for replacement soldiers to come from these same regions. This meant provincial units that had started in the war with locals soon became a conglomerate of accents and faces. Yorkshire men now fought alongside troops from Liverpool, Victorians stood by Tasmanians, and men from the Yukon lived and died next to troopers from Newfoundland.

This mass of humanity, moving, dying, being captured, wounded, or buried without a trace, all meant an enterprising man could go missing without much effort. He would then be free to do just about whatever he wanted as long as he stayed out of view of the authorities.

One of these men had risen to become the kingpin of crime in the trenches. No one was sure of his real name, but everyone had heard of the Great King Rat. Though he wore the uniform of an English soldier, his accent was more Scottish—though even that was cut with something else, suggesting he had only been born in Scotland and had spent some time in the much larger world. Was he Australian? Canadian? A New Zealander? Was he South African, Rhodesian or, rarer, a white soldier in the Indian regiments? No one who'd met him could tell, and those who had met him likely didn't care that much—to get close to the Great King Rat meant you were part of his growing empire, you belonged to the trench mafia.

The name had originated with a New York soldier who, like many adventurous Americans, had joined the Canadian army to fight, and he had baptised the black market that sprung up along the front after criminals from his home town. The trench mafia were a group of men who'd abandoned their military service for something far more profitable: the goods they could buy and sell on the black market.

Food and souvenirs such as weapons and uniforms were their obvious trade, but the organisation was capable of finding almost anything for the right price. Women were no problem, and the mafia ran one of the most profitable brothels anywhere in the war. It was this business that allowed the Great King Rat to remain autonomous; he created an officer-only house of ill repute, then immediately blackmailed the officers who enjoyed themselves within its walls.

The trench mafia soon had a network of spies and informants that put the Germans to shame. These men ensured the Great King Rat and his men were left alone, and that any attempts to enter the trenches they used as their headquarters were diverted, or the mafia were forewarned in time to make themselves scarce.

With time and enough military power to employ engineers, the mafia had even dug their own system of tunnels and subterranean warehouses, created to hide their activities from prying eyes. With an ingenious play of trickery and diversion, the entrances to these tunnels could be quickly hidden or, in case of a German attack, key structural supports knocked down to cause a collapse and bury their contents, to of course be dug back out at some later date.

The Australian MP moved into the lost trenches now ruled by the pirate kingdom of the Great King Rat. Beside him walked Tommy Kirkland, the man considered the greatest of the Australian black marketers. Kirkland and the Rat were not exactly friends—their relationship was more one of mutual ignorance; the Rat didn't bother with the small-time efforts of Kirkland, who repaid the compliment by staying out of the markets the trench mafia controlled.

Though Ash had no real time for Kirkland and would be happy if the man disappeared forever, he was aware his only chance of getting into the underground world of the black market was through the scavenger.

Kirkland was at first uninterested in helping out someone wearing the hated MP armband, but with a little persuasion, along with a promise Ash would make it his mission to end the black marketeer's career, the scavenger had come around. Ash also had to promise not to start a turf war by bringing any heat down on the Great King Rat, as Kirkland was sure neither would survive that.

The entrance to the lost trenches looked like so many disused and abandoned breastworks. Giant rifts in its wall had been torn apart by shell fire and eroded by weather. A single grizzly hand protruded from a mudslide, the body buried too deep to excavate without pulling down half the trench wall, so the appendage was just left, hanging out in the open, subliminally forcing any onlooker to turn away.

There was no reason for anyone to head down that ruined path, and even if they did, Kirkland pointed out the hidden mafia guards posted around the entrance. One was a soldier with bandages covering most of his face and hands, and when Ash thought about it later, he realised the man didn't seem to be in any pain whatsoever. Wounded soldiers moaned and squirmed uncontrollably, yet this man just sat with his back against a duckboard, seemingly awaiting a medic who would never come.

'Just how many men does the Rat control?' Ash asked as they stepped into the trench.

Kirkland gave a little nod to the wounded man, then answered, 'I'm not sure. Locally, he likely has about twenty guys around him, but in all, scattered amongst the armies in the region and the rear lines, maybe a few hundred.'

'And no one ever comes looking for them?'

'Not really. Either they've been reported dead, missing, or in the case of a specialist the King really wants to employ, their officers have been blackmailed or bribed into forgetting about them.'

'What do you mean by specialists?'

'Well, one guy I know about speaks fluent German and French, which as you can imagine is a boon to someone in the Rat's line of business.'

'Why would he need someone who speaks German?'

'Sometimes a prisoner comes their way, maybe a deserter from across the lines. The Rat takes him in and turns him. He actually has a few men now working in the German lines, and that's where his real profit comes from. German officers will pay a lot for a decent bottle of schnapps, you know, and the Rat's contacts are more than happy to sell it to them.'

'You're telling me he's conspiring with the enemy?' Ash

couldn't believe the words coming out of his mouth, even as he spoke them. The MP band was coming off the second he was done with his mission.

'Not really conspiring. More exchanging, or profiteering if you want it to sound sinister. Its only goods they deal with here, and they only deal with soldiers on the other side, not the officers. I'm pretty sure any German officer would shoot himself, and then everyone else, if he discovered his naughty bottle of schnapps had come from our side of the lines.'

'Still, I'm not comfortable dealing with someone who is supporting the enemy in any way.'

'Dealing? Look, you ain't dealing with shit. The King calls the shots here. We'll be lucky if we leave with our shirts, if we leave at all, so get it outta your head that you have a lot of choices here. You want information, you're gonna have to deal with some down and dirty folk, and none come downer and dirtier than the trench mafia ...'

'Right,' Ash said resolutely.

'Oh, and one last thing,' Kirkland whispered over his shoulder as armed soldiers seemed to melt out of the very walls about them, weapons pointed at the two Australians. 'Don't call them mafia, and don't call the Rat "Rat" ... got it?'

Tied together, with hessian bags over their heads, both men were yanked, tugged, and pulled through a twisting set of trenches, a route clearly designed to hide the exact location of the Great King Rat's current headquarters. After what seemed like hours, but more likely was mere minutes, the bags were suddenly yanked off their heads, and both men stood blinking in a pool of bright light.

'Really, King, is this necessary? I thought we were friends,' Kirkland said, clutching at his sore wrists from where the bindings had just been removed.

'It's because I know you that such practices are necessary,

Kirkland, so don't play the innocent bystander. Get on with why you're here.'

'Well, King,' Kirkland said, trying to shade his eyes from the blinding lights. 'I'm not actually here for myself. I've brought you a visitor.'

'How sweet. Throw them out!' the disembodied voice ordered. Instantly the shadows that had been hugging the small room's walls moved forward with hands full of rope.

'I asked Kirkland to find you. My name's Ash and I'd like to have a private word with you, King.'

'Ash ... as in the Ash who cut down that soldier on the wheel, then decked the pompous British prick of an officer who put him there?'

'The one and the same,' Kirkland said.

In some unseen movement, the guards resumed propping up the wall with their backs.

'Well, this is interesting. I owe you some thanks, Sergeant— the man was actually one of mine, and his punishment meant I was about to do something necessary, but likely stupid.'

'Stupid?' Ash asked.

'I was going to either rescue or kill him. I trust my men, but four months crucified like that would make the hardest man talk, I'm sure.'

'Would you go so far as to agree that you owe me a favour then?' the MP asked brazenly.

Kirkland tried to take a step away from Ash. No one wanted to be in debt to the Great King Rat, but only worse than being in his debt was having him owe you a favour. It meant the King took a special interest in your career, and that was never a healthy thing.

The dugout fell quiet as the marketeer pondered the question. In the semi-darkness, with the only light the one shining in his eyes, Ash swore he could hear everyone in the room thinking. The tension ratcheted up and up, until with a heavy breath the Great King Rat finally spoke.

'It would seem I may well owe you a favour, but I will need some information before making my decision. Why should I be dealing with an MP?'

Ash felt he was now on safer ground. This was one question he knew he could answer, and hopefully satisfactorily enough to engage the services of the Great King Rat.

'I'm only an MP for the short term, and I'm not actually attached to the provosts at all. I'm part of a small international team investigating the rumours of the crucified soldier, and that's what I'm hoping you can help me with.'

'And nothing else?' the Great King Rat asked.

'And nothing else that could affect you or your business as far as I'm aware.'

'Everything affects my business, but I understand your point.'

Somebody entered the room and moved up to the marketeer. Both Australians could hear the men whispering, and then, with a click, the light went out and a small square of sunlight opened at the far end.

The Great King Rat stepped into the light. 'Follow me.'

CHAPTER TWENTY

LIEUTENANT COLONEL JEAN DANJOU WATCHED THE AUSTRALIAN MP and another Australian trooper he did not recognise enter an older, crumbling trench and seem to disappear. From his own blind corner, he quickly decided that the 'wounded' man sitting along the trench wall was a guard for the entrance, and came to the conclusion that no one here was up to any good. With a single flick of his hand and a finger pointed like a gun, five brawny gendarmes entered the trench and jumped the supposedly wounded soldier.

After a few hard blows, the soldier was in need of a real doctor.

Danjou stepped quickly into the false trench, followed by his guard. Though the ruined trench was deserted, it was still easy for the Frenchmen to follow where the Australians had gone thanks to the footprints on the muddy floor. He had been astute enough to work out the pattern on the sole of a right boot— which had an odd little nick out of it—was perhaps where the Australian had stood on something sharp like barbed wire. This mark made his footprint as individual as a fingerprint, so the Frenchman could follow him as long as there was wet soil to carry the boot mark. Luckily no duckboards had been placed here or, if they had been, had long since been torn up to fuel cooking fires or shore up tunnel excavations.

The gendarmes moved silently through the trench, though never fast enough to blindly step around a corner or walk past an off-shooting dugout without first inspecting it. Most carried nasty looking truncheons, while two of the Frenchmen had rifles slung on their backs, just in case they came across trouble a foot-and-a-half piece of weighted oak couldn't overcome.

* * *

Someone from the trench mafia once more yanked the bags from their heads.

'You were followed,' one of the Great King Rat's men said as everyone shuffled down yet another trench.

'We were not,' Kirkland argued, with a certain amount of pride.

'You most certainly were. There are five French gendarmes on your tail. They took out our guard and marched right into the trench behind you. We have maybe a three-minute lead on them.'

'You're going to let them follow us?' Ash asked.

'Certainly not. We are going to let them follow you, right into a little surprise we have for stickybeaks like these idiots.'

'I don't like the sound of that,' Kirkland noted under his breath. It was never a good idea to come down heavy on a cop, even a French one.

* * *

Though the path was clearly designed to disorientate, by simply following the marked boot print, Danjou kept on their trail. Soon the path entered a much larger and better maintained trench section, located well behind the front lines. The flatness of this part of the countryside hid these trenches far better than any shrub or forest could have, as no one would be unwise enough to stick a head over the top to see what else was in the region.

In his head, the Frenchman made a list of things to do once he returned to his own headquarters, and one of those was to find out why such a large section of trenches near the frontline had been abandoned.

The footprints moved toward a small tunnel entrance, and Danjou gestured to his troopers to prepare to storm the entrance. The first guard swung open the canvas flap to the small shelter and leaped to the side. The second charged through the opening and moved to the right, while the third followed and moved to the left. Both men were counting on the sudden light through the door to temporarily blind anyone inside, but they found no one awaiting them.

After they called the all-clear, Danjou followed them through, stopping briefly to allow his eyes to adjust to the dark room. About fifteen feet long and eight feet wide, this proved to be an impressive little hole for an abandoned part of the trench system. Here and there were slats shoring up the walls and roof, made from what he assumed were the missing duckboards from the trench floor. One of these boards even had a large piece of cord tied around it, something of a luxury along the frontlines —starving men had been known to boil and eat rope. As if on cue, the piece of hemp suddenly drew taught, then went slack again as though someone was pulling it.

Realising what was happening, Danjou screamed a warning, but before anyone could move, the rope went taught with a loud twang and ripped the wooden slat away. With a roar, the entire alcove collapsed as the single support beam buttressing the roof was pulled away, burying the Frenchmen alive.

* * *

In a world where explosives that could leave craters the size of football fields went off on almost a daily basis, the tremor and noise from the collapse of a small tunnel went by unnoticed.

The trench mafia ran their guests through a series of short channels to a second hideout. Though the entire system was ingeniously designed, Ash knew its time was almost up, and the Great King Rat and his merry band of misfits would soon be caught. A recent innovation to the battlefield was now buzzing overhead, and the photos that the Royal Air Corp and the French Air Force had taken of the battlefield would quickly reveal the truth of this trench system.

Someone at HQ would understand there was a large section of the frontlines left relatively undefended, and no amount of corruption was going to stop soldiers from occupying these lines and ending the reign of the Great King Rat once and for all.

Such a move could be months away though, and right now Ash needed the connections and information these marketeers possessed.

'Through here,' said one soldier with a thick Australian accent. Before the MP could turn and glimpse the man's face, a big hand pushed him square between the shoulder blades and he stumbled into yet another dugout. This one smelled musty with disuse.

Once inside, lugers and bayonets were drawn, all pointed at the two Australian captives.

'Give us one reason we shouldn't gut you right now?' asked one of the men holding the weapons.

'Because I'm Military Intelligence, you idiots. If you think one of us is going to be murdered with no investigation, you got another thing coming.'

'Put the weapons down, lads. These boys didn't have nothing

to do with those Froggy coppers. It was just one of them coincidences,' the Great King Rat said, continuing to hug the shadows to hide his features.

'Actually, I'd say the guy *was* following us, we just didn't have anything to do with it,' Ash admitted, pushing away one of the blades pointed at his chest. 'The French consider this murder to be theirs to investigate since we are all on sacred French soil. The gendarmes back there were likely just covering all the bases by having everyone in my team followed, so I do owe you an apology for that. I never thought they'd go that far.'

'Little harm was done,' one of the soldiers said with a smirk. Ash felt even more concern for the fate of the gendarmes.

'What is it I can help you with exactly?' King Rat asked.

'I'd like any information you have about the crucifixion, preferably the name of the soldier, or at least the name of someone who actually saw him out there.'

'Gee, I dunno about this, boss,' someone said from the rear of the dark room. Ash had no clue what sort of accent he had. 'You start dealing with MPs, you never know where that's gonna lead. They say we ain't of interest today, but tomorrow ... well, there's always a tomorrow.'

'Very true, but I think we're going to help our friends here.'

'Hey, as important as this is, I was just hired to make introductions,' Kirkland said, throwing his hands up to show they were empty.

'As I was saying,' King Rat continued, 'I think we're going to help these gentlemen. Someone murdered one of our boys out there, and strung them up like a piece of meat. Nobody deserves to go out that way.'

The shadowy figure then turned toward Ash. 'I don't have any personal knowledge of the crucifixion, but leave it with me and I'll find out what I can.'

'How do we get back in contact with you?' Ash asked.

Both Australians were suddenly jumped and hogtied once more, with the hessian bags slipped back over their heads.

'Don't worry too much about that. We'll find you when we need to,' King Rat said.

Both men remained tied up on the floor as the marketeers bustled about. Soon everything grew quiet, and after ten minutes the Australians began to squirm about. They discovered the ropes hadn't been tied too tightly and soon had their hands free.

They stepped out of the small hole, back into the trenches and was greeted with a sky filled with the bright reds, deep purples, and dark blue of a French sunrise.

'How fucking long were we in there?' Kirkland asked, 'and where the hell are we?'

CHAPTER TWENTY-ONE

ONE BY ONE THE SURVIVING MEN OF THE STRAFBATTALION slipped back into the German trenches after their night-time patrol. They had timed their arrival perfectly, returning just as the sky above began to lighten with the coming dawn, making their movement hard to spot from the Allied lines.

All the goods the troopers had brought back with them went into backpacks, while the papers and letters were dumped into a satchel and sent to the forward post office of the Abteilung IIIb.

Though the German office of Military Intelligence had achieved little success in its overseas operations, their work along the trenches of France and Belgium had so far been exemplary. Working with well-trained units, they had managed to create an effective web of information gathering cells along the western and eastern fronts, and helped blunt numerous local moves of the enemy.

Hauptmann Hans von Papen had hoped for a more glamorous role overseas, maybe helping to sabotage war efforts in England or India. Instead, he had been sent to a forward post and charged with controlling and collecting information from the French line.

Most of the time this meant tediously reading through the unsent letters dead or captured enemy soldiers had written to their loved ones, along with any mail they had received. The hope was some important piece of information may have been missed by the military censors, and only an intelligence officer knew enough to recognise that rare nugget for what it was.

Flicking through the contents of this latest harvest of blood-stained correspondences, family photos, routine military orders, and other worthless paraphernalia his soldiers returned with from their patrols, one note caught his eye. It was a folded picture postcard that had been carefully smoothed out and placed inside an envelope marked 'urgent'. Sliding the postcard out, von Papen noticed one corner had been clipped away, a flaw that indicated this was something more than a simple message home.

Collecting a small glass brown bottle, von Papen dipped a clean paintbrush into the liquid it contained and painted a single, clear wet streak diagonally across the reverse side of the postcard. Instantly, previously hidden text appeared.

He dipped the brush again and this time painted the entire card. Following the swipes of the brush, words, numbers, and a small diagram appeared. Working quickly, the intelligence officer transcribed the note before the liquid evaporated and its message disappeared again.

Job done, he signed the copy, placed it with his daily report, and forwarded it up the chain of command. If nothing else, the German army was always efficient with their paperwork, even the secret kind.

CHAPTER TWENTY-TWO

WOLK STOOD BY THE DOOR, NOT EXACTLY AT ATTENTION, BUT not slouching either. The officers in command of the Highlanders gathered around a large map, poring over the orders they had just received. HQ was demanding a small diversionary push by the Canadians to relieve an attack the French had planned further south.

Runners were despatched to all junior officers, ordering them to prepare their men for the upcoming action the next morning. Wolk found himself sent by a winking Darcy to the furthest perimeter of the Canadian zone, carrying orders for a squad that didn't seem to exist.

Clearly the English officer was hinting at something the MP might want to investigate. As night fell and he passed through the Canadian lines, Wolk's suspicions grew even greater when he requested directions. Everyone he asked claimed to have never heard of the 14th. Finally, he was pointed to an outer trench marker, where a corporal and two seedy-looking privates were laying up inside a large perimeter foxhole supporting two entrenched machine gun positions.

'Gentlemen, could you point me toward the 14th?'

The corporal leaning against the trench wall grinned. 'Certainly, all you have to do is hop over the top here, go about two hundred feet toward the Hun, call out nice and loud, and I'm sure you'll find the 14th scattered all about you.'

'They're dead?'

'Hell no, boyo,' the corporal said with a thick Irish accent. 'They're manning the forward listening post.' Then, as if to a deaf friend, the soldier jokingly threw a thumb at the MP in disguise as a runner. '"Dead", he says.'

'Is there a safe way to get to them?' Wolk asked, ignoring the joke at his expense.

'Sure is. We haven't seen much action around here for days and not had a sniper in these parts for maybe two weeks. Just keep your arse and head down as you go and you'll be all right.'

The Mountie followed the man's gesture toward the German lines. Of course, he could not see anything from his position, but all he could think was that it looked far too dark in that direction to be natural. Wary, he picked up a nearby trench glass leaning against the wall and lifted the box up to his eyes.

The makeshift periscope, with opposite facing mirrors set at a 45-degree angle at the top and bottom of the purpose-made wooden box, allowed one to peek over the top of the trench wall without exposure. Wolk peered into no man's land, taking a slow scan of the entire region in front of the trench. Nowhere could he see signs of the German lines, though he did spot what he assumed was the Canadian forward listening post manned by the 14th. He could even see one of their soldiers lying behind a jumbled pile of sandbags, listening in to the German lines with an audio trumpet.

The style of post was unusual to others the Mountie had seen, which were usually constructed of a deep slit trench. These were often not so much to listen for movement in the enemy trenches but for tunnelling deep underground.

'Off ya' go, sweetheart,' one of the soldiers jibed.

'Yeah, watcha waiting fer, an invitashun?' the other encouraged.

'Ignore the lads, it's perfectly safe,' the corporal told him with a slap on the shoulder. 'Just creep over, be quiet, and you'll be fine.'

Wolk gave no man's land one last look through the periscope. Nothing had changed. 'Well, I guess there's nothing for it. Wish me luck.' And with that he slid over the trench top and began crawling his way forward.

He was relieved to find that, unlike most of the front at the time, the ground here was relatively hard—a sure sign that very little action had occurred in the area recently. With distant gunfire flashes occasionally illuminating the ground about him, the MP began to inch forward.

CHAPTER TWENTY-THREE

HAVING EVENTUALLY FOUND HIS WAY BACK FROM THE MEETING with the Great King Rat, Ash entered Fitzhugh's office to find himself the only one there. An MP sergeant—not the burly monster that was always yapping at the heels of their commander—leaned in and explained that the captain was out and wouldn't be back until at least the following day. Fitzhugh had left orders that the MPs should keep at it and, if need be, send messages to the office. He would get them eventually.

Needing a sounding board to figure out his next move, the Australian marched over to the censor office and pulled McGavin away from his desk.

To keep the Englishman's identity a secret, and perhaps have more than a little mischievous fun, Ash charged into the office and arrested him in front of everyone. When McGavin asked why he was being detained, Ash pointed out that men who slept with generals' daughters should expect this kind of treatment. Not only would this give everyone something to talk about once they left, it would give McGavin a certain amount of popularity amongst the other censors and may even help them open up to him.

Once both men were outside and out of view, Ash let go of his prisoner's arm and allowed McGavin to compose himself.

'So, what have you got that's so important?'

'I made contact with the Great King Rat and his troop of bastards. If anyone is going to know anything about a murdered soldier, I figured it would be them.'

'I thought that guy was a myth? How did you find him?'

'I have contacts,' Ash boasted, then at the sceptical look from McGavin admitted, 'All right, I have *a* contact, but it proved enough to get me in the door. I'm also a famous rogue soldier, don't you know? The beater of scoundrel officers, so that certainly helped.'

'Learn anything?' the Englishman asked, rotating his shoulder to make sure the Australian had not broken anything vital.

'Not a thing, though I did get a promise he would look into the matter.'

'That's disappointing. You trust him?'

'Not really, though I think he will come through if he uncovers something that doesn't affect business.'

'How so?'

'He seemed genuinely angry about how the man died.'

'If he died,' McGavin reminded him.

'Yeah, yeah, "if" he died. That crap is getting old.'

'Actually, I do have news on that front, but I might wait for Fitzhugh to pass on what I found. Meanwhile, nothing else?'

'Well, the meeting didn't go for long. We were raided,' the Australian said, intrigued at the mysterious comment.

'Raided? MPs?' A light went on in the Englishman's head. 'Oh, the French.'

'One and the same. But I think the little Froggy prick is out of the way for a while. I'm not sure what happened, but Rat's men mentioned they had taken care of him.'

McGavin ran a phantom knife across his throat and stuck his tongue out.

'I don't think so. Killing a copper isn't something Rat and his blokes would do. They'd likely bribe him, or maybe just beat the shit out of him, his wife, and kids—but no, I don't think they killed him.'

'So, if we bump into him again, he's not likely going to be nice.'

'He's French, so was he ever nice?'

Smiling at the joke, McGavin asked, 'So what's next?'

'Well, I figure we need to really start looking into this Canadian outfit, and as our captain has gone walkabout, I'll wander off and try to find our Mountie … unless you need help?'

'Right now, I'm sorting through letters trying to find a few things Fitzhugh put me onto. So far, no luck, but if you want to pull up a desk and help, I'm sure we can come up with some sort of excuse.'

Trying not at all to hide the horror of sitting at a desk reading other people's mail, Ash backed away from the Englishman, his hands raised in mock surrender. 'As fun as that sounds, I may just go find that Mountie and see if he needs a hand.'

'I figured as much,' McGavin said, mussing up his hair and pulling his jacket half off one shoulder. At the quizzical look the Australian gave him, he explained, 'I need a reason why you let me go. Just gonna say you beat me and left.'

'Good thinking.' Ash punched one fist into the other. 'Want me to help make it a little more real?'

CHAPTER TWENTY-FOUR

THE OFFICE FLOOR TO THE GENDARMERIE NATIONALE SHONE IN the afternoon sunlight. Freshly mopped and kept free of clutter, this care helped impose the belief that, although France was under siege, the country was still maintaining a level of dignity and hoped the example would help the rest of her allies do the same.

Lieutenant Colonel Danjou stormed through the front doors, resembling nothing less than some medieval bog monster. Mud and debris clung to his uniform and hair, with only his eyes, blazing white hot with fury, shining out of the morass to prove there was indeed a man under that mess.

Drying dirt flaked off him with every footstep and went bouncing and sliding across the marble floor. Soldiers either scuttled out of the creature's way to keep their own immaculate uniforms clean, or watched open-mouthed as the mass lurched past, moving deeper into the building.

Muttering curses to itself, the bog-beast staggered past the numerous secretaries and NCOs that had been positioned there to stop just such unheralded incursions into the offices of their commanders. No one knew what to do, so most just watched

Danjou as he walked directly into his superior's office and snapped off a salute, which flung more mud about the room and a small grass clod onto the desk between them.

Général de Brigade Anthoine Guillaumat was seated behind the desk, and the old soldier didn't bat an eye as the bipedal garden before him sat and, with a sigh, slumped back in the chair, exhausted.

'Lieutenant Colonel Danjou, I presume?'

'How could you tell, sir?'

'Just a guess. So how can I help you? Perhaps a glass of water?'

'I'm fine for now.'

'Lieutenant Colonel, you seem to have, how shall I say this, got something on your uniform,' Guillaumat remarked with a sympathetic smile. He then leaned down from his chair, collected his wastepaper basket from the floor and, with two fingers, picked up the tiny patch of the Somme from his table and dropped it into the receptacle.

As Danjou shrugged his shoulders, this only threw more dirt about the room, and angry as he was, any sympathy the man before him might have would quickly dissipate if he continued soiling the office. Some sense finally took grip and the gendarme stopped moving and stated, 'They tried to kill me, sir.'

That got a reaction, if one could call the raising of a single eyebrow a reaction.

'Not just me either. I had three of our men along, and they tried to kill us all.'

'And that explains your current state?'

'Yes, sir. I followed the Australian into some suspicious looking trenches, which I need to also make a report about.'

When the Général de Brigade waved that fact aside as though a bothersome fly, Danjou took that as a suggestion to stay on point.

'We followed close behind when he entered a large dugout,

yet when we pursued and found the room empty, they collapsed the entire structure on us.'

'Deliberately?'

'Sir, they waited until we were inside and then yanked the support beam holding up the roof.'

'The Australian MP did this?'

'I'm certain it must have been him … I mean, we were following him and never saw anyone else, well, except the wounded soldier.'

'Wounded soldier?' Guillaumat asked, confused.

'Yes, sir. The trench I mentioned had a guard posted, disguised as a wounded soldier. We took care of him and chased after the Australian.'

'You "took care" of this wounded soldier? You mean you physically assaulted him?' the Général de Brigade asked, leaning forward dangerously. 'And where did this occur?'

'He wasn't really wounded, sir,' Danjou added, realising the ground beneath him had just shifted. 'We could tell.'

'By carefully examining his wounds, I take it?'

'Well, not really.'

'By taking the advice of a medical officer?'

'No, sir.' Danjou grimaced.

'I see,' Guillaumat said, taking notes on a form before him. 'So how did you determine this wounded soldier was indeed faking?'

'He looked suspicious,' Danjou said, realising as he said it that this was entirely the wrong thing to say.

The Général de Brigade didn't reply and continued writing.

'I think we are getting off point, sir,' Danjou suggested, trying desperately to get onto any point that didn't make him look like an idiot who'd just beaten up an invalid. 'Sir, what of the attempted murder?'

'Of the wounded soldier?' Guillaumat asked pointedly.

'No, sir,' Danjou squeaked.

'You're telling me you don't care about this wounded man?'

'No, sir. I mean, of course, sir. Wait—he wasn't a wounded man, sir. He was a posted guard for whatever was going on down in that trench.'

'The trench where you were almost killed?'

'Yes, sir.'

'By someone you never saw?'

'Well, I wouldn't put it that way ...'

'I have heard the way you put it, Lieutenant ...'

'Lieutenant Colonel, sir ...'

'Well, that is still to be decided. I'm just telling you the way I hear it.'

'Sir?' Danjou pleaded, trying to get his thoughts back in order.

'Do you have anything else to report?'

Picking up on the clearly unveiled warning, the gendarme leaped to his feet. 'No, sir.' He then saluted, spun about, and retreated from the room.

'Oh, and Lieutenant?'

'Yes, sir?' the junior officer said, noting his demotion yet again.

'Pick that up, will you?' The Général de Brigade indicated to the dirt left in the chair and across the floor.

Danjou dropped to his knees and began anxiously cleaning.

CHAPTER TWENTY-FIVE

FOUR MONTHS EARLIER

WITH THE BRIGHT MORNING SUN GLITTERING ACROSS THE unusually calm Baltic Sea, Lieutenant Spindler made his way to the bridge of the guard ship. Positive he was in trouble for some infraction, and racking his brain to figure out what that might be so he could prepare an excuse, the German sailor was pleasantly surprised when the captain read out his new orders. Because he could speak some English and had experience sailing the Atlantic, he was being offered his own command. This was no warship; that was an impossible dream for a junior officer on a vessel classified only a little higher than a fishing trawler with a canon stuck on the bow. He was now the commander of a small merchant ship called the SS *Castro*.

Ordered to select another officer and a dozen men who could speak some English, Lieutenant Spindler and his crew reported to their new charge. At 220 feet, the *Castro* had been a workhorse for the Wilson Line shipping company of England before the war, but had been captured by the Imperial German navy early during the conflict as she passed through the nearly 100km Kiel Canal that cut though Germany, linking the North Sea with the Baltic.

All but useless to the navy, the captured *Castro* sat moth-balled until the High Command had come up with a plan to create a new front for the war and hopefully divert some of the allied army away from the French trenches.

Spindler's handpicked crew helped rechristen the merchantman as a Norwegian vessel, the *SMS Libau*, and Germany's newest captain then met his mysterious passenger and the reason for this ruse.

Both men began discussing the plan, and what the passenger explained brought dreams of promotion to the young German officer. Here was the chance he'd been waiting for his entire career: an opportunity to make his mark on world events and possibly help Germany win the war.

If they succeeded, fame and glory awaited everyone involved in this glorious adventure.

CHAPTER TWENTY-SIX

McGavin scanned a letter from a soldier who clearly had left school, or *skool* as he would have spelled it, before crayons were put down and pencils picked up. Every third word was spelled phonetically, and even then it took several reads and actually saying the word aloud to understand what the writer was trying to say.

It was as he was attempting to sound out *konstanbularyly* that one junior censor, who had taken a real shine to the MP after his apparent 'arrest' for keeping with a general's daughter, brought him a letter.

'Thought you might find this interesting.'

Most of what the younger man had brought him so far was decidedly uninteresting, often full of sex descriptions, which, while amusing and helped break the monotony, were unhelpful.

This time, however, the young man had struck gold.

To Mrs Brand,

I am sorry to say that I am writing to you with terrible news about your brother. During an attack last Easter, your brother, a fine man who I was happy to call friend, was captured by the Germans and killed. Though there are many rumours about Charles's death, some of which I hope may never reach your ears, I feel it's my duty to report the grizzly news of his end. Though I nor anyone I know actually saw his death, we did discover his body afterward.

The Germans had crucified Charles to a barn door—and please believe me when I say our medical officer claims he was most likely already dead when they did this despicable act to his body. Though our world is one of daily horror, this act has disturbed many men who have seen more horror than any individual ever should. By telling you the truth of what happened to your dear brother, I hope this is just one small burden I will be able to remove from you, who may still question his death, and also from our men, who feel the guilt of holding on to the secret of his passing.

Sincerely

Lance Corporal William H Smike

14th Highlanders

The MP leaped from the table, clutching the letter and messing the hair of the young censor officer. 'Well done, lad. Very, very well done.'

Grabbing his coat, he ran out of the office, only to run back in and ask, 'Anyone know where the 14th Highlanders are stationed at the moment?'

CHAPTER TWENTY-SEVEN

HAVING SPENT THE LAST HOUR CRAWLING ACROSS THE battlefield, expecting at any time to have his arse shot off, Wolk's tension was high and he could hear little but the blood pumping through his ears. The idea that any noise he made would bring a terminal response from the Germans just feet away was making his imagination run wild. Every shape was an enemy taking aim, and every noise was someone approaching, ready to bayonet him to death.

This all got worse when the sun began to rise and he still had some distance to go. He was now dangerously exposed, so he slid down into a large shell hole, pulled a small mirror out of his jacket's breast pocket, and angled it in such a way he could see over the dirt lip and past where the listening post lay. It was bright and he squinted hard, allowing his eyes to adjust to the glare of the day. He could make out a faint line running just below the horizon, a tell-tale sign of a trench system.

He watched this line for a long time, and when he was certain there was no movement, he decided the three men back in the trench had been correct.

'Runner coming in,' he whispered, preparing to move the last few feet to the listening post. Keeping his silhouette as low as possible, Wolk pulled himself out of the hole and jinked back and forth to ensure no eagle-eyed sniper got a straight bead on him, expecting to be shot at any moment. With a sigh of relief, he dived into the foxhole that made up the forward listening post.

The space was cramped as it held the five-man squad from the 14th. But none of the men there cared about his intrusion—they were all dead. Looking back to the rear, the Mountie tried to get the attention of the three men he'd just left, only to see one of them taking careful aim with a rifle.

Wolk never heard the shot that hit him in the head.

CHAPTER TWENTY-EIGHT

CAPTAIN FITZHUGH STEPPED OFF THE PUFFING TRAIN, SERGEANT Andrews following close behind carrying both their bags. A row of horse-drawn cabs was waiting out the front of Edinburgh's train station and, once their luggage was safely stowed on the first vehicle, Fitzhugh barked at the driver, 'The Peacock Hotel, my good man.'

With a crack of a whip and a jolt, the horse stepped forward and the cab was away.

'Could I now please ask why we're in Scotland?' Andrews asked, continuing a long-time conversation.

'Of course, you can ask, Sergeant,' Fitzhugh answered, watching intently as Edinburgh slipped by outside. 'Did you know this is my first trip here?'

'You may have mentioned it once or seventy times on the boat over.'

'Did I? Sorry about that, my mind is a little preoccupied.'

'With the reason we suddenly dropped everything and came to Scotland?' Andrews prodded.

'Quiet right, quite right. I knew you would understand.'

'Understand what, sir?'

'Exactly,' the captain said, stroking his nose with a forefinger. 'Hush hush and all that.'

Giving up, Andrews mirrored Fitzhugh by staring out the other side of the cab as it clip-clopped along the ancient cobblestone street.

An hour later they arrived at a small stone building. The Peacock Hotel was built in the 1800s, a time when people were much shorter. Fitzhugh found himself ducking through the building's low front door. Behind him, the much shorter Andrews, despite once more struggling with the combined weight of both their bags, entered with little trouble.

Manning the counter inside was an older gentleman, who was anchoring the front desk from floating away with his sleeping head. Before Fitzhugh could stop him, Andrews gave the desk a thump with one booted foot.

Instantly the clerk was awake, and he eyed the captain standing before him with confusion. Fitzhugh hinted in the direction of his sergeant with a flick of his eyes and a raised eyebrow.

Understanding the message, the clerk gave the sergeant a scornful look and asked, 'Can I help you, gentlemen?' The last word he heavily stressed with his out-of-place brogue.

'Not Scottish?' Fitzhugh asked as he picked up a pen and, unbidden, signed his name in the registry book.

'Most Scots are off fighting your stupid war. However, we Irish are far more civilised than that, and we're quite happy to take all the jobs you lads have vacated, thank you very much.'

'Civilised, except when it comes to each other?' Andrews bit.

'And the English. Don't forget how "civilised" we are to you buffoons,' the Irishman replied with a pasted smile. 'Now, one room, is it?' he asked, hinting at the closeness of the relationship between the two soldiers.

'Two rooms,' Andrews said.

'Your finest for me and whatever you have left for him,'

Fitzhugh added, repeating the same motion he had used earlier to give away who'd woken up the clerk.

Fitzhugh's room was typical for this part of the country. An elevated view of the countryside, a large bed, a single armchair, and a sideboard holding a washbowl and water jug. All the rooms shared a bathroom, and after a brief freshening up, he headed downstairs to the hotel's lounge room to wait for Andrews.

Eventually the sergeant arrived, having enjoyed his first real bath with hot water in months. Fitzhugh couldn't really complain, but of course, that didn't stop him.

Tapping his watch, he said, 'At least you no longer smell like France.'

'Sorry, sir, but I noticed those of the gentry were starting to move away from me on the train. I thought I should get a good cleaning before we got on with the day's business.'

'Enough of your excuses, Sergeant,' Fitzhugh said with a wave. 'Now, if you would be so kind and sit, we can begin.'

Taking up the armchair opposite his captain, Andrews leaned in like a conspirator.

Fitzhugh matched his stance. 'We are here to find a spy, Sergeant. Now I have some things to do, sightseeing and such, so I would truly appreciate it if you could camp your arse in that chair and keep an eye on the front desk.'

'A spy? Really? And what should I be keeping an eye out for?' Andrews asked excitedly.

'Oh, I dunno, the usual thing. Someone with a German accent, perhaps with a large moustache, which they continually twirl the ends of. They may walk around on tiptoes a lot and look real shifty, perhaps dramatic music appears every time they walk into a room ...'

After a year of service to this peculiar master, Andrews didn't bother replying; he just waited until the captain had made all his little jokes and got to the actual point.

'… they will probably be wearing a top-hat and a black cloak, which they will try to hide their features behind …'

Sometimes it took the captain longer to get to the point than others.

'Honestly, Andrews, we are looking for a spy. They will likely be hiding in plain sight, so it really could be anyone. Just use your imagination and keep an account of everyone who enters and leaves and anything that is said.'

'And where will you be, sir?'

'I have my own errands, Andrews. Ministry business and all that.' From the wall behind his chair, Fitzhugh pulled the fishing rod he'd managed to procure.

'You know me, always busy, Sergeant.'

CHAPTER TWENTY-NINE

WITH THE SKY DARKENING AS NIGHT APPROACHED, MOVING through the unknown trenches had become hazardous to the shins and ankles, and not for the first time Ash considered turning around and heading back to his own quarters. It had taken the Australian only a few minutes to discover where Wolk, in his disguise as a runner, had gone when he visited the Highlanders' HQ. He was starting to enjoy the power the MP armband carried. Even senior officers seemed to get a little nervous, and a hell of a lot more polite, when an MP was in their midst.

The section of the trenches the Mountie had been sent to was closer than if he turned around, so Ash decided to continue on. The early night sky was clear and, though not exactly warm, the usual cold that made life so miserable along the lines seemed to be holding off thanks to a day of sunshine. Despite the lack of a moon, the sky was bright with a thousand stars, and not for the first time the Australian found it hard to believe men were slaughtering themselves under the sparkling canopy.

'Halt! Who goes there?' asked a sharp voice from the gloom

in front, instantly snapping Ash's thoughts back to more terrestrial matters.

For a few brief seconds of terror, he couldn't recall the day's password, then finally it came to him. 'Four and twenty,' he said loud and clear.

'Blackbird,' said the voice. 'Come on in.'

The trench ended in a protected alcove with a machine gun embedded behind a heavily sandbagged wall covering one section of no man's land. Three men were inside this segment of the trench, with two of them seemingly asleep under a pile of ratty blankets.

'Can I help you there, cobber?' the guard asked, noticing the rising sun badge on his collar.

'Maybe. I'm looking for a crazy Canadian runner who came down this way sometime this afternoon.'

'Friend of yours?'

'As much as one can ever be friendly with a Canadian,' Ash said playfully.

'Right,' said the Irishman wearing a Canadian uniform. 'Well, your mate was here looking for the 14th.'

'The 14th? I was under the impression this was the end of the Canadian lines.'

'Right, except of course for the men out there,' the guard said, flinging a thumb over his shoulder. 'What's left of the 14th is holding down our last listening post.'

'And that idiot is out there with them?'

'Seems his message was really urgent,' another soldier explained.

'When did he go?'

'Mmm … about an hour or so ago. Not sure how long 'xactly.'

'Expect him back soon?'

'I would say not till morning at least,' the first soldier said. 'That way they can sneak in under the glare of the first sunlight if she's a clear morning. The Germans will be looking right into it then. You can wait with us if ya want.'

Ash thought about it. In the end it came down to the maths. A quick trip out to a listening post and back meant he could be asleep within a few hours. Waiting here meant a night out in the cold, huddled up against a dirt wall, freezing his arse off.

'Much activity around here recently?'

'Almost none. We went out last night and captured one wounded bosch,' the soldier admitted, indicating a pair of boots sticking over the edge of the rear part of the trench. 'Poor fella didn't make it. But as far as we can tell, we think the Hun has forgotten about this end of the line.'

Looking to kill time while he made up his mind, Ash asked, 'You're Irish?'

'Yeah, me and a bunch of lads from our city tried to join up at the start of the war, but they weren't letting any of us Paddies join the mainline units.'

'Well, it's not like any of you potato kissers can be trusted now, is it? This way they can keep you in yer place,' Ash said, jokingly referring to the long history of trouble between Ireland and her masters in London.

Luckily, the Irish were as well known for their sense of humour as the Australians.

'True, though most of the worst Irish lads were sent to Botany Bay. Seems the place was in desperate need of a little class and culture.'

Ash tipped his hat in appreciation at the Irishman's quick answer. 'So, how the hell did you end up in a Canadian regiment named after a bunch of hairy-arsed Scotsmen?'

'It's a short trip from Ireland to Canada, and laugh if you want, but we really were keen to do our bit for king and country. There was a leaflet handed out around my town on how we could join a Canadian regiment, and at the end we would have the chance to take out Canadian citizenship. Seemed like the perfect solution to all me troubles.'

'A long way to come straight back,' Ash said.

'Not as far as you lads've come for a fight that has less to do with ye than it does with us.'

'You have a point,' Ash admitted. He had also made up his mind. 'Can I borrow one of these?' he asked, picking up a rifle from a pile of weapons.

'We won't be using 'em, so go fer it,' the Irish Canadian soldier said.

Ash completed a quick inspection of the gun. The action was smooth, the barrel was free of debris, and the clip full. He then grabbed a bandolier of spare ammunition, secured it on his uniform, stuffed a hand grenade deep into a pocket, and then in one easy motion he slid over the trench and began crawling his way forward.

'I love them Australians. 'Fraid of nuthin',' the soldier said, moving over and waking one of the men under the blankets.

'Leave me alone, Wilkes. I'm awake and I heard everything,' Corporal Robert Keogh said before sliding back under his warm blanket. 'Fire the damn flare gun.'

* * *

The stars were bright enough to give a small but dangerous amount of illumination, and Ash used this to inch his way toward where the Irishmen had indicated the listening post was situated. Having been part of more than his fair share of trench raids, he knew exactly what to look and listen for. Pausing while a shell screeched overhead, the MP counted a few seconds, then slithered forward as quickly as he could as the distant explosion muffled any noise he made.

Refusing to be greedy and go for too much distance, he stopped and listened for anyone nearby who might be reacting to his presence. When no noise came, he waited for the next shell to sail past. This time he didn't move; instead, he remained still and listened for any Germans nearby, using the same tactic to patrol the area. When he detected no one, on the next shell he began crawling again, confident he was alone.

Moving in this way it took the Australian nearly an hour to reach the listening post. Just outside the crater he whispered, 'Four and twenty.'

There was no reply.

Looking toward the opposite side of the ditch, he whispered again, just in case he'd missed his mark and those in the post hadn't heard him.

'Four and twenty.'

No reply.

Ignoring the rifle on his back, Ash pulled the Webley pistol he always carried from its pouch. Its shorter barrel made it easier to wield in the confined foxhole, while its six rounds would easily handle two, maybe three enemy soldiers. Firing all six chambers as fast as possible would give him time to either get away or pull another weapon if needed.

Taking one last, deep breath, Ash got up and sprinted the last few feet to the now clearly visible listening post. In the darkness, his right foot snagged on something heavy, causing the Australian to tumble head-first into the pit.

Air exploded from his lungs and stars blinded him as his head struck something hard. Cursing quietly, Ash rolled onto his back, lifted his weapon, and prepared to shoot anyone who came at him. He lay that way until he began to regather his senses.

When his vision cleared and the blood in his ears quieted from a cacophony to a dull roar, Ash sat up and looked for what had tripped him. Beyond his feet he found the prone body of Wolk.

CHAPTER THIRTY

CORPORAL KEOGH SNUGGLED DEEPER INTO THE LITTLE HOVEL HE had dug for himself earlier in the day. Though useless against a rainy night, the alcove kept the wind out and the night's falling dew off his blankets. In a world of wet and cold, these excavations offered a brief escape from the misery.

After waking up and listening quietly to the Australian MP arrive, then go over the top as per instructions, he had managed to get back to sleep. It felt like only another minute had passed before Wilkes woke him again and presented him with another MP—this one was English.

'Come on, Corporal, I'm not really sure what to do here.'

Keogh cracked open a single eye and stared at the grimy face before him. The overwhelming stench of tobacco wafted from Wilkes's breath.

'Following orders would be a start. Did you fire the damn flare?'

Wilkes shook the weapon in front of his nose, then turned and smiled at McGavin standing at the far end of the trench, his MP armband clear even in the dark. 'I don't think that's going to work now, Corporal. Plus, I think he knows.'

A cold shudder ran down Keogh's spine, as though someone had just dumped a bucket of ice water on his head. Any thoughts of sleep were burned away by the terror of being discovered before the final plan could be sprung.

Disentangling himself from his blankets, Keogh pulled himself to his feet, then stepped over to the MP, who was busy looking about the almost abandoned trench with a worried expression.

'There's really only the three of you defending this entire sector?'

'No, sir,' Keogh said, wiping sleep from his eyes and stifling a nervous yawn. 'We also have five men forward and a patrol that's expected back any second now.'

'And the MP looking for that other fella,' Wilkes added unhelpfully.

'Yeah, and those two,' Keogh agreed, giving the private a nasty look when the MP's attention was diverted.

'Still, I'd expect at least a company to be holding down a trench this size.'

'We were a company ... but then we got hammered during our last knock. They promised to move us back to rest and resupply, only we were forced to stay forward when that last big attack began and drove away the Frenchies who'd been just up on the corner there. It didn't help that they used gas too.'

The recent use of poison gas had come as a great surprise to all, especially the French, Canadian, and African units that had been forced to stand and hold as the very first toxic cloud had slowly drifted over them. Though many fled in terror when they realised what the gas was, enough stood their ground to hold the line. The following German attack was halted, partly thanks to these men, partly thanks to every reserve unit the Allies had thrown into a counterattack. Later it was learned what had won the day was the fear the German soldiers had of the gas, and their refusal to move in until it had dissipated, unless they too got caught in its deadly embrace.

'Seems to be happening a lot at the moment,' McGavin said, relenting. 'Well, if you like, I can point out your circumstance when I get back to HQ. Maybe we can get you pulled out for some fresh troops, or at least get some newbies up here.'

Relieved the MP had swallowed his horseshit, Keogh moved on. 'So, how can we help you, Corporal?'

'As your man here said, I'm looking for a fellow MP and a missing runner.'

'Sure, they're out there,' Keogh said, tilting a head at the distant German lines. 'The runner showed up with a message for the 14th. They're currently manning our forward listening post. The MP—an Aussie, I do believe—went out there after him. I warned him not to bother as they'd all probably be back with first light, but he seemed intent on finding that runner. The guy must have done something really wrong to warrant ducking out into no man's land to catch him.'

Carrying on his earlier lie, McGavin grinned. 'Yeah, he was caught screwing a general's daughter who came to one of our rear posts to visit her old man. I think they're gonna line him up against a wall and shoot him.'

'The way he did the daughter, huh?' Wilkes added.

Keogh glared at the private, who stepped over the bedroll still containing a sleeping soldier and retreated to the rear of the gun emplacement.

'Well, if you're that desperate to find them, they're just over the top about two hundred feet forward of us. It's been so quiet here, I don't think you'll have any trouble reaching them.'

'How long before dawn?' McGavin asked.

"Bout three hours,' Wilkes said.

'Screw that, I'll go out after them. Which way's this post then?'

'Here,' Keogh said, handing the MP a periscope.

With a few quick instructions, McGavin had the box lined up on the listening post. 'There they are. I can even see one of them moving about.'

That cold shiver returned to the corporal. He had not thought about what would happen if the MP saw his quarry dead out there or somehow sent a warning back. Moving quickly, he put a hand on the periscope and dragged it back down.

'See, safe as houses. If there were any Hun about, they'd have taken a pot-shot at them for sure for moving that much.'

'Right,' McGavin said, handing the looking glass back. 'Will see you in a minute then.' And with that, the MP climbed over the trench wall and disappeared into the night.

Keogh grinned at the back of the departing Englishman. These idiots were making it far too easy.

CHAPTER THIRTY-ONE

CLEAN AND WITH A NEW UNIFORM ON, DANJOU MARCHED TO where he'd last seen the Australian. After the gendarmes had excavated their way out of the collapsed dugout, they discovered not only that part of the trenches but the surrounding alleys and strongholds were completely abandoned. Even the phantom wounded soldier had disappeared.

Understanding that criminals often returned to the scene of a crime, Danjou headed to the collapsed dugout where he had escaped death. Passing through the extensive military works built behind the trenches to support the men on the frontlines, he noticed one of the other MP investigators—the British one if he remembered correctly—walking toward a different section of the front. Figuring the man was either on his way to rendezvous with the Australian, or at least may know where he might be, the gendarme decided to take the chance and began to follow the man.

He watched as the MP removed what looked to be censor battalion markings from his uniform, then pull his armband from a pocket and slip it over his arm.

Something was clearly up.

The Englishman made his way into the lines held by the Canadians and stopped to question a gaggle of officers. Before Danjou could approach and listen in, the MP began quick-timing it toward the front, and the gendarme scrambled to catch up. This time he would not make the same mistakes. This time there would be no set up, no ambush. If they were really trying to kill him, Danjou refused to make it easy for them.

At each corner the Frenchman stopped, only moving on when he was sure there was no ambush for him on the other side. He just had to make sure he stayed close enough to see which trench his quarry turned into.

Jinking from side to side, then sprinting like a lunatic with his arse on fire down each straight section, the gendarme continued to track his man.

Eventually he came to one final section of trench where he was confronted by three soldiers manning a machine-gun post. One was asleep, the rest were standing about chatting. One of the men held a flare gun and looked like he was going to fire it into the air. When Danjou stepped toward them, the soldier with the flare gun astonishingly rolled his eyes in frustration at the tense-looking lieutenant and groaned.

Before any of them could speak, Danjou barked, 'The MP who was here before, where did he go?'

A private simply pointed over the top of the dirt wall beside them in the direction of the German trenches.

'A traitor, I thought so.'

Pulling his pistol, the gendarme jumped over the trench wall without even checking to see if it was clear and duck-walked away into the night.

CHAPTER THIRTY-TWO

As Ash's rough hands fumbled over Wolk's body in the dark, trying to feel for a wound, he heard someone approaching. Quietly, he unslung his rifle and took cover. Cocking his head to the side to detect any noise, he confirmed the sound was coming from the direction of the Canadian lines. This did not mean he was out of danger, though, as the experienced soldier was aware trench raiders had learned a long time ago that the safest way to approach such outlying posts was from their own lines.

Chambering a round, Ash pointed his rifle into the gloom before him, looking for any movement revealing where the attack was coming from. As time dragged by, his finger nervously started to squeeze the trigger as every shape in the darkness morphed into a phantom enemy soldier.

Then one of those phantom shapes whispered from the darkness, 'Fish and chips.'

Recognising the voice, but rolling his eyes at the use of yesterday's call sign, Ash whispered back, 'Vinegar. Get your arse in here, McGavin.'

A figure that was much closer than the Australian had

realised rose from a dark pool of shadow on the ground and squat-ran toward the listening post.

'Just watch out for …' he whispered, too late as the Englishman's foot snagged on Wolk's body and he tripped headfirst toward the trench. Dropping his rifle, Ash did his best to catch the plummeting MP, and the impact sent both men crashing into the dugout.

The soldiers untangled themselves quickly and began scouring the darkness, certain the enemy had to have heard the noise and would now be approaching to investigate.

After several long minutes, McGavin whispered, 'Where's Wolk?'

'You just tripped on him,' Ash answered.

'He's dead?'

'Well, he ain't moved in ten minutes, so yeah, he's dead.'

'What are we going to do with him?'

'I figure we're gonna have to carry him outta here.'

'Seriously?'

'If it was you, would you want us to leave you here?'

There was a long pause.

'Well?' Ash asked.

'I'm thinking … hell, I suppose not. So how are we going to do this?'

'I've been waiting here for something to happen, maybe a barrage or something to help disguise the noise of dragging him.'

'Good idea.'

'But I don't think we'll see one until dawn, else it would likely have started by now. That will be too late, though, as it'll be way too light by then to be caught walking around this place carrying a body.'

'You're saying we're going to leave him here and head back?' McGavin asked hopefully.

'Nope, now that there's two of us it will be easier and

quieter. We're gonna grab him by his shoulder webbing and haul him out of here.'

'I was afraid you were going to say that.' Looking at the destroyed listening post about them, McGavin asked, 'Any idea what happened here?'

'By the smell of 'em, these ones have been dead for some time. I can't be sure, but I think those fellas back in the trench may have just set us up for something.'

'Those Irish guys in the Canadian lines? They did seem to be acting weird,' McGavin agreed.

'Yeah, I think it's a good idea for us to get out of here fast, before whatever little surprise they have planned for us shows up.'

'Well, then,' the Englishman said, holstering his pistol, 'let's do this.'

'Keep an eye on me as we near our lines. I don't want to just come charging out of the dark, in case those boys are a little trigger happy.'

'Right, I'll follow your lead then.'

At a nod from Ash, both men crept out of the hole and, feeling their way in the dirt, found the prone Canadian. They each grabbed hold of one of the material braces all soldiers on the front wore, and as quietly and as low as possible began dragging Wolk's body back to their own lines.

Both men had not moved more than ten feet when, with a small pop, what looked like a firecracker shot into the night sky from the trench before them.

'Shit!' Ash snarled and, grabbing McGavin, pulled him to the ground just as the flare ignited high above. With a loud sizzle, the bright white light illuminated the countryside in a strange, sterile, swinging glow as the shadows across the battlefield danced and rocked back and forth to the motion of the drifting flare.

If the sudden light had been a surprise to both men, the image of a French gendarme standing before them, holding a pistol and looking up at the sky in confusion was almost comical.

* * *

Danjou heard voices and could just make out the silhouette of men approaching him, carrying something between them. Careful not to make a noise, the gendarme aimed his sidearm and prepared to arrest the MPs when they came closer.

The soft pop and sudden explosion of light high above, however, was something the inexperienced Frenchman was not prepared for, and he automatically looked up into the night sky to see where the light was coming from.

No sooner had the flare illuminated the area than Danjou was hit by something heavy and hard. He fell to the ground face-first and was held down as bullets tore through the air where he'd just been standing. Whatever the weight was on his back, it kept up the pressure, forcing his head deeper and deeper into the earth, until the countryside fell into darkness once more.

* * *

Ash dropped the body of the dead Canadian, pushed McGavin to the ground, and then charged toward the little French gendarme. Behind him, a number of German Maschinengewehr guns, sighted specifically on the listening post, cut loose with a long burst of fire. Capable of firing five hundred rounds a minute, the portable machine gun had changed the face of warfare forever. No longer would waves of soldiers have to charge forward without paying for such an effort with hundreds, if not thousands of lives at a time. Now an entire division could be held off by a few men, a maxim gun, and a good supply of ammunition.

The Australian hit the Frenchman in a rugby style tackle and drove him to the ground, just as the Germans took advantage of the light and began firing in their direction. He could feel the Frenchman struggling to stand, but Ash kept his weight firmly on the man's shoulders, pinning him down while they waited for the flare to die out and the battlefield to fall into darkness once more.

Keeping control of Danjou, Ash turned and watched McGavin lift his rifle to return fire. Exasperated, the Australian flung a dirt clod at the Englishman's head to catch his attention. The clod burst on the man's helmet, terrifying him as he thought he'd been shot. When his fellow MP finally looked in his direction, Ash shook his head, then mouthed, 'Let them think we're dead.'

Nodding that he understood, McGavin returned to scanning the surrounding countryside for an approaching enemy, but never fired a shot.

A short time later the flare died out and, not wanting to be caught in the open again, Ash tapped the shoulder of the Frenchman under him and whispered, 'We're safe for now. Stop struggling and follow me.'

Together both men frog-ran back to McGavin. The two MPs then grabbed Wolk and all three ran from the battlefield.

Returning to their initial plan, the two MPs dropped Wolk's body once they approached to within a few dozen feet of the Allied trenches. When Danjou went to call out to the Canadians inside with today's password, the Englishman caught him, held his hand over his mouth, and put a finger to his lips to indicate silence. The Australian gestured the two to stay and crept away into the night.

After a few minutes, McGavin heard Ash call him forward and, punching the Frenchman in his bicep, he indicated the body at their feet. Both grabbed Wolk and together charged the last few feet to their own lines, dropping the body as they dived in.

CHAPTER THIRTY-THREE

THE SUDDEN JOLT OF HITTING THE GROUND SNAPPED WOLK BACK to consciousness. The first thing he knew was how cold he felt, though he had no idea why. Having lain on the ground all night in the cool air only exasperated the loss of body temperature from his wound. As he lay there shivering, the pain in his head grew, and he reached up and touched his temple. His hand came away with sticky, drying blood.

Sitting up, he was amazed to find he was still wearing his helmet. Gingerly removing it, he began prodding his head where the pain was worst. Though nothing seemed soft—an indication the bone underneath was damaged—his investigation caused the wound to start bleeding again. A check of his helmet revealed where the bullet had pierced the steel, and at the opposite side was a second, far more jagged hole where the round had exited. Wolk couldn't help but smile at the thought of a bullet tearing through both sides of the helmet, yet somehow missing his head—well, mostly missing it. The smile dropped just as quickly when he recalled who had shot him.

Ice water suddenly flowed down his spine as the realisation struck of how exposed he was, sitting on an active battlefield playing with his head. Wolk lay back and began patting himself down, looking for a weapon. His rifle and bayonet were gone, but still attached to his hip was his pistol. Drawing the revolver, the Mountie rolled over and began creeping around, getting a good long look at his surroundings. Somehow, he was back near the trench holding the men who'd just tried to kill him. How had he got here? Perhaps he'd managed to crawl his way back before passing out. Doubtful, but anything was possible.

He slowed down and waited to see if he could detect anyone inside the nearby trench, specifically the guy who'd tried to kill him. That thought made him grip the revolver tighter, and a determined grimace settled on his face. His fellow soldiers should have had his back in this situation, not be trying to stick a knife in it.

Wolk replaced his revolver and drew his own knife. This was no military issue blade, like the standard Ross trench knife. Nor was it one of the ugly serrated blades many soldiers had been originally issued with. Almost all of those had been filed down once news got out that the enemy was shooting prisoners captured with one of the vicious blades—they were considered unsporting.

What he unsheathed was a sharper, far larger bastard Bowie knife, given to him by his grandfather as he prepared to leave for the war. His grandfather had used the blade when he first began pioneering in the Canadian wilds and promised the knife would always bring Wolk good luck and keep him from harm.

Looking at the enormous naked blade in his hand and feeling its great weight, he could not help but think that the knife was a far better idea … and would be far more satisfying.

* * *

Picking themselves up from the trench floor, McGavin and Danjou found Ash holding his rifle on the three Canadian soldiers. The privates seemed content to remain quiet, but the corporal, doubled over in pain, kept shooting the digger with daggers of hate.

'What did you do to him?' McGavin asked.

'He got a bit lippy, and we had a disagreement.'

'That help make your point?' the Englishman asked, referencing the butt end of Ash's rifle.

'Yeah, I think he sees my point of view now ... though he don't seem to appreciate it.'

Danjou looked from one man to the other, and then at the Canadians cowering in the corner. 'If I may ask, what the hell is going on here?'

McGavin shrugged his shoulders. 'Don't look at me, I just got here myself.'

Taking up the challenge, Ash answered, 'I'm not entirely sure what's going on. What I do know is these idiots just tried to get us killed by setting off a flare so the Germans could catch us out in the open ...' He stopped as a thought struck him. He looked at McGavin quizzically, who returned the Australian's look with a raised eyebrow as the same thought occurred to him.

'You don't think ...' the Englishman asked.

'I'm pretty certain,' the Australian said, levelling the gun with a little more determination at the corporal. 'Did you idiots kill our mate?'

'They tried,' Wolk answered, sliding down the lip of the trench behind the Canadians. His bare blade was soon at the corporal's throat. 'But these idiots couldn't even do that right.'

'Jesus, we thought you were dead,' McGavin said with relief. 'We almost didn't drag your body back here.'

'That was you guys who dropped me then?'

'Sorry about that. We had a bit of a situation,' McGavin said, pointing out the still dazed and now completely confused Frenchman.

As though everyone turning to focus on him brought him

back to life, Danjou asked, 'Would you like me to look at your head? I have some medical training.'

Wolk's knife never wavered as he answered, 'Maybe in a minute. I think I have some taxidermy to complete first.'

'Taxidermy?' asked one of the Canadian privates.

'Cut off the skin, stuff them with straw, and make a statue,' explained the second private.

The corporal glared at both men, suggesting their help at this time was not appreciated at all.

'Now that is a good idea,' McGavin agreed, pulling his own standard issue, less impressive knife. 'I'm not sure I'd be all that interested in keeping the skin of someone who tried to kill me though.'

Despite his position, or maybe because of it, the corporal managed to croak, 'You clowns won't be skinning anybody and you're not scaring anyone. You're MPs. You'll arrest us and take us to the stockade. You won't kill us.'

'Normally that would be a good point you're making, my friend,' McGavin said, taking a menacing step forward. 'But you see, we're not really MPs. We're on a temporary assignment. My Australian friend here was about to be sentenced for life after beating an officer, and my Canadian friend with the knife is a Mountie—and they always get their man ... just not always alive.'

'Or gift-wrapped,' Wolk added, sliding the dull edge of his blade along the skin of his prisoner.

'And you?' the corporal scoffed.

'Me ... well, you just tried to kill me, and that fucking pisses me off.'

CHAPTER THIRTY-FOUR

DANJOU WAS CONFUSED.

The men he'd believed to be traitors had just saved his life, yet now here they were holding guns on some of their fellow soldiers, threatening to turn them into museum exhibits ... whatever that meant.

Standing behind the Canadian machine-gun squad that he had run past what felt like only minutes ago, he decided to contemplate the information he had before making a decision on what to do next. Looking at the men before him, he realised that what he thought he knew was pretty much useless now. Maybe a better approach was to consider what he didn't know. He didn't know why the MPs had saved him, nor why they were now threatening to kill the Canadians, nor why they had been carrying a dead body.

And now the dead body had proven to be not so dead. Danjou decided he needed more information, and the best way to get it was to stand quietly in the corner and listen.

He watched on attentively as the three MPs discussed which of the Canadians they wanted to try to make talk. As the former Mountie continued to play with his knife menacingly, the

Australian and Englishman occasionally dropped phrases like 'shoot one' and 'no man's land'.

The gendarme was unsure how serious these threats were, or if he had any right to try to intercede. These men were part of the Canadian forces that had come to fight for France, and that alone gave him some moral authority to take charge of the situation. Yet on the other hand, the three MPs looked like they would have little care for his moral authority. They were hard men fighting a hard war, and if what they said was true, their prisoners were traitors and unworthy of his help.

Looking at the very large, very sharp knife, Danjou came to the conclusion that this entire affair had nothing to do with him …

… and then he became involved in a most disturbing way.

CHAPTER THIRTY-FIVE

SERGEANT ANDREWS SAT IN HIS CHAIR, FAST ASLEEP.

After nearly eight years in the military, and the last ten months continuously serving near the frontlines, how could anybody expect the old soldier not to fall asleep when seated in a comfortable chair near a window with warm afternoon sunshine streaming through?

This was, of course, exactly what Andrews wanted everyone to think.

Eyes closed, sitting in his chair in his worn out uniform, he played possum. He'd noticed on the first day that the few guests to enter the hotel's tiny foyer gave him a wide berth or looked at him nervously, as though he were a spider in a web waiting to pounce, which, now that he thought about it, was exactly what he was.

He'd come up with the idea of faking being asleep after he actually did fall asleep one afternoon; the chair was extremely comfortable and the day's sunlight warm and toasty. He'd awoken with a start and caught the last snippet of a conversation between the cleaning maid and an elderly woman standing behind the counter. Of course, he could not recall a word they had said—he had just woken up, after all—but the fact they seemed happy to chat quietly while he slept was the very key he needed to open this lock.

So far, he had overheard three conversations, and a carefully cracked eyelid had revealed who those conversations were between.

It seemed one of the guests was unhappy with the small pile of mud the sergeant had left in the hallway between their rooms. Though the uniform he was travelling with was clean, his boots were not and, along with some old French clay, he'd managed to bring in the remnants of an ancient cow pat he'd stood in while carrying Fitzhugh's bags. Pretending to be asleep proved a boon here too, as it also garnished sympathy from the hotel staff—and eventually the complainer—as such exhaustion must surely have meant he'd recently been serving on the front-lines … which of course he had.

Later he discovered one of the maids was really fond of a boy who'd just left for the war, and she was now nervous because the night manager of the hotel—the Irishman they had met that first night—was a lecherous old fart and she didn't feel safe around him.

The old lady behind the counter agreed, admitting she didn't like the Irishman either, but what could they do? Men were in short supply and he was needed here.

This was a situation many workers were now finding them-selves in. Temporary jobs, employment that would only last until war's end, when supposedly everything would return to normal. Andrews was well aware nothing would ever be normal again. A lot of boys would never be returning home, and of those who did, a good percentage would not resemble the man who left. He'd visited the hospitals and knew the war was imposing itself on the flower of Europe's young men in ways no one could fully understand—not just on their bodies, but on their minds as well.

As the captain was fond of saying, 'One could not look into
the abyss without the abyss looking back.'

Fitzhugh lay on the river bank soaking in the day's warm sun,
while his fishing rod, its butt embedded into the earth beside
him, bobbed and swayed with the movement of the water and
the light breeze blowing across the meadow. On the far side of
the clearing stood the local train station, and opposite this, still
clearly visible from his position, was the Royal Mail post office.

So far, only the usual suspects had entered the building: old
men, women, and the occasional boy running errands and
picking up or dropping off mail. Ever since the war began, the
country just didn't have enough employees to run the post
office effectively, and very few places still had mail delivered to
their houses. Instead, people now had to visit the post office
themselves—a small sacrifice compared to the one their former
postmen were now paying.

In a small notebook, the captain kept a running tally of who
visited the office and how often. Next to these tallies were
descriptions like 'old man with a Kaiser moustache', or 'woman
with baby and boy'. A single notch indicated only one visit.

Next to this column was a similar one for the train station.
So far this afternoon, only two trains had stopped there and
only one person had got off. This morning, no passengers had
disembarked from the three trains that passed through the
town.

Tugging at the line that had nothing more than a rock on the
end of it to supposedly entice a nibble, Fitzhugh lay back in the
green grass and took a bite out of an apple he'd earlier snagged
from a tree.

This was certainly the way to fight a war, he thought.

CHAPTER THIRTY-SIX

The MPs had a problem.

To go back the way they came meant moving through Canadian lines, and though the majority of the men were most certainly loyal, they had no way of telling who was friend and who was foe. For some reason, these three Irish Canadians seemed to be working with the Germans, and McGavin had supported the idea. The Englishman hinted that he might know what this was all about, but he could not explain anything until they heard from Fitzhugh. The others agreed that there was something very suspicious happening here and they needed to get help.

The men decided to head back to HQ in a different direction, but stuck as they were at the far end of the trench system, it was proving near impossible to figure out how.

'What lies behind us here?' McGavin asked the prisoners, none of whom seemed that interested in talking.

'Maybe just one of us can head back and get help?' Ash asked, thinking the Australian lines were too far to reach, but someone from a friendly unit may be stationed nearby.

'No good,' McGavin answered, shaking his head and

thinking about who had sent him here. 'Whoever is leading these idiots is likely the one who sent us down this way in the first place. If one of us shows up alive back there, they're going to know something is up and either investigate or just get rid of us another way.'

'You really are a cop, aren't you?' Ash mused. 'I hadn't even thought of that.'

'I could go,' Danjou offered.

'You they'd especially shoot, Frenchie,' the Australian said. 'Ever since the little mutiny in your countrymen's lines, the other men in the trenches haven't been happy with you boys.'

'Maybe we wait here 'till morning?' Wolk suggested.

'That's a good idea, you should do that,' the Canadian corporal encouraged.

All four men looked hard at the prisoners, as though they could telepathically read their thoughts. Snapping out of it, Wolk grabbed a rifle and took guard at the entrance to the trench system.

'What are you doing?' Ash asked.

'These guys have been here a long time. I figure their relief is going to be here soon, or at least someone with food and water might show up.'

Danjou noticed there was indeed no stores in the area and slapped his head in frustration. 'Merde!'

'When are you to be relieved?' Ash asked, kicking at the boot of one of the prisoners. 'So help me, if we get bushwhacked here, I'm using you as a human shield.' When none of the prisoners answered, he grabbed the trench telescope and started peering over the walls. Forward, back, and on both sides, he could not see if there was any avenue out.

'See anything?' McGavin asked.

'It's too dark. I can't see a thing.'

'Allow me,' Danjou said, and before anyone could stop him, he picked up one of the Canadian's discarded flare guns and fired a round into the air above them. With a screech, the projectile streaked high into the night, and with a pop, it flooded the area before the trench in red light. Still looking through the telescope, Ash caught sight of several spike-topped helmets worming toward their position.

'Fuck,' he yelled, dropped the telescope, and reached for a rifle. Within seconds he had fired an entire charge into the countryside beyond. The others, realising something terrible was happening, snatched weapons and joined him on the wall.

'Watch them!' Wolk called to Danjou, who dropped the flare gun, pulled his own pistol, and trained it on the prisoners.

Between shots McGavin asked, 'How many did you see?'

'No idea!' Ash answered, slamming another clip into his gun and firing.

Incoming bullets whistled above the men's heads and buried themselves in the dirt wall, proof that what had spooked Ash was not just a figment of his imagination.

When his rifle had fired its last round, McGavin pulled his handgun and began firing it blindly over the top of the trench as he ran along the length of its wall.

'Where are you going?' Ash called after him.

The Englishman did not answer; he just moved and fired until his revolver clicked on empty chambers. Tossing the useless gun aside, he sprinted the last ten feet before leaping behind one of the two vacant Maxim guns protecting the trench.

Pulling back the lever to chamber a round, he pushed both thumbs onto the twin triggers located at the rear of the weapon. Instantly, the gun started bucking and the long belt of bullets began feeding through the side. The barking gun sent dozens of bullets down the small gulley that had been hiding the approaching Germans, but thanks to the slightly higher vantage point behind a protective wall of sandbags, McGavin could see everything, even the faces of the men he was gunning down.

Between short bursts he screamed out, 'There's maybe thirty of them.'

'Scouting group,' Ash yelled back. He then picked up a Mills bomb from a case he had noticed earlier and tossed it high over the wall. Before the first one had even landed, the Australian had two more bombs in the air in quick succession. Not five seconds later, the ground shuddered with a loud explosion and pieces of earth and German soldiers rained down over them. Hand grenade after hand grenade flew across the trench wall, adding to the constant stream of death spitting from the machine gun.

The combined defence proved too much, and within minutes what few Germans had survived began to back away from the gulley and retreat to their own lines.

'What the hell was that?' Wolk yelled, his ears still ringing from the battle.

'I'd guess we just interrupted something of a rendezvous with these idiots,' Ash shouted, bowling one last Mills bomb, cricket-ball style, after the fleeing Germans, just in case they considered regrouping and coming back.

Shocked at how close they had just come to death, and finally understanding who was who here, Danjou pointed his pistol directly into the eye of the corporal. 'Speak or I will shoot!'

The Irishman sat there, resolute, literally staring down the barrel of the gun.

It was one of the privates sitting next to him that chose the better part of valour. 'They were coming to take some paperwork we've been collecting for them.'

'Paperwork? What paperwork?' McGavin asked, fishing out a fresh belt for the Maxim.

'It's behind the sideboard with the empty candleholder nailed to it,' the prisoner offered.

Wolk reached the indicated section of wall and yanked on

the loosest board. It pulled away with little effort, and behind it he found a large satchel. Inside were maps, lists, and other official papers.

'Is that the plan for our upcoming attack?' McGavin asked, peering over Wolk's shoulder.

'The dates certainly match up—but what is this?' he asked the prisoners.

'It's what you think it is,' the corporal spat.

'What, are you idiots Bolsheviks?' Danjou asked.

'Yup, got it in one. Free the worker and all that.'

'Shut up,' the former Scotland Yard investigator said, firing a kick at the corporal. 'They're Irish,' he said, then turned back to the prisoners. 'Please tell me this isn't yet another attempt to free yourselves from the Empire again.'

'Shit, this is getting a lot bigger than a single murder,' McGavin said when no one answered. 'We really need to get out of here and warn someone ... and definitely not through the Canadian lines.'

Ash completed an inspection of the trench to see what resources they had left. With his bandolier full again, and the last of the Mills bombs at arm's reach, he turned to the others and grinned. 'Right boys, now I'll show you how we do this Down Under.'

And with that he climbed over the trench wall and was gone.

The other MPs looked at each other and, as they prepared to follow, the Australian's smiling face reappeared over the edge.

'And don't forget to tie and muffle those idiots and bring them along.'

CHAPTER THIRTY-SEVEN

MORNING'S FIRST LIGHT CREPT ACROSS THE BATTLEFIELD AND found the MPs, Danjou, and their prisoners sitting deep in a crater, nearly a mile from the trench. During the night they had cut a parallel path along the Allied and German lines, trying to clear the Canadian sector and reach someone friendlier. Above their heads, shells and bullets whined and roared, but they were safe enough here.

They all shared the two tins of bully beef Wolk had found earlier. The cold, jelly-like meat was hard to swallow, but for men who hadn't eaten in nearly a day it was never going to be enough.

'Any idea where we are?' McGavin whispered.

'About five hundred feet from our lines, which means we're about one mile from the German lines. This area is renowned for snipers, so we'll be sitting right here until nightfall,' Ash replied.

'This was your great plan for our escape? Take us into no man's land in daylight?' the Englishman asked, nervously watching the skies as though he could spot the shell with his name on it.

The Digger slapped him on the back warmly. 'It's genius, boys. They won't be looking for us here now, will they?'

'But what about the trench we just left wide open?' Wolk asked.

'You mean the trench the Germans thought was full of sympathetic Irish soldiers? The one where they just got their arse kicked? I figure any survivors from last night will be busy explaining to their superiors that they were lied to. I also figure their officers will think their men are stupid and just got the wrong trench. Either way, we are good while it's daylight, and I am pretty sure the Canadians would have changed the guard by now and noticed our three prisoners are missing.'

'That's going to be a problem, isn't it?' Danjou asked nervously.

Ash thought for a minute before answering. 'No, I don't think so. Soldiers along the frontlines go missing all the time, either killed or captured in a trench raid … and the fight will indicate that's what happened. If, however, we are talking about compatriots to these arseholes,' he said, indicating the prisoners, 'they might think they just left with the Germans willingly and the short battle was just a ruse to hide their defection.'

Keeping low and quiet, waiting to be discovered or for nightfall, the men took turns sleeping or guarding the prisoners —who seemed to have resigned themselves to their fate and slept most of the day away.

As it does every day, the sun finished its slow arch overhead, and then seemed to stand still, before dropping low to the far horizon. The lapis blue French sky turned bright red, then deep purple and orange, and McGavin woke the sleeping men in preparation for the last stretch of their journey. The darkening sky was stitched by the appearance of stars and the slightest sliver of a moon began to hang just above the horizon.

With care, Wolk lifted the trench periscope they had brought with them and inspected the surrounding countryside to see if it was clear. What he saw stopped him cold.

'I don't think we're going anywhere,' he whispered.

'Germans?' Ash asked.

'Worse. We have Germans coming at us from one side, and what looks like New Zealanders coming from our own lines.'

'Yup, we're not going anywhere,' Ash agreed. 'Either side would shoot us right now. I think it's best to wait and hopefully the Kiwis will reach us and we can catch a lift back to our lines with them.'

'What if the Germans get here first?' Wolk asked, inspecting his rifle.

'Then we'll give them something to remember us by,' Ash answered, climbing the crater wall and digging himself a gun pit.

'What do I do?' Danjou asked, never having been in this situation before.

'Sit there, watch them!' Ash snarled. 'And shoot anything that comes over the pit lip.'

The gendarme looked in the direction the Germans were coming, but his pistol never wavered from the prisoners.

With very little time, the MPs dug small parapets into the crater wall closest to their own lines. This allowed them to fire accurately out of the ditch without lifting their heads above their rifles, and helped keep their heads low enough that only the most eagle-eyed sniper could pick them off.

'When do we fire?' the Englishman whispered.

Ash slipped closer to the lip and raised the telescope to spy on the New Zealanders, who were currently a little further away but moving faster than the closer Germans. Ducking back over to his gun slit, he explained, 'This is going to be close, and I think we're going to have to fire a few shots soon to warn the boys behind us of what they're walking into.'

'What do you mean by that?' McGavin asked.

'Haven't you seen what's coming this way?' the Australian asked incredulously.

This time, McGavin took the periscope and looked for himself at the soldiers creeping toward them. They were clearly moving more slowly and stiffly than a soldier should. He then noticed that some of the Germans were carrying large shields, while others wore chest plates made of metal. Behind them were men who looked a lot like turtles, carrying large cylinders on their backs.

Moving back to their trenches, he asked, 'What the hell are those?'

'Stormtroopers. These guys are specially trained to attack trenches, and those big tanks are flamethrowers, in case you were wondering.'

'What the hell is a flamethrower?' Wolk asked. But before anyone could answer, he sheepishly added, 'Oh, right.'

* * *

Traversing no man's land, the stormtroopers continued to creep toward the enemy lines. Their plan was simple: the men with shields would take point by moving forward, plant their heavy screens on the ground, and allow those following behind to hide behind these mobile strongpoints. This method of attack meant the entire unit was only as fast as their slowest troopers—the ones encumbered by their armour and the heavy flamethrowers. Each move was designed to get the soldiers as close as they could to the enemy trenches before unleashing the hell they carried with them.

These troopers were relatively new to the battlefield, but Ash had encountered them before. He'd seen the great gouts of flame that screeched across a field like some dragon of old when those weapons were triggered. Everything that wicked blaze touched caught fire: trees, sandbags, ammunition boxes, and men. Even standing at a distance, he recalled feeling the intense heat, along with the noise those who caught fire made as they squirmed and thrashed about, hopelessly trying to extinguish the flames. Instead, these moves fed the fire and made them burn even brighter and hotter. The flamethrower was an evil weapon … and approaching now were at least a dozen of them.

Ash and the Australians were not unique amongst the Allied troops on the frontline—all who had met these special shock troops had a specific hatred for the weapons and the men who carried them. He lay down on the cold dirt, but any discomfort disappeared as his focus shrank into the small iron sights at the end of his rifle. At the other end, a German soldier carrying one of those monstrous tanks on his back followed the man holding the actual firing mechanism. Both moved in and out from behind a pair of shield-lugging storm troopers.

The Australian calmed his breathing and waited, and then he waited some more. The careful zigging and zagging of the Germans meant any shot was going to be a tough one, but he paused and mirrored the movements of the stormtrooper until he moved into a gap between the shield carriers.

Squeezing the trigger, the .303 bucked and the bullet raced down the battlefield and hit the large tank on the back of the soldier. For a moment, Ash thought he'd missed, and then a large orange mushroom of flame erupted into the sky, catching several German soldiers in its fiery embrace.

All three MPs opened fire, with the Canadian knocking down man after man with some highly accurate shooting. The far less accurate English MP hit three stormtroopers, two through the shield, and one on the chest armour, who toppled over backward, only to immediately begin struggling back to his feet under the weight. The Englishman fired three more times, making sure the German never rose again.

Ash pulled his remaining Mills bombs and pitched them down the field. The first landed before one stormtrooper, who simply ducked behind his shield until the bomb went off. Realising his mistake, the next few went sailing behind the Germans, so when they exploded, they caught the men from behind.

Knocking the first few troopers down, behind them came hundreds more, filling the gaps in the line the MPs had carved open.

'Well, this isn't looking good,' Wolk yelled, firing and hitting another German.

With no bombs left, Ash remembered the hand grenade in his pocket. He squirmed about, fishing for the bomb while keeping his body low. Finally, he retrieved the explosive, pulled the pin, and flung it as far as he could.

Almost instantly the countryside beside the shell hole was illuminated by an explosion far larger than a single grenade could generate. About them, the New Zealanders had arrived and were bringing the weight of their own weapons to the battle. Not only did the Kiwis add rifle fire and Mills bombs to the fight, many were carrying Lewis guns, and these handheld machine guns began dropping the Germans like dominoes.

Their armour and weapons were great for a sneak attack, but in an open battle like this in broken ground, the stormtroopers tired quickly and often stood about the battlefield like tree stumps. As the New Zealanders entered the fight, a second, and then a third flamethrower was hit and erupted, burning many soldiers around them.

These detonations helped silhouette those stormtroopers still on their feet, and the New Zealanders, many of whom were farm boys who'd grown up with guns in their hands, shot them down.

From the rear of the crater, men from the island of the Long White Cloud poured in and took up position on the far lip. The MPs moved out of their makeshift ditches and joined their saviours, and their combined fire forced the Germans back once again.

Unlike the earlier trench raid, here normal German forces were following close behind the stormtroopers, ready to rush forward to keep pressure up when needed, or dart back to the rear to explain what was happening and call in reinforcements. What had begun as a diversionary attack was now coalescing into a full-blown battle, one the New Zealanders were currently winning.

Once the fighting was done around the bomb crater and the New Zealanders moved forward again, stretcher bearers snuck in and started collecting the wounded and dead. With the immediate danger past and the way clear, Ash gathered the rest of their little troop together and everyone headed back to the rear, prisoners still in tow.

CHAPTER THIRTY-EIGHT

ON THE THIRD DAY OF HIS FISHING TRIP, FITZHUGH THOUGHT HE finally got his hook into something unusual. When the morning train entered the station, a man disembarked and marched directly over to the post office. There he picked up a few letters, then followed the road all the way around the creek and began heading in the direction of the hotel.

Though the man and his errands were not themselves suspicious, he was the first passenger Fitzhugh had seen in days. And the next train wouldn't be for a few hours, so even if nothing panned out investigating the passenger, Fitzhugh had plenty of time to get back to his fishing spot before it arrived.

Waiting until the man had walked past him and onto the last stretch of the small path leading to the hotel, Fitzhugh packed up his fishing rod and what remained of the lunch he'd brought with him and began following at a leisurely pace.

Though the man didn't seem to be in a rush, the captain began to fall behind. Quickening his pace to at least match his quarry, Fitzhugh was soon almost at a full march. It was his experience that only those who'd gone through military training were capable of this kind of pace without looking as though they were pushing hard. During basic training, recruits quickly learned to internalise their pain and fatigue to escape the unwanted attention of a trainer.

Fitzhugh's suspicions were growing, but he was so deep in thought that when he came around a blind bend, he did not notice the four men on the other side until he almost bumped into one.

'Pardon me,' he said as he jovially took an exaggerated step to the left.

'No problem, Captain,' the rear-most man said in a thick Irish brogue, mirroring Fitzhugh's path with his own exaggerated step so that he was once more in the way. 'We've been waiting for you, as it turns out.'

'Waiting for me? I could hardly think so. I only arrived a few days ago on leave, and all I've been doing is fishing.'

'Fishing in a pond renowned for having no fish, at a spot where you can see whoever arrives on the train? My, how convenient. Or is it coincidental? I'm not too sure which suits better.'

Looking at the four men, Fitzhugh realised he was in serious trouble. Though he felt confident he could take the man he assumed to be their leader, the other three were thuggish types, like those from some potboiler crime novel—all broken teeth, cauliflower ears, and twisted noses.

As the first man approached, Fitzhugh brought his fishing rod around and struck at the man's face, the thin rod snapping across his features like a whip. The man cried out in pain as a thin line of blood ribboned out from where the rod struck. The captain wasted no time tossing his lunch at a second man, buying time for him to strike out at the third.

'I wouldn't do that if I were you,' the leader said, brandishing a shiny Luger in his hand.

'Now, that's an unusual gun for someone in Scotland to

own,' Fitzhugh said, and regretted saying it the second the words passed his lips.

The man's face turned stone cold, losing all its Irish humour.

'I really have to learn one of these days to keep my mouth shut.'

'You really do,' the Irishman agreed, flicking the pistol in such a way as to indicate the other men should close in on their quarry.

'Really unfair of you to outnumber me *and* have a gun,' Fitzhugh said as the man he'd struck with the fishing pole stepped in and threw a haymaker at his head. Fitzhugh didn't remember much after that.

* * *

Sergeant Andrews sat in his chair and tried hard not to react when a new guest entered the hotel foyer. Though nothing was said, he could sense something was wrong. Normally, the old man behind the counter would make a derogative remark if it was someone he knew, or a half disguised derogative remark if it was a customer.

This time, however, the Irishman seemed all business when the new guest entered. Cracking an eye, Andrews could only just make out an older gentleman, who stood ramrod straight and wore perfectly clean shoes and a well-pressed suit. When he spoke, he revealed that though his English was fine, it was clearly not his first language.

'I was hoping you could put me up for the night.'

'We're pretty booked up, but I'm sure I can fit you in,' the Irishman answered.

Now that is odd, Andrews thought. Sitting here as he had been for the last few days, he knew the hotel was nowhere near capacity. Besides himself and the captain, there were only four other people staying: an old couple, who seemed to be Polish or Hungarian by their accents, and two single women, one he fully intended to have a crack at taking out one of these nights if the captain kept them on station for a while longer. Knowing his luck though, he'd organise a date and Fitzhugh would suddenly get a hankering for hunting butterflies and they'd be off to the Isle of Skye, or worse, Wales.

It took a few minutes for the guest to complete his paperwork and sign in, and through it all the sergeant kept up the pretence that he was asleep.

'Catch the morning train in, did you?' the Irishman asked, taking a key from the pegboard behind the counter. Almost every room's key still hung there, again adding to the oddness of his previous statement.

'Err ... yes,' said the guest, a little uncomfortably.

If the man had caught the train and came here from the station, then where the hell is the captain? Andrews thought. He then stifled a very real yawn, mentally shrugged his shoulders, and nestled back into his comfortable chair as the manager took his new guest to his room.

* * *

Fitzhugh hurt.

He could also tell he was bleeding badly—as he had that horrible iron-rich taste in his mouth. He could also tell he was being carried by at least two of the thugs, and he did not know where to.

Running his tongue around the inside of his mouth, Fitzhugh could feel where his cheek had been cut from the punch. On the left lower side at least one tooth was loose enough to wiggle with just a little pressure. On the right, things were far worse—one tooth was gone, likely swallowed or drooled out, while another half hung out of his gums.

Feeling sick, probably from the amount of blood he was

swallowing, Fitzhugh carefully opened his mouth and let the fluid building up in his throat just pour out. This proved a mistake, however, as no sooner did the pressure ease on the back of his throat than he retched and vomited.

Incapable of stopping himself, Fitzhugh spasmed and his eyes snapped open as his body heaved and everything that had been collecting in his stomach fountained onto the ground. The two men carrying him instantly let go, and he only just managed to cushion himself with both arms before he struck the ground. The violent motion didn't help any and, now on hands and knees, he began uncontrollably vomiting. Blood and mucus and, yes, there was his missing tooth, pooled on the ground and he felt worse than when they had been carrying him.

Once he had ceased and the dry heaves went away, Fitzhugh rolled onto his side and lay in his misery. From this position he looked up and caught the four men standing above him. They looked disturbingly pleased.

'Well, well, look who's awake?' one of the Irishman said.

* * *

Stifling a yawn, Andrews sat up in his chair and looked about the hotel's sitting room. No one was behind the counter, and the window outside had grown dark with the coming night.

The captain would be back any minute and the two would retire to a meal in the hotel's restaurant, likely something with wild rabbit as this was the only meat available to those not fighting the war. If the captain ever had the sense to start fishing for real, they could enjoy a nice trout perhaps. The chef-maid-cleaner had offered to cook up whatever he brought back, but the captain insisted to continue his ruse, adding to this the sergeant's frustrations at rabbit stew three nights in a row.

His dozy wait ended when the front door exploded and two

men ran inside. One of them pointed at the sergeant and yelled, 'That's him,' then stepped out of the way and let the second bruiser through the door.

Recognising the danger, if not the reason why, Andrews jumped up, grabbed a nearby chair from a writing table against one wall, and whirled it over his head, bringing it crashing down on the first man, who dropped to the carpeted floor with a thud.

'It's about time this assignment had some fun,' the sergeant said, grinning and dropping into the worst fighting stance in the world. Andrews was no boxer; he was a leg-breaker from way back, and this was not his first brawl. 'You comin' in, boys, or do I have to come out there and get you?'

A third man entered the room from the hotel's rear door and the second, uninjured thug grinned a wicked grin. 'Was just waiting for some help, sweetheart.'

Andrews blew the man a kiss and attacked.

CHAPTER THIRTY-NINE

AFTER A HOT MEAL AND SLEEP, ASH, MCGAVIN, AND DANJOU woke up late the next day and rendezvoused at the New Zealand corps stockade, where their prisoners had been deposited for safekeeping. All were asleep, and Ash was more than happy to take a little piece of revenge and wake them from their slumber.

'Up you get, sleeping beauties. We have an appointment with a firing squad ... and when I say "we" ...'

Over the squawks of the privates, the Canadian corporal growled, 'They ain't gonna shoot us, you idjuts. We ain't had a court-martial yet or nuffin'. These boys now have to do everything by the book after they put us in this here gaol. There's a proper trail now, so we can't just be disappeared.'

'Well, you'd be right if we had catalogued you as prisoners, and to be fair the Kiwis here were all for us doing that, us storing prisoners in their stockade and all ...'

'What I tell ya?' the Irishman crowed.

'... but we then explained to the lads how you intended to bushwhack them with that little trap last night and how you had been giving away their positions for weeks to the German artillery. They weren't so sympathetic after that. In fact, they insisted in, shall we say, helping expedite your court-martial in any way they could.'

'What does expedite mean?' one of the privates asked.

'Rush or push it forward,' McGavin said helpfully.

'You serious?' the second private asked, his nerves clearly fraying.

Before anyone could say another word, a New Zealand sergeant stepped forward and unlocked the door holding the men inside. He then gestured to the line of armed guards awaiting them.

'But you can't do this, we're prisoners.'

'Terrorists, you mean? You know, you would be right if it wasn't for the fact that you've been charged with treason,' McGavin explained. 'Treason, you see, holds an execution order, and if warranted this sentence can be carried out in the field if there's overwhelming evidence and an immediate danger to the war effort, and if there's a chance the sentence might not be carried out, if you get what I mean.'

'Excusez-moi, I am in the French army,' Danjou added. 'We shoot cowards and Bolsheviks and complainers every day, and if we do that to our own people, what do you think we're going to do to a foreigner who tried to sell away our nation?'

'But there's no danger. We're behind the lines and unarmed,' one of the privates pleaded.

'Ah well, behind the lines you are, but unarmed … well, I think you have information that could save lives and obviously we need that information as quickly as possible. So, me and the lads here have decided to shoot each of you and spare the first one to talk,' Hank said with not a hint of mirth.

'Collateral damage,' McGavin added as he moved behind the prisoners and started shuffling them toward the door.

'But this is against the Hague Conventions. You cannot just shoot prisoners.'

'Again, that would be true if you were enemy soldiers, but you're not. You, my friend, are wearing a Canadian uniform,' McGavin explained.

'That's right, we can do pretty much whatever we want to a prisoner from our own side,' Hank said, mimicking the Englishman's accent.

'But we're not on your side! We are enemies!' the first private blurted, and was immediately kicked by the corporal.

'Shut it, you idiot!'

'Piss off, Gibbs, I ain't dying for your stupid cause. We are Republicans, sir, free Irishmen and thus not English citizens. That makes us soldiers of Ireland, and an ally of Germany, sir.'

Though the MPs were sure that's what this had been all about, it was like a slap in the face to hear it. What had started out as a simple, if not somewhat bizarre murder case had just turned into part of the English empire siding with Germany.

'You're Irish revolutionaries?' Danjou exclaimed, catching on.

'That's right, making us allies of Germany and therefore enemy soldiers, so you have to follow the Hague regulations and put us in front of a court-martial,' the second private boasted.

'That would be true, soldier, except for one thing,' Ash said, ruffling the hair of the closest private playfully. 'As admitted enemy soldiers, you've been caught wearing British uniforms and are clearly spies ... and you know what we do to spies, matey?'

'Idiot,' Gibbs snarled, rolling his eyes.

'We're fucked,' the second private said, the weight of what just occurred finally getting through. 'We're really fucked.'

'That you are,' Ash said. 'That you are.'

The three prisoners were marched into a small quad at the rear of the New Zealanders' HQ. Along one wall was a line of soldiers at parade rest, their rifles slung over their shoulders. As the MPs pushed the prisoners along the wall opposite, the Kiwis stood to attention.

'You can't do this,' one private pleaded. 'I told you the truth.'

'No, you told us some of the truth. We still need to know who you've been passing information to, where you got the information from, and how you've been doing it—you know, little items like that.'

'But we don't know that stuff,' the second private pleaded. 'We told you that we were just following his orders.'

Corporal Gibbs did not look pleased at being singled out.

'And why were you doing that?' Ash asked.

'Are you fucking kidding me? Have you not seen what happens to people who get in these guys' way? You saw what they did to Sergeant Band when he discovered what they were up to.'

Confused, Ash said, 'Who the hell is Sergeant Band?'

'The guy you've been asking about,' the first private said, as though talking to an idiot. 'The soldier that was crucified. He was a Canadian who didn't like the way the Irish were pushing their way into the unit and changing things. They figured he'd guessed what they were up to and they got rid of him before he could squeal.'

'That was the man's name?' Ash asked.

'I have no idea—he was from a different battalion. I only know what Gibbs told me, and what happened if we didn't do what he says. It could be one of us standing the lone post out in no man's land during a stormtrooper raid. Don't you see? We had to do what they wanted us to do or else they'd kill us.'

'I don't think I believe you. Amazing how you are only now just starting to remember all this, right before you're about to be shot. Do you have any proof of what you're telling us? Do you have anything to back up your story?' McGavin asked.

'No, sir,' the private admitted, crestfallen.

'What about you?' the Englishman asked the other private. 'Got anything that can help save your traitorous neck?'

'No, sir. We only ever had the corporal tell us what was going on and why. For all I know, everything he said was a lie.'

'Everything he said *was* a lie,' McGavin stated.

Gibbs ignored the jibe and continued to wait, stone faced, for the firing squad to take its mark.

'Shame you have no proof. Looks like you're going to be shot after all,' Ash said, taking an exaggerated step away from the prisoners.

'Wait,' the first, clearly most troubled private yelled. 'We don't have proof, but Gibbs does. He has orders and a plan hidden in his little notebook.'

'And where would this little notebook be now?' McGavin asked.

'He always hid it.'

'Yeah, you showed us your stuff, remember?' said McGavin. 'There was no notebook there.'

'No, not in the trench. He'd always have his secret orders passed on to him whenever he returned to HQ, but he never seemed to have them with him once he came back. I figure he has another stash somewhere, maybe hidden in his kit or near his bunk.'

'That true?' Ash asked Gibbs. 'You been holding out on us?'

Gibbs continued staring at where the firing squad had lined up.

'Tough guy, isn't he?' Danjou asked.

'"Course he is,' Ash answered. 'He thinks he's dying for a noble cause, that his sacrifice will help free his family from the tyranny of merry old England. Of course, he's wrong. The Germans don't care about Ireland and will happily run over his little rebellion if they take power. If that sad day ever comes, all this will be for naught. His effort will be despised. Instead of under British rule, Ireland will become German, and if you don't think they will suppress the Emerald Isle with brutality, you haven't been paying attention to our own little reality here!' McGavin said. He then turned away from Gibbs and faced the other prisoners.

The Irish corporal in the Canadian uniform remained silent, though the pride was gone, and his stone face looked far more worried now. Having been betrayed by the French and half a dozen other countries throughout the centuries of occupation by the British, the men of Ireland were naturally wary of anyone pretending to be their ally, so this information was nothing new.

'The Germans won't want us. They're after France and England,' Gibbs finally said.

'They're after everything, you idiot,' McGavin snapped. 'They're hungry for power, and desperately jealous of what England and France have always had … an empire. They won't stop until they've reached their supposed destiny, to be the most powerful empire the world has ever known.'

'Bullshit, they're just after the head of England, and we're more than happy to help them cut it off. Maybe we'll even bring back the guillotine—that was one thing the French did right.' This last comment was directed at Danjou.

'You're fooling yourself. They're going to crush Ireland like a soft-boiled potato. With France and England out of the way, who do you think's going to protect you from the German bear? The Russians? The Ottomans? Who else would be left?' the Frenchman replied.

The three Irishmen looked on in silence as that thought sunk in.

CHAPTER FORTY

FITZHUGH LAY ON THE STONE FLOOR OF WHAT HE ASSUMED TO BE a wine cellar in a cottage, perhaps even an abandoned factory. It was the smell that gave his location away—that damp, musty smell of age and disuse. What he wasn't expecting to find when he finally sat up was the arc shaped wall of light at one end of the room. He somewhat groggily noticed the two lines of steel running out of the opening, and his pain-addled brain took a moment to register they were railway tracks leading out of what was clearly a tunnel and, judging by the amount of foliage that had grown inside, a long abandoned one.

What had woken him up was approaching footsteps and voices. His head swooned and his stomach lurched violently, so he lay back down and tried to find a position that, if not comfortable, was far less excruciating.

'Seems our little birdy was trying to fly away again,' said the voice of the bastard who'd hit him. He'd know that voice anywhere … and he would remember it.

'You hit like an Irishman,' Fitzhugh croaked, unsuccessfully trying to keep the pain out of his voice.

'Ah, English bravado,' said a second voice, one he didn't

recognise. This one, however, had a different accent to it. Taking a stab in the dark, he asked, 'And how are you today, Mein Herr?'

'Told you he was a smart cookie,' the Irish voice said.

'Perhaps too smart for his own good,' the second man said, his voice dropping into a far more obvious German accent. 'Now it seems I need to find out what you know, and as Mr Casement's form of persuasion doesn't seem to have an effect on you, I may have to get, how would you English say, inventive.' He said the last word with a hard 'T' and 'V', so common in the German language.

'Well no, actually, that's how you would say it if you were German. We English would say "in-ven-tive".'

'Humour, that's good. You will need that soon because where we are going will not be humorous at all ... at least, it won't be for you. Turn him over for me, will you, Mr. Mallin?'

'Should you be using my name?' Mallin asked.

'It will not matter, Mr. Mallin. Our friend here will not be leaving this tunnel, at least not in one piece.'

Fitzhugh now had the name of the man who had hit him.

'Tough words for a man with only one friend to back him up,' Fitzhugh managed to groan as he tried to get to his feet. The noise was from the pain and nausea, not the terrible criminal banter that sounded like it belonged to some Boy's Own villain. If this was the way he was going to die, he was determined to at least be standing long enough to spit in the eye of his murderer.

Mallin's boot came flashing out of the darkness and caught Fitzhugh in the stomach, doubling him over with pain and creating a loud *whuff* as the air in his lungs was evacuated by the blow.

'Stay down, Captain. It will be better for your health.'

This time Fitzhugh didn't have anything humorous to say.

* * *

Andrews pushed his jaw from right to left with one bleeding hand, hoping nothing was permanently damaged. On the floor before him lay the man he'd hit with the chair, who was laying next to the Irish innkeeper.

Both men were tied together with electrical cords the sergeant had ripped from the lamps on the hotel's lower floor. In another room lay the two bruisers who'd followed the first man into the fight. Neither needed tying down as they would never move again.

When it came to fighting, Sergeant Andrews did not play around. He fought to win, and if this meant using a seventeenth-century antique table as a club, or throwing an assailant into a mounted deer head on the wall and then using its broken antlers as a stabbing implement, well, so be it.

Now he intended to use something far more refined than furniture to get his way. From the fire he had lit in the waiting room, he pulled a poker sitting in the smouldering coals. Its end glowed bright red with heat and, realising time was ticking away, he pressed the glowing piece of metal to the exposed heel of the innkeeper's left foot.

No sooner had the flesh begun to sizzle and blacken than the man woke up screaming in pain. His flailing and yelling woke up the bruiser next to him too.

'Good, you're both awake,' Andrews said through a snaggle-toothed grin. Most of the damage to his teeth had been done years before he'd even joined the army, on the rough streets of his childhood. 'Now we get to play "where's the captain?"'

Replacing the poker in the fire, he inspected the innkeeper's foot. The heel was red and already had a nasty blister.

'Now that looks painful,' he said. 'My ma always said the best thing for a burn like that is vinegar. Sure it'll hurt like the blazes, my ma admitted, but it will keep the wound clean and that's the important thing.'

Andrews ducked into the hotel's kitchen, and re-emerged

with a bottle of vinegar. He removed the lid and prepared to pour some of the liquid over the man's wound.

'Anything to say yet?' he asked.

'Do not say a word,' said the bruiser.

Sliding to the side, so that only the groaning innkeeper could see him, Andrews pointed out, 'Now, he's being awfully cavalier about your wound. I mean, it's easy enough for him to say "don't say anything", 'cause it's not his foot that's blistering and ...' taking a look at the wound, the sergeant winced, 'bleeding rather profusely.'

'I won't talk, you English bastard,' the innkeeper spat. 'Do your worst.'

'Wow, an invitation. Well, I'm pleased to announce I accept your offer. I know you don't think you'll speak, but believe me, boyo, everyone sings in the end.'

With that the soldier poured some of the liquid onto the man's foot, nowhere near the burn. The innkeeper screamed at the anticipated pain, then slowed and finally stopped when he realised the pain hadn't increased with the liquid.

With a sigh of relief, the innkeeper looked up at the grinning sergeant.

'Just kidding,' Andrews said, then poured the vinegar directly onto the wound.

There was only the shortest, sharpest yelp of agony before the innkeeper passed out.

'Expect you don't intend to talk either?' Andrews asked the thug, moving back to the fire and stoking its depths with the poker. Sparks and crackles greeted his machinations, the fire grew, and his face was bathed in orange light.

After a few minutes, he retrieved the tool from the flames and, holding it so his prisoner could see its glowing end, said, 'Ready or not, here I come.'

* * *

Fitzhugh awoke once more to find he was breathing a lot easier, as though a great weight had been removed from his chest.

'Morphine,' the German said, moving into his field of view. 'I realised your injuries meant any sustained punishment we subject you to would simply cause you to faint, and we cannot be having that. The little bit of morphine I injected you with will help keep you awake, though I'm afraid to say it won't take away much of what you are about to feel.'

Fitzhugh tried to move, but found one arm was pegged to a rail sleeper.

'Now, now,' Mallin said from behind his head, 'if you wiggle I might miss.' Arching his head to see what the Irishman was talking about, Fitzhugh managed to turn just enough in time to see the hammer slam down on his little finger.

The pain was so intense that, for a blissful moment he felt nothing, then it struck deep into his brain like a lightning bolt and didn't go away. He already figured he had a number of broken ribs, maybe even internal bleeding, but none of this could match the white-hot searing agony of his shattered little finger.

'I'm not going to ask you what you know because you're a tough, funny Englishman and you likely won't tell me anything. We are just going to work our way across your digits until you start telling us what we want to know.' Before the last syllable had even left the German's lips, Mallin brought the hammer down again, this time crushing the Englishman's thumb.

The German leaned close and whispered, 'If you recall, I said this wouldn't be humorous.'

* * *

Andrews ducked under a tree, careful to take his finger off the trigger of the shotgun he'd found in the hotel's office. Though the shells were only buckshot and good for hunting little more than rabbits, just the presence of the gun made him feel better, and he hoped it could help him bluff anyone he came across.

He had to admit the hotel keeper was a tough old bird. After everything he tried, the old coot never said a word. By the time he had finished, the room smelled like a Sunday roast had been in the oven all day.

After a while, one of the hotel's maids entered through the front door for the start of her shift. At first, she was horrified at what Andrews was up to, but then she noticed it was the creepy manager suffering under his efforts, so she shrugged her shoulders, gave a little curtsey, and backed out the door. Andrews loved country girls; it took a lot to distress them. Still, he thought, it was time to get moving.

The old guy refused to talk, but then Andrews he never expected him to. Most people either start talking straight away or take each blow as a badge of honour and double down on the stubborn. The intent was never to force the clerk to talk; it was to terrify the thug so much that when it came his turn, he'd sing like a canary.

With the hotelier passed out once more, Andrews retrieved the glowing poker again and started looking at the thug's bare foot, tied as it was to the clerk's. This not only kept it in place, it meant the thug had felt every twitch and spasm the suffering man had gone through while conscious. To hear someone in pain is hard; to feel them struggle and shiver as agony washes over their body—well, no one with blood in their veins could ignore that for long.

'Right, as he won't be stirring for a while, I think it's about time you and I had a chat,' Andrews said, waving the poker in the face of the thug so he could feel the heat radiating off it.

'You wouldn't dare,' the man said without a lot of enthusiasm.

'I wouldn't? I think your unconscious friend here would indeed be surprised at that statement.'

Standing on the rope binding both men's legs together, thus keeping the thug's bare foot in place, Andrews didn't mess about with over-exaggerated theatrics. Instead, he just matter-of-factly moved the poker toward the man's heel.

The thug winced and stiffened for the coming pain.

Andrews stopped and slapped the man's bare heel. 'Don't flinch or I might miss and burn off a toe and you'll never walk straight again.'

When he had the foot in place, he lowered the poker.

'Wait!' the man pleaded.

Andrews didn't look up, just waited to see if the man followed up the plea with information.

'Wait, I'll tell you …'

'Go on,' Andrews prompted, keeping the poker in position, its heat radiating against the bare skin of the thug's foot to show he meant business.

'We captured your captain.'

'He still alive?'

'Last I saw him, though he did take a fair beating.'

At this, Andrews moved the poker closer to the man's foot. Even at such a short distance, the heat must have been almost unbearable. 'He fought us, we had no choice.'

'And …?'

'We took him to an abandoned railroad tunnel we found. He was going to be interrogated there.'

'By who?'

'What?' the prisoner asked, playing deaf.

'Who? Who was in charge of the interrogation?'

'Some guy, who knows? I didn't know. We were just told to help him out and do whatever he asked.'

'You saying you don't know what this is all about then?'

"Course I fucking do. I ain't stupid.'

When his prisoner did not go on, Andrews said calmly, 'You gonna make me ask?'

'This lot.' The man squirmed, nodding his head as best he could toward the hotelier. 'The fucking paddies. They're trying to break away from the crown again, and this time they're getting help by the friggin' Boche.'

'You serious? And you're helping these arseholes?'

'What do I care who's running the damn country and who's in the empire or not? I get paid, I'm happy. It don't really matter who's footing the bill.'

'Funny you should mention foot,' Andrews said, lowering the poker once more.

'Wait,' the thug cried, tensing his entire body again. 'I told you everything.'

'No, you told me just enough, but I ain't no idiot either. You're holding onto something.'

'I told you everything.'

Vindictively, Andrews brushed the man's foot with the poker for just an instance. The contact was brief, but long enough for the thug to feel the heat and get a jolt of pain for his troubles. He immediately began babbling.

'It's the attack, they're planning an attack.'

Andrews let go of the man's foot and turned around, brandishing the now dull red poker in his face. 'If you don't want this slipped under your armpit, or perhaps inside your pants, you better start fucking talking.'

'There's going to be an attack on the front. The Germans are going to move an army through the Canadian lines right where the Irish are stationed. There's also going to be a bombing of Parliament after the king returns from visiting the war.'

'And the Irish think they'll get away with this?'

'The Irish ain't stupid. Why do you think they've got so chummy with the Germans? They're gonna blame them for everything.'

'How do you know all this? How can I trust a word you're saying?'

'I care what you believe?' the man said, then squawked when Andrews reached for the poker he'd put back in the fire. 'Information is power, and to play in this game you gotta know when to stand, when to run, and when to shut up and act dumb and listen like a hawk.'

'Right, well, thanks for being truthful,' Andrews said, cracking the thug over the head with the poker as hard as he could. The big man was tough though, and it took two more blows to knock him out.

Before Andrews left, he gave the innkeeper a shot too. The man groaned and slumped back onto the floor, proving despite the pain he'd been awake and playing possum.

Leaving the hotel and running further into the village, Andrews searched about the train station, looking for someone who could tell him where an abandoned old tunnel might be located.

CHAPTER FORTY-ONE

THE NEEDLE PIERCED THE SKIN ALMOST PAINLESSLY. THE GERMAN wasn't being gentle; Fitzhugh was just in such agony that a minor pinprick bypassed his overtaxed nervous system without any registration. After about a minute, his pain receded and his eyes fluttered open.

'You done?' he managed to mouth.

Four fingers on his left hand were now little more than meat and, as if for a change of scenery, the Irishman had started working on the toes of his left foot. The first impact had been so hard, his little toe had been removed entirely, the small appendage proving incapable of standing up to such a violent impact. The second toe hadn't fared much better, though at least it was still there.

'I would like you to explain why you were waiting for me at the train station. I also want you to tell me who has been informing on us, and exactly what it is you know.'

Fitzhugh managed to raise his head a little and look deep into the German spy's face. 'All right, you win ... It was your mother, she sold you out. But if it helps, we didn't have to beat it out of her or anything—she gladly did it for a bottle of peach schnapps and a bar of Belgian chocolate.'

'Amusing,' the German said, sounding not amused at all. He then nodded at Mallin, who lifted the hammer again and, as he brought it crashing down on Fitzhugh's third toe, a bullet caught the Irishman in the shoulder and sent him spinning away into the darkness.

The German turned about to see where the shot had come from, pulling his own luger from his pocket.

'I wouldn't do that if I were you,' Wolk said, holding his revolver on the man's chest. 'Drop the gun and step away from the annoying and rather condescending captain or I'll be forced to shoot you.'

The spy let the weapon fall from his fingers to the ground. He then took three large steps backward.

Wolk looked at the bloody mess of the captain's face and then inspected his ruined hand and toes. Shaking his head in disgust, he turned toward the German and shot him in the knee. The man screamed and fell to the ground. The Canadian waited until the man stopped yelling and, taking careful aim, shot him in the other knee.

Wolk looked down at Fitzhugh and said, 'Well, Captain, it's good to see you again.'

'How did you find me?' Fitzhugh asked, struggling to sit up.

'How many times do I have to tell you, Captain? I'm a Mountie; this is the kind of stuff we do all the time … though normally I'd be tracking a moose or grizzly.'

'Tracking? You mean you tracked us here?'

'It wasn't that hard, to tell the truth. You left a hell of a blood trail along the way.'

As Wolk reached out and helped Fitzhugh get to his feet, Sergeant Andrews, two police constables, and what looked like a railway worker brandishing a coal shovel ran into the mouth of the tunnel. Seeing his captain standing with Wolk's assistance, the Sergeant snapped a salute.

'Just like you, Andrews. Never around when I need you,' the captain said, leaning into the Mountie.

Moving under Fitzhugh's other arm, Andrews helped carry the wounded officer out of the tunnel, leaving the police to clean up the mess behind them.

CHAPTER FORTY-TWO

ASH AND MCGAVIN SAT IN FITZHUGH'S OFFICE, SENDING OUT what runners they could muster to anyone they thought would listen. There had been a heated argument between the MPs and Danjou as to what to do next with the information they had gathered. Sending a message to GHQ was next to stupid—no one would believe it. The generals would contact the Canadians and, in all likelihood, ask Major O'Connell what he and his men were up to. As they were certain the Irish major was the spy and organiser of the attack, O'Connell would of course lie, and nothing would change except the MPs would be classified as time wasters and likely be demoted, or at worst, arrested.

Danjou decided to headed into his own office and try to drum up support there, but he was in the exact same boat. There was no proof or any specific details, like where and when the attach would occur, that he could share.

The New Zealanders had been helpful, but could do little. They understood the importance of the information and began trying to get help by sending back messages of possible intelligence they had also been collecting. Of course, they could not come right out and say what they knew because GHQ would ask how they got this information.

Few officers would admit to setting up a fake firing squad to scare the information out of soldiers on their own side—the generals had some sort of standards, after all. There was also the issue of proof. Other than their three prisoners, they had no evidence besides the papers the Irish had been hiding, and there could be any number of reasons information on allied troop movements and numbers had been found in Allied trenches. The Irish themselves had already shown they knew their fate once they were arrested, and their long, drawn-out court proceeding would end well after the likely coming attack.

Sometime within the next week, a German army was going to punch through the weakened Canadian lines, thanks to help from an unknown number of Irish traitors, and there was little the Allies could do to stop it. The future of the war was now hanging on this one battle, one the Allies were going into unaware and unprepared …

At least, that's what the situation was before the MPs really started putting their heads together. After an evening arguing and bitching, a plan began to form between them. It wasn't much of a plan; in fact, it was barely more than a scheme, but it was something.

McGavin filled out one of the coded telegram forms he had found on Fitzhugh's desk and sent a message to their commander, one camouflaged enough to not be understood by anyone who intercepted it.

Using the captain's office as both a front and a HQ, the MPs set about trying to save the war. They issued orders, not to unit commanders or general staff, but to men they knew who really had power. Sergeants, field commission NCOs, MPs—and Ash also reached out to cash in a favour.

They spent the next nervous night near the front trenches, watching for any sign of a German attack to begin, and when dawn's first light broke over the horizon and the day began, they knew no attack would be coming for at least another twelve hours. Twelve hours to win a battle and save a war.

* * *

With a crisp salute, the runner stepped up to the table and deposited the message he was carrying. Seated behind Captain Fitzhugh's desk, Ash took the note and read its contents.

'Well, at least that's something,' he said, standing up and grabbing his helmet and coat. At McGavin's confused look, he said, 'Wait here, this shouldn't take long.'

It was a twenty-minute walk to the location the note listed, an all but abandoned ammunition station where three men, smoking against a wall of sandbags, were waiting.

When the Australian arrived, they simply nodded for him to follow, and they started off into the labyrinth of trenches. Here and there they passed men who at first glance seemed to be just lounging about, but the attitude between these men and the three leading Ash suggested they knew each other very well.

It was becoming clear to the MP just how large the Great King Rat's organisation had become, as well as how he'd been getting away with everything, even the occasional murder according to some rumours. He had men deposited throughout the trenches, who kept an eye out for any suspicious movement coming his way. If someone ever tried to investigate the trench mafia, a warning was soon sent so Rat and his hierarchy could move location before the investigators could get anywhere near him.

It so happened the size of the organisation was a saving grace. Here was an army, albeit a very small one, that could be used to plug the Allies' defences until Fitzhugh arrived. It was doubtful they could halt a large German attack, but they didn't need to stop it, they just needed to slow it down long enough for GHQ to realise what was going on and send real reinforcements to the area. Once these units arrived, King Rat and his men were then free to melt away and go back to business as usual. All Ash had to do now was get a commitment from the marketeer to do exactly that.

Moving into a small alcove filled with cartons of tin peaches, the party was met by a number of men standing around the enclosed space. Though he couldn't see their faces, Ash recognised the voice of the Great King Rat and so he laid out his plan. The crime lord's answer was short and simple.

No!

Ash considered pleading his case, he even thought of appealing to whatever patriotism was left inside the man, but finally he decided a far more direct approach was needed.

Before anyone could stop him, he pulled his pistol and aimed it at the King Rat's head.

'And now you're going to shoot me?'

'No, now I'm going to ask you one more time to reconsider. I'm dead, you're dead. We're all dead if we can't stop this attack. The Germans won't care and won't be playing nice when they come. You marketeers will be the first put against the wall and shot once they take over. Even if you do survive, just how much money do you think you'll make supplying underground goods to people under a German regime?'

King Rat stood in his shadowy corner. He never flinched from the cold barrel of the revolver. After a few minutes he raised his hand, opened it flat, and then lowered it slowly. His guards followed suit, lowering their weapons.

'All right, you have my attention. Explain this plan to me again.'

Ash lowered the gun, placed it back in its holster, then pulled a map from his top pocket and began describing what the MPs were organising.

CHAPTER FORTY-THREE

FITZHUGH LAY IN HIS HOSPITAL BED, LISTENING WITH HORROR AS Wolk reported why he had travelled across the English Channel. It was all starting to sound terribly familiar.

'You believe the Irish are planning yet another rebellion?' he asked.

'We're pretty sure about it, and we think they've been coordinating with the Germans and have something pretty substantial prepared.'

'Funny you should say that,' Andrews said from the wall he was propping up with his back, 'I found out pretty much the exact same thing. The Irish are going to rebel, but there's something you both have missed.'

'And what's that, Sergeant?' Fitzhugh asked.

'They're also planning to bomb Parliament when the king presents his findings after his tour of the front. They're gonna blame the Germans for it.'

'Where the hell did you hear that?' Wolk asked, looking at the man suspiciously.

'I have my ways.' The sergeant counted the Canadian's stare with one of his own as he returned to leaning on the wall.

'He does, you know, he really does. It's one of the reasons I keep him around.'

'Well, it ain't for my looks,' Andrews put in before the captain could say it.

'He's a man of nasty talents is our Sergeant Andrews, and once more it seems my faith in him has borne fruit.'

'You trust what he found out?' Wolk asked.

'Explicitly. Now all we have to do is work out what we can do about it.'

'We still have the Irish Canadians we captured, so maybe we can get the location out of them.'

'I doubt it, they're gonna shut up now that they've had time to shore up their resolve. They may have spilled the beans, but if no one ever stops the plan, they'll likely feel they're still going to be seen as heroes for the cause. It's only if the plan fails that they'll have really big trouble ...'

'In their minds,' Andrews added.

'Yes, in their minds. In reality, I am going to nail them to the wall, no matter what happens in this stupid war!'

'So, what are you doing lying about?' Wolk asked, slapping Fitzhugh on his shoulder, one of the few places not covered with a bandage or plaster.

'Sergeant?' Fitzhugh asked.

'Sir.' Andrews saluted and then marched out of the room. A few minutes later, he returned with a wooden framed wheelchair.

'Your chariot, sir.'

With both soldiers' help, the captain managed to get out of bed and slide into the chair. All three then headed out of the hospital ward, with Wolk carrying the officer's belongings. They even managed to slip past most of the staff on the floor, except for one nurse, whom they escaped by simply running out of the hospital and down the street before she could stop them.

It took a few hours, and one very uncomfortable clothes

change in the train station men's room, but all three men managed to make it to their train without further incidents. In no time, they were safely chugging along toward London.

By the time they got off the train at Paddington, Fitzhugh was feeling very much the worse for wear. Sitting up had allowed blood to circulate and the pain began to increase. The cramped, rattling conditions on the train had done little for his upset stomach either. Waves of nausea washed over the captain as they rolled into greater London, and only by some well-timed deep breaths did he manage to keep from vomiting.

After rural Scotland, where few soldiers could be seen, the three stepped into a chaotic world of men in uniform pushing and bustling through one of the world's busiest train stations. Soldiers were arriving on leave from the front, while others were departing for France. Wounded men were being ferried to one of the hundreds of hospitals that had sprung up over the last year throughout the nation. These were places of quiet and solitude, where the true cost of the war could be hidden away from a public whose goodwill was helping to fuel the fires of the conflict. If the public ever got sight of what was actually occurring—the ruined bodies and minds of their children and husbands; the uncontrollable shaking, violent outbursts, or hysterical screaming from the shell-shocked; the men scratching at phantom limbs, long cut away by some over-worked medic under a canvas roof on a battlefield—they would demand an end to the war.

The military had organised the train system so that these men flowed through London's main arteries with barely a whisper. Taken from train to train, they would soon be deposited in warm beds and sterile rooms in sanatoriums miles away from everyone.

With the burly Canadian strong-arming a path through the crowd and Andrews following close behind to ensure the captain's ruined foot wasn't stepped on, the trio managed to exit

the station. Out front they hailed a horse-drawn cab and were
soon trotting their way toward the Houses of Parliament.
Everywhere, the results of the nation's war industries filled the
streets. Armed soldiers were either resting, arguing, eating or
drinking, while police constables swarmed every street corner
in numbers large enough to suppress trouble if, and more
inevitably when, it began between these groups of highly
stressed military men.

The chilly evening had stoves belching black smoke into the
heavy atmosphere above, adding to the gloominess of the
nation's capital. This contrast was especially vivid after the
vibrant colours of the countryside. Women, something
Fitzhugh rarely remembered seeing on London's streets before
he left, were everywhere. Some wore nurse's uniforms, but most
seemed employed in the jobs their husbands, sons, and brothers
had vacated. At one point, the war had been the greatest threat
to the suffragette movement, and possibly its saviour. Though
here and there women stood under their banners calling for
equal rights, the need for women to work meant most no longer
had the free time to keep up political pressure on the government. There was something of a ceasefire between the two
warring parties, and the support of the women's movement to
the war was something that had not gone unnoticed.

The large square before the House of Parliament held the
usual numbers of tourists as it did before the war, the only
difference now being that almost every visitor was a soldier
wearing a uniform from some distant part of the Empire. South
Africans, Australians, and New Zealanders mixed it up with
Indians and faces from half a dozen other nations.

Helping Fitzhugh from the cab, the two sergeants moved to
stand on either side and helped carry him through the grass
square to the edge of the road.

Towering high above them stood the face of Big Ben, its
honey-coloured limestone surface and Victorian clock looking

down on the guardians of the free world. The three men moved along the perimeter of the building, making their way down to the Thames, with the river in front and the Victoria Tower Gardens on the right. Even with most of the country's manpower in France, the three men noted there was still a large number of soldiers patrolling the fenced perimeter.

'Sorry to trouble you, but we heard the king will be addressing Parliament soon?' they asked one of the guards stationed at the main gates.

'He ain't. Sorry to tell you but 'is majesty's over in France at the moment on an inspection tour.'

'But we heard he was back and coming here to pass on what he'd learned to Parliament.'

'Well, if he is, he never told me of his plans, us being so close and all,' the guard said, then moved away from the fence and returned to his patrolling.

'So that means we're off the hook?' Andrews asked as they carried Fitzhugh back across the street.

'Nope, I'm now more convinced than ever that the information we got is accurate. If everyone knows when the king is coming to Parliament, then there was nothing to corroborate. But if not even the guards know when he'll arrive, that suggests the information is true—otherwise the Irish would have told us a time when everyone knew he was coming. They're smart enough to know we'd check their story.'

'Maybe they're just screwing with us,' Wolk suggested.

'No, the Irish are pretty angry about the Home Rule Act the king promised to implement and then suspended because of the war. I also have information that there are Irishmen carrying German Mauser rifles currently patrolling parts of Dublin. The Irish are getting serious about their freedom once more, and the most militant are willing to fight rather than argue for it.'

'How'd they get the rifles?' Andrews asked.

Fitzhugh and Wolk looked at him like he'd just grown a

second head. The sergeant eventually caught on that they were German rifles.

'So, how are we going to do this?' the Canadian asked.

'We're going to get some help,' Fitzhugh said, hailing another cab.

CHAPTER FORTY-FOUR

McGavin and Ash stood along the trench closest to the Canadian lines. Behind them, men were starting to move into position, and though they were all trying to be as quiet as possible, there was enough noise from the group to concern the Englishman.

'Don't worry too much about it, trenches are like houses. Men may be wondering what's going on when they hear something from another trench, but rarely will they investigate unless ordered. People get shot for desertions like that,' Ash explained, sensing the nervousness of his compatriot.

'But these guys don't care about being shot for desertion. They're probably more worried about being shot just because they're at the front.'

Ash didn't have an answer for that. When someone made too loud of a whisper, however, he was the first to tell the man to be quiet.

As the night dragged on, more and more men arrived. Though they would never have enough to turn an entire German army away from the trenches, that was never the point. Things could become a lot different if the help the Great King

Rat promised arrived, but for now they just had to make do with what they had.

The MPs had to believe most of the Canadian unit was still loyal, otherwise why the apparent secrecy? They decided not to take the risk by alerting them though; the men they had captured were obviously not the only members of this traitorous cell.

They also believed they had worked out how the Irish intended to let the Germans in. Through simple logistics, the MPs figured the Irish sympathisers did not need great numbers to achieve their victory. All they required was enough hand-picked men to stand watch, allowing the rest to bivouac on the night of the attack. These men would help mask the German advance and not raise any sort of alarm. They'd then simply stand aside when the enemy units approached their section of the trenches. Before anyone could react, the leading German elements would be in the lines and taking control. The rest of the army following behind would then move forward unhindered, and with no one to halt their progress, it would not take long for these troops to take over the entirety of the Canadian lines and silence whatever Allied troops they found there. The Germans could then keep pushing forward, and with enough men and supplies it was possible they could roll back the Allied defensive line in the region. The chaos this single event could cause would possibly be enough to end the war.

With no time to find anyone high enough in the Allied command structure that would believe their wild theory, the MPs had come up with their own plan to save the war, and though it was still a longshot, they felt strongly it was their only shot.

If only Fitzhugh would answer any of the dozen or so emergency cables they had sent him. He surely had the connections to warn someone who could help, yet they had heard nothing from him, nor the gullible Mountie they had sent after him with their findings. They figured both were dead, because if they weren't, they soon would be once Ash got his hands on them.

Things would be different once the attack began. When a German army finally arrived before the trenches, Ash had runners ready to deliver news to HQ that the line was under assault. The great military mechanism the Allied command had created would then swing into action, and reserves would be sent forward to help hold the line.

This was their hope, but the hard history of the war had taught the MPs never to trust generals to do the right thing.

* * *

Danjou also arrived, leading a few dozen men, mostly armed gendarmes, as he'd had the same trouble finding anyone who would listen to him without official corroboration. The question, 'How would a gendarme know anything about a secret German attack?' would be hard to answer. The Frenchman explained to the MPs that these were the men under his immediate command from his own office.

The plan the MPs devised was then explained to everyone. They would watch the Canadian sentries like hawks and, when it was clear they were either signalling for the Germans to move forward or completing preparations that would allow the Germans to enter the lines, flares would be fired and everyone would charge forward. The aim was to hold the Canadian trenches long enough until the Canadians themselves were alerted and those still loyal entered the fight, or GHQ could respond. Ash and McGavin would then take their rescue force and hunt down the Irishmen and hopefully capture them before they could do anymore damage.

And if the Germans do not show up tonight? Ash pondered. The MPs would do it all again tomorrow night, and the night after, and they would remain at their vigil until it was clear the danger had passed.

The mixed force of cooks, supply workers, and a large number of supplementary forces who were never really trained to fight may not have been the greatest army in the war, but they were there. The MPs had called in every favour and contacted everyone they knew to get anyone available who could carry a gun into their tiny army. It is claimed that Napoleon had once called England a nation of shopkeepers; the French emperor may well now be rolling in his grave knowing that was exactly the army that was about to try to save France.

Midnight came and went, and nothing happened. Ash could see many of the men with him were starting to fall asleep in the cold French night air, and one of those asleep was McGavin lying next to him. To wake them up would be appropriate, but the very act would likely warn anyone paying attention. Instead, he let them sleep and kept watch.

Three hours later and even he was starting to doubt the sanity of their plan. What if they were wrong and there was no attack? What if the men he had were incapable of holding off the Germans? He had rolled the idea around so much in his mind that he was even starting to consider calling the entire enterprise off.

Watching the dark, hour after hour, alert for even the smallest motion, started to play tricks on his eyes. Shadows took on familiar shapes, the differences between light and dark began to create the illusion of movement.

But it was not an illusion.

Having spent nearly two years in the trenches, it wasn't a noise that set his neck hairs standing on edge, it was the lack of noise. Men not only made sound, they absorbed sound, and men mobbing through an area generally sent wildlife scurrying. However, there were very few living things along the front, and those that remained had learned to go quiet if anything started moving about them.

Absolute silence was as telling as a bell being rung to an experienced ear.

Straining his eyes, Ash tried to peer through the gloom blanketing the countryside as though sheer force of will could see what dangers it contained. He then reached out and tapped the shoulder of his fellow MP until he awoke.

McGavin was ready to whisper a mouthful of obscenities into the ear of the Australian when he noticed how tensely the MP was looking into no man's land. He watched his friend with growing alarm, then, realising what it meant, started grabbing the shoulders of the men closest to him and pantomiming that they in turn should wake those next to them. Very soon everyone was awake and ready to go.

Across the field, Ash's vigilance paid off when he caught the tell-tale flash of a weapon in the moonlight deep inland. 'They're coming,' he mouthed to McGavin, and both men lifted their weapons and prepared to charge forward. The Australian looked about, and when he saw that everyone was now awake and hefting a weapon, he lifted a small pistol and was about to fire a flare when, to his right, a small streak of red shot into the air, blossoming into a miniature sun.

Stretching across the ruined countryside before them, Ash saw at least one hundred Germans creeping in the direction of the Canadian front lines in the flare's red light. In the nearby trenches he could even make out men he assumed were Irish troopers in Canadian uniforms, waving them hurriedly in.

'GET 'EM,' McGavin cried, and from both sides of the Canadian trench their small army charged forward. As planned, the first of these took out the few Irishmen holding the strong point and the rest manned the trench wall.

Ash had found a few experienced gunners with the Australian troops he trusted who had answered his call, and they ran up and took control of the heavy Browning machine guns at the corners of the trench. With a simple ratchet motion, they chambered rounds from the long ammunition belt feeding into the weapons and began firing into the night.

The commotion alerted Danjou, and the men with the MPs were soon joined by these French soldiers and gendarmes. All stood side-by-side, adding their fire to the trench's defence.

No sooner had they begun fighting than the well-trained Germans recovered from the surprise attack and sprang into action. Men with stick grenades hurled them toward the trenches, and though most fell too short and others too long, enough landed to start tearing holes in the Allied defensive line. These explosions were also enough to get defenders to duck, and so were no longer able to fire at the Germans rushing forward behind this cover.

'We're gonna need a miracle here,' McGavin yelled over the din of battle between chambering a round and sending it off toward the enemy. Far to the right of the Englishman a grenade exploded and killed five men.

The Germans were too experienced to remain in shock at the appearance of the enemy where they had been promised no enemy would be, and they were fighting their way through the tiny MP force. Things got even more dangerous when some of the Germans began laying down covering fire for smaller groups, who continued to dart from one piece of cover to another, inching their way forward.

Ash screamed at one of the machine guns to suppress these men, but his orders went unheard in the thunder of battle. Returning to his own rifle, he squeezed the trigger again and chambered another round as his first bullet hit one overly eager German in the chest.

Behind this man he could now see in the dying flare light what looked like a countryside starting to flow toward them. The initial hundred or so men were just the breach-head, sent forward to open the way for an entire German division. Thousands of men strong, they were now moving forward while the initial screen of soldiers at the front of their advance occupied the enemy trenches.

Loading and firing in a mechanical fashion, Ash started cursing King Rat, who clearly had abandoned them. All along the trench, the few men left continued to fight on, but they were far too few and, minute by minute, the accurate Germans ensured they were growing even fewer.

No sooner had the curse left his lips when a single shell screamed overhead, fired from somewhere behind their own lines. The shell exploded close to them with a thud that rattled the teeth and rang the ears. As his hearing recovered, Ash caught a voice talking into a field telephone.

'Short eighty, fire one for effect.'

Incapable of looking for whoever was calling in those coordinates as the enemy was so close, Ash slammed a fresh clip into his rifle and emptied it as fast as possible. There was no longer any need to even aim—the wall of enemy soldiers before him was that thick. When he saw one of the Browning gunners get shot in the head, he took a precious second to grab the arm of a man who, judging by the apron hanging down the front of his uniform, was likely a cook, and hauled him along as he ran to the gun.

Taking position at the trigger, he yelled, 'Keep the ammunition coming. While I'm firing, open the next box of ammo. When you see the last bullet in the belt go through, I'll open the breech, you lay the next belt across, and we keep going until all those boxes are empty—got it?'

Ash did not wait to see the wide-eyed cook nod yes and start to open a box of ammunition; he thumbed the triggers of the water-cooled machine gun and began knocking down the closest figures to the trench. He then swung the gun about and hunted out the largest gaggle of Germans, firing short, controlled bursts into these units.

As he fired again and again, he thought he felt the cook tugging at his shirt, perhaps to pass on a message, but soon realised the tugs were from bullets passing through his uniform. One even grazed his ear and, refusing to duck, he continued firing.

All too soon the Browning rattled empty as the last of the belt fed through the gun. In one smooth, practiced motion, Ash levered the top of the gun open and the cook instantly ran a new belt through the breach. Once it was lined up, he slammed it closed, re-cocked the weapon, and began firing again.

Bullets from the gun stitched across the countryside, catching a few Germans who had stopped to snipe at the Allies, but most just passing over their heads or hit soldiers moving up to join the attack. He continued firing until the belt ran empty again.

As the pair once more began reloading, the countryside before them blossomed into mushrooms of mud and trees of fire as units of unseen artillery, miles behind the battle, zeroed in on the fight and started laying down suppression fire. The dirt flung into the sky from these initial explosions had not even landed when a second salvo shrieked by overhead. It appeared the artillery commanders at the rear had received their warnings and begun a counter offensive.

This time, Ash felt his jacket being tugged for real. He turned and faced a soldier with black teeth pulling him from behind the gun and moving into his place. Ash looked about and noticed a stream of Canadian soldiers pouring into the trench to join them. Though these troops would likely not be enough to blunt a full attack, their appearance at least gave the MPs' ragtag army a fighting chance.

Remembering there was still another job he had to do, Ash grabbed two soldiers nearby, then duck-ran through the now cramped trench to McGavin's side. He slapped his fellow MP on the shoulder to get his attention, and the four of them ran off toward the rear of the Canadian lines.

They were hunting the man who could give them the answers they needed, possibly the only man who knew the extent of this entire revolution: Major Daniel O'Connell.

CHAPTER FORTY-FIVE

WATCHING THE FIRST WAVE OF GERMANS FALTER IN FRONT OF THE Allied lines, the Great King Rat lowered his binoculars and started clicking his tongue against the roof of his mouth in a nervous gesture.

'We goin' in?' one of his men asked.

'He's thinking, so back up and let him think,' another voice said nervously from the surrounding gloom of the trench.

King Rat continued to click and think, and then the decision was taken out of his hands.

'Holy fuck! You guys seeing this?'

The marketeer returned to looking across no man's land. Behind the first wave of Germans were thousands of men, charging across the battlefield as fast as they could and threatening to swamp the few defenders standing against them.

'Seems they were not lying,' Tommy Kirkland said.

'Seems like,' King Rat agreed. 'Well, boys, looks like we didn't get dressed up in our best party clothes for nothing.' Though most of the men had painted their faces, uniforms, and weapons in coal dust, their teeth and eyes against this were so bright they seemed to be glowing. 'Weasel!'

Through the gathered men, a smaller soldier with rodent-like features pushed his way forward. 'Boss?'

'Your man ready at the phone exchange?'

'If he isn't, he's going to wake up tomorrow with his balls on his pillow.'

'That would make an uncomfortable night's sleep,' Kirkland said.

King Rat put his hand on the smaller man's shoulder. 'The second we're there,' he said, pointing to a section of no man's land, 'get the wire connected and start calling in help.'

'I got it, boss, don't worry about it.'

'Don't worry about it, he says.' Kirkland gulped as the wave of Germans grew closer and closer.

As the battle raged before them, the black-market army pushed their way forward, taking up positions at certain strong points to create an enfilading effect by catching the enemy in covering fields of fire. The startled Germans found themselves attacked from new directions, effectively making much of the cover these soldiers had been using for protection from the Canadian lines now totally ineffective.

Moving his men forward, King Rat stationed them like a string of beads, with small gaps between pockets of soldiers supporting each other. This effectively allowed fewer men to hold a much longer line, but was dangerous as there were obvious gaps between them.

In this way, he managed to reach the very edge of the Canadian trenches, where he could hear more than see the MPs and their men fighting. With his few remaining uncommitted troops, the King Rat pushed on into the main defensive trench, where those troops with him began to plug the obvious holes in the firing line. He then called out to his secret weapon.

'WEASLE.'

The short man ran forward, this time leading a dog on a leash. The canine did not look happy at the noise about him, but remained at his master's side. On his torso was a strange coat contraption that ended in a small spindle of wire.

'Do it!' King Rat ordered.

Weasel kneeled next to the dog and unclipped the lead. He then grabbed the end of the wire poking out of the harness.

'Hansel, EXECUTE!'

With that command and a point in the right direction, the dog ran off, bounding out of the trench and toward the back lines, the wire unspooling fluidly behind him.

Weasel turned and attached the end of the wire he was holding to a field telephone. He then picked up the receiver and leaned an ear into it, trying to block the noise of the battle for the tell-tale sound of the phone line going live.

King Rat watched everything occurring about them. The Allies were only just holding, and if help did not arrive soon, the entire front was going to collapse.

'Well?' he urgently asked Weasel.

Weasel shook his head in the negative.

Pulling his own pistol, King Rat considered joining the line and adding his almost ineffectual firepower to the massacre unfolding about him. He aimed and fired at a German who managed to get into the trench near him, killing the man, and was about to crack open the gun and reload when Weasel tugged at his pants leg and gave him the thumbs up.

Hansel had arrived. Using speed and a low profile, the dog had managed to run the one hundred or so feet to a radio post stationed behind the trenches. There, Rat had stationed a man to look for the dog and connect the wire into the main lines once it arrived, thus bypassing the Canadian phone operators, which most likely were manned by Irish traitors.

'NOW FER CHRISTSAKE!' King Rat yelled.

Weasel, who had spent the time waiting for the line to go live by observing what was happening in the battle and matching it to the chart he held, yelled into the phone receiver, 'Short eighty, fire one for effect.'

This order arrived at the artillery unit that King Rat had bribed to be on standby in case they were needed. It cost several cases of whiskey and a box of raunchy pictures from Paris, but he now considered that a price well worth paying.

Seconds later, a single artillery shell sailed overhead and impacted deep in no man's land. The resulting explosion sent dirt and men flying into the air. He turned, gave Weasel a thumbs-up sign, and the little man began calling in more coordinates.

Soon dozens of shells were falling before them, shredding the exposed German army with the devastating effect of shrapnel and high explosives.

Though the artillery was helping to stem the flood, they were a long way from safe. There were still thousands of German soldiers out there, and if even a fraction of them made it into the trenches, they would be enough.

The black-market soldiers had helped hold the front, but attrition was taking its toll and now there were dangerously large gaps in their defensive line. Not for the first time, the Great King Rat considered calling out to his men to pull back, but then he caught a strange sound. At first, he would have sworn he could hear the sea, like the crashing of waves on sand, but that roar grew louder and louder until a flood of Canadian soldiers ran into the trench and joined the fight. These tough, experienced troopers filled the gaps and began pushing the Germans back.

Recognising the immediate danger had passed, the marketeer called out to his men, and those who could began pulling out of the firing line. And just like that the Great King Rat's army dissolved into the night as quickly as it had appeared.

With so much chaos, there were now opportunities to

exploit, and King Rat felt he had well and truly earned these spoils of war.

CHAPTER FORTY-SIX

As the MPs moved through the front trenches, someone called out that the Germans were beginning to pull back, and Allied soldiers from their own lines were charging into no man's land after them. Those new to the front gave a cheer, while the more experienced soldiers knew this could just be a lull before a renewed attack. They began looking about to repair defences, reload weapons, remove the injured, and take a drink.

Ash at first thought the men haring after the enemy might be some over-enthusiastic soldiers with their bloodlust up, but this all changed when McGavin found one of the Canadian captains leading the men who'd just arrived.

'Warm work today, sir. Could you tell me where Major O'Connell is?'

'Our Major O'Connell?' the man asked, confused. 'Funny you should ask that, he just took a few men and ran out after the Germans. He said something about getting maps back, but there have never been any maps stored in our front trenches.'

'He's making a run for it,' McGavin said.

'What do we do?' Danjou asked.

'We follow him,' Ash said, grabbing a fresh ammunition

bandolier from the supplies the Canadians had brought with
them.

'We?' the Frenchman asked.

'Yes, err, "we",' the Australian said. 'That's the spirit.'

'I was not volunteering,' Danjou stammered. 'I was asking
what you meant by "we"?'

'We are heading that way,' Ash said, pointing toward the
Germans. 'Who the hell knows what secrets that idiot O'Connell has stolen. We need to get him back before he can hand
anything off.'

The Australian gathered a few of the men he'd brought with
him and completed a quick inspection to ensure the trench was
now secure and that the fresh troopers moving in replaced the
fallen and injured. Things had already settled down so much
that hot food and strong tea was appearing.

Everyone devoured as much as they could, and from
around a mouth of hot bacon and bread, Ash managed to
croak, 'Eat up, fellas. We need to get moving and catch that
Paddy before he can get away. This might be the last meal we
see in a while.'

Picking up a Lewis gun and checking its round ammunition
cartridge was full, Ash hefted the weapon over one shoulder
and gestured at the trench wall. 'Gentlemen.'

Following the line of devastation into the battlefield, the
Australian led his team onto a path defined by lost equipment
and the shattered bodies of the dead and injured.

Because of their previous experience in this section of no
man's land, the motley crew of soldiers made good time, and for
a time even looked to be catching up with O'Connell.

Despite the German attack having faulted, their path
forward to this point had been far too easy, with not a single
shot fired their way. As they closed on the slow-moving Irish, it
soon became obvious why. O'Connell's men carried an Irish flag
above their heads, clearly a prearranged sign for them to pass

through the enemy lines without being shot. They were also walking to appear unthreatening.

The Germans likely believed the MPs, following so closely behind O'Connell's troop, were part of the same group, explaining why they met no opposition. This was still a dangerous trip though, as the region was full of unexploded bombs and entangling barbed wire—despite most of it having been cut or destroyed thanks to the shelling, there were partially buried strands everywhere that could entangle a boot or tear and infect skin.

Rusty barbed wire could kill a soldier as easily as a bullet on the Western Front.

Staying on the same path as the Irish helped them evade most of these dangers, but Ash was starting to think that their quarry was moving unnecessarily slowly because they expected to be followed. Having spent the last few years fighting for his life, the soldier's instinct in him suspected they were now walking into a trap.

This was not as unlikely as it sounded. The Australian army were by far the war's greatest souvenir hunters, and the fearless Aussies were known to sneak out at night, cross no man's land, and duck into the German trenches to steal anything not tied down. It became so bad that German troops began complaining when they found out Australians held the lines opposite them. One wrote a letter home, claiming the diggers 'were like cats, and were often discovered sneaking into their own trenches to steal everything and take prisoners'.

There was even one ANZAC, a man called Barney Hound, who had a dead-or-alive price placed on his head by none other than the Kaiser himself. It seems Barney was so good at sneaking over to the German trenches and 'souveniring', he managed at one point to steal a grand piano. Hound was also on the Allied watchlist as there were rumours that, while on weekend leave, he had robbed a bank in Amiens.

This experience at trench raiding became evident when the force reached the first stretch of German siege works. Ash and the other Australians gestured for everyone to stay put while they snuck ahead. It only took them a few minutes, but eventually they recognised a blind spot in the trench's defences and moved behind it. Once in position they leapt inside and subdued the small squad of Irishmen and their German allies who had been left behind to lay in wait for them.

They did this all so quietly, the rest of the motley Allied force were not aware what was happening until it was all over and the Australians began waving them in. As McGavin led his men forward, they entered the German trenches and were horrified at what they found.

Unlike the Allied fortifications, which always seemed to be made in a haphazard fashion, built from whatever was at hand at the time of construction to shore off the French mud and clay, the German trenches had concrete walls and well-built outposts to look after the men. They even had toilets.

'First time visiting Germany?' Ash asked.

In one of these bunkers, McGavin found what remained of the Germans and Irishmen who had been manning the trench. The bodies lay in one small alcove filled with smoke. One uniform was even still alight from the gunfight.

'What happened here?'

One of the Australians, who had been part of the attack, peered over his shoulder. 'Them? No time for prisoners, mate. Let's just say we just locked them in with Mr Mills.' The group then started heading down the corridor, and it was only later that McGavin realised the prisoners had been locked in that room, and a Mills bomb had been tossed in after them.

The group moved quickly through the German trenches, following O'Connell and what remained of his team. The few enemy soldiers they encountered, not expecting danger from the direction of their own lines, were easily subdued. Their unexpected success meant there was a real opportunity here, so the MPs stopped, penned a quick report, and sent a runner back to their own lines to ask for an immediate push forward to exploit the situation.

That done, everyone continued the pursuit of the Irish before they could reach a German communication post and forward on whatever information they were carrying.

'I think we can do it,' Ash whispered.

'I think you're a madman and we are all going to die here,' McGavin whispered back.

'*I think* we should head back before the Germans notice there is something strange happening along their trenches and send someone out to investigate,' Danjou added.

'We're doing this,' the Australian said adamantly.

Light was just starting to peek over the horizon, and before the three men was their worst nightmare. The Irish had reached a point where the Germans felt safe enough, and had space enough, to start interrogating their supposed allies. The MPs recognised Major O'Connell and a toady looking little sergeant, along with a dozen other soldiers in Canadian uniforms. Around them were twice as many Germans in varying states of alertness. Some held their weapons in a way to indicate they did not trust the Irishmen, others had their guns slung and appeared relaxed.

Time was against the Allied force and they desperately needed to move fast, so, just like the earlier attack, the men spread out and came at the German rally point from several directions. On Ash's signal they were all to lead with bombs and grenades, then under strict instructions from the Australians, they were to charge into the trench with bayonets on their guns. The reason for this was simple: the weapon terrified the Germans.

This simple piece of steel was reminiscent of battles from days gone by, when knights in armour ruled the battlefield. All armies were issued the weapon but they were almost never used in battle, more often evolving into a handy can opener or fire prod than used as a weapon. The Australians, however, drilled with the bayonet constantly, and they had learned early on that its appearance on a battlefield often brought more compliance amongst their enemies than any other weapon.

To start their charge, three grenades were tossed into the trench, with the Allies warned to not even get their heads up until the last one had detonated. Inexperienced men all too often enthusiastically ran into their own bombs, suffering losses that just the smallest amount of patience could have spared them.

After the grenades detonated, the Australians led the way into the trench, shooting, bayoneting, or clubbing anyone who had survived. The few Germans that had escaped unscathed were quick to respond, but the shock and awe tactic of the attack meant they were easily subdued. Dozens lay dead or wounded, the screaming and bleeding men, including a number of the Irish, pleading for help. When the attackers checked though, there was no sign of O'Connell. Somehow, he and his sergeant had managed to escape.

'We did this for nothing,' Ash spat angrily as he collected weapons and tossed them into a growing pile in the middle of the trench. His men took up positions to ensure they could not be assailed in the same way as they had just used.

'We stopped the attack and possibly saved the war. We most certainly saved that Canadian division, maybe even France itself,' Danjou argued, 'and that is certainly not nothing.'

Filing out of the dugout toward the Allied trenches came a line of surviving German and Irish soldiers under armed guard, their hands on their heads.

McGavin walked up to the first man and started searching his pockets. 'We may not have lost everything. We need to collect every scrap of paper, every map, anything not tied down, and then we need to get out of here.'

Ash stepped over to one Irish soldier he recognised from earlier in the line. 'And we need to make sure this arsehole is under guard until we can throw him in a deep, dark prison.'

CHAPTER FORTY-SEVEN

FITZHUGH STOOD NEXT TO SIR NEVILLE CHAMBERLAIN OUTSIDE the offices of Augustine Birdell, chief secretary to Ireland. Both had been told to wait, while Birdell went over their report with his under-secretary, Sir Nathan Matthews.

Returning from the wilds of Liverpool, Fitzhugh had received some thirty-five messages from his men in France about what they had uncovered. As he was working his way through these, a new and urgent wire was handed to him, fresh from the Western Front. The information this contained tied into what he had already learned, and he immediately called everyone he knew to get an interview with the one man who would understand its significance and be in a position to help. The three men then got on a train, then another train, and then a boat, followed by a third train to Dublin.

By the time they arrived, Fitzhugh was a hobbling bag of bruises and agony. He really needed to see a doctor about getting some morphine, but not until the job was done. For now, scotch was his painkiller of choice.

The men caught a cab directly to the office of the Inspector-General of the Royal Irish Constabulary, Sir Neville Chamberlain. The man had agreed to the call for an urgent meeting, and as Fitzhugh presented his evidence and theories, Chamberlain shook his head in doubt that the information was correct, but he was also not foolish enough to simply ignore it. There was always a chance it could be true.

The Inspector-General rang the office of his commander and organised an emergency meeting. Fitzhugh then left to tell his story to the Chief Secretary for Ireland, located at the rear of Dublin Castle. As always, Andrews followed, while Wolk begged off to take a walk around the ancient city and catch some sights. When was he ever going to get the chance to visit Dublin again? Understanding the urge, and realising they didn't need the Canadian until the next day, Fitzhugh agreed, and they all promised to meet up later at their hotel.

Dublin Castle was founded by King John of the Magna Carter fame in 1204, and over the centuries had been modified and rebuilt into the current seat of the English government in Ireland.

Items of interest were pointed out to the men by the soldier tasked to escort them to Birdell's office. Amongst the titbits he proudly revealed was that the imposing structure of Bermingham Tower was the only piece of the original fortification remaining, and that at one time it had been the prison where General Joseph Holt and his United Irishman were locked up during the Irish uprising of 1798.

Fitzhugh was hoping this was not some sort of universal sign of impeding doom, while Andrews was pleased to find out the Irish rebels were sent to serve their term in Botany Bay. He would remember that for the next time he had to deal with Ash.

Long minutes ticked by, punctuated by the occasional civil servant running to or from Birdell's office. Feeling the weight of what may be occurring as they stood there, Fitzhugh and Andrews nervously looked at each other, knowing the precious time they had left to stop a massacre was gone. Even now, free

Ireland supporters could be gathering in their thousands, about to initiate a rebellion to end the rule of the United Kingdom over their country.

Ireland was going to rebel, and Germany was about to take a step closer to winning the war by opening a second front against the king from a direction far too close to home.

CHAPTER FORTY-EIGHT

CAPTAIN SPINDLER STOOD ON THE BRIDGE OF THE CONVERTED SS Castro and watched the two Irishmen march onboard. With the arrival of this final element of his shipment, he issued orders for the vessel to begin preparations to sail.

The mysterious man who had arrived all those weeks ago and been sitting in his small passenger cabin awaiting their arrival had turned out to be the Irish born British politician, Roger Casement.

The entire plan was then explained to the newly minted captain. And he was tasked with sailing to Ireland with Casement, some former Canadian soldiers, and a shipment of weapons to help spark a new Irish revolution against the English monarchy.

Spindler, Casement, and their cargo were all set to sail and were just waiting for a small army of Canadian/Irish troops to arrive when things on the Western Front forced everyone's hand. Somehow the British had caught wind of the revolution and had even managed to block part one of the plan: an attack on the trenches in France.

Everyone flew into a panic, both Irish and Germans. Casement refused to sail with the ship, preferring instead to catch a much faster ride on a U-boat to Ireland to help prepare for the arrival of the weapons shipment. Spindler was then ordered to stow the guns and keep the *Libau* ready to sail for when the Canadians arrived.

Spindler was surprised to discover the weapons were Russian rifles, a handful of older-model machine guns, and piles of ammunition for both. The soldiers that had transported the weapons explained they had been captured when Germany first attacked the great bear in the north and overran entire sections of their lines—including Russia's vast supply dumps. Before he sailed on the U-Boat Casement had also inspected the guns and complained bitterly, believing the revolution was being issued inferior weapons. The German officer in charge of the procurement explained they were perfectly useable, the rifles just took a different type of ammunition to their own, and so for sake of uniformity these were being issued to the Irish as they were useless to the uniformity-loving German army.

Spindler watched on as Casement explained he understood, but now he had to wait and explain this to the Canadian troops they were waiting for before he left on the U-boat. This change of plan meant some of the Canadians would now be required to help retrain the men waiting for the shipment back in Ireland. They had been expecting German Mauser rifles, not Mosin—Nagants, Russian hand-me-downs from the turn of the century.

* * *

Major O'Connell and his sergeant no longer wore their Canadian uniforms, but the new and, more importantly for them, clean uniform of the German Irish Brigade. The pair had managed to escape the unexpected attack by the MPs on the German trench and had subsequently been rushed through the German lines to Berlin. Here they received their uniforms, new papers, and were sent on to the Baltic port of Lübeck to catch the disguised merchantman.

They were also given new names: Major Robert Monteith and Sergeant Daniel Beverley, and before departing for the coast they were issued a portable explosive device and tasked with placing it along the route King George V would take when he visited the Palace of Westminster.

Awaiting them at the top of the gangplank was the man who had designed the entire plan, Sir Richard Casement.

Instead of greeting his fellow countrymen warmly, Casement took the soldiers aside and, once he was sure no Germans could hear, gave O'Connell his news.

'We have to get home and stop these idiots.'

'The uprising? You want us to stop it?' O'Connell asked incredulously. 'After everything we have sacrificed?'

'Maybe not stop it entirely, but most certainly get them to postpone the thing until I can drum up more support. The Germans are cooling on us, and they most certainly are not giving us the weapons we asked for.'

'What's on the ship then?'

'Oh, they've given us guns and ammunition. Not enough, but some ...'

'Then what's the problem?'

'They're older Russian rifles called Mosin—Nagants, and we only received a handful of machine guns and explosives. No grenades or cannon, and they most certainly are not supplying the men to train us in how to use them and help create an effective army.'

'So, we'll train the men then,' the sergeant said, not recognising the point or the danger.

Luckily O'Connell did. 'We need to delay the attacks. Without German support or training, our people will be going up against an army with weapons they have no idea how to use.'

Casement agreed. 'I feel that if the Germans knew I'd uncovered their betrayal they would cancel the shipment and arrest us all. We need them to think everything is fine, so we'll get them to sail with the guns, and I have organised a U-boat to drop us in Ireland to get everything ready for their arrival. This way I believe we can beat the shipment home and stop the uprising. If we don't, then I'm afraid Ireland will be lost forever.'

'What about this stupid thing?' the sergeant asked, waving the suitcase full of explosives at his commanders.

'If that's what I think it is,' Casement said, 'give it to Captain Spindler for storage. There's no way I'm taking a bomb with us on a submarine.'

CHAPTER FORTY-NINE

'WHO IS HE?' DANJOU ASKED.

McGavin, the long-time Scotland Yard investigator, gave his companions a knowing smile.

With him in Fitzhugh's office stood Ash, Danjou, and the Australian who had recognised their prisoner. It had taken them nearly three hours to get back to their own lines, and their decision to leave had proven a wise one. Just as they began filing into their own trenches, German reserves arrived behind them and opened fire into no man's land, hoping to catch anyone they could out in the open. As the sun was now up, if the group had waited a minute longer, they would have been massacred.

After handing off the majority of their prisoners, the MPs had taken the German officer and deposited him in Fitzhugh's office for interrogation. Sitting in their absent commander's chair, Ash gave their prisoner a good once over. The German's uniform held no insignia other than his rank, and beside his slightly older age, he looked exactly like every other German they had captured in the trench.

One thing and one thing only had given him away, and it

was something the professional French sleuth had missed, but the digger hadn't. His boots.

Every soldier in the trenches wore the standard hobnailed jackboot, with metal rivets in the sole to add strength and durability. This man wore handmade boots that must have cost more than a soldier's yearly wage—boots that did not spend a lot of time in the trenches as they would never have survived.

'Mein Herr?' McGavin said, 'Anything to say for yourself?'

'You sure he speaks English?' Ash asked.

The Englishman lowered his face, placing himself at the prisoner's eye level. 'Not only does he speak English, I am certain he was there to meet Major O'Connell and debrief him, isn't that right, Count Casimir Markievicz?'

It was only there briefly, but McGavin caught it. That flicker of shock and recognition at hearing his own name.

'I should introduce myself. I am Sergeant Malcom McGavin, former inspector at Scotland Yard. I knew your wife very well.'

'My wife?' the prisoner said in almost perfect English.

'The Countess Markievicz. You know, the first woman to be elected to the House of Commons and a prominent Irish rouser and founder of Fianna Éireann …'

'Fianna Éireann?' Ash interrupted, struggling with the unfamiliar Irish word.

'They're pretty much the armed force of the Irish freedom army,' McGavin explained, then returned his focus to the prisoner. 'Why are you here? Waiting to meet the Irish traitors? Exactly what's going on?'

'I think you can work it out,' the count said, his voice now tinged with a Polish accent.

'The Irish are about to rebel?'

'Yes.'

'And the Germans are about to throw their weight behind them, successfully opening a second front.'

'No,' the count said. 'And I need your help to end what is

about to happen. The Germans have betrayed us all, and I now have no way of saving my wife.'

McGavin grabbed a wire slip and began furiously penning a message to Fitzhugh, transcribing everything the German officer told him. An open wire was not the best way to send a communication like this, but there was no choice.

They were all out of time.

CHAPTER FIFTY

FITZHUGH HAD LOOKED IN SHOCK AT THE WIRE FROM FRANCE. IT was almost unbelievable, so he read it three more times before contacting the office of Sir Neville Chamberlain. It was from McGavin, who laid out in detail everything Count Casimir Markievicz had explained. He now knew what the entire affair was about. Even as they stood there, free Ireland supporters were gathering to initiate a rebellion they believed would be supported by Germany.

The Germans had already supplied the Irish with a few weapons, and right now a shipment containing thousands of guns and over a million rounds of ammunition was on the way. The Irish believed this was the first step of a far larger plan, but what they didn't know was the guns were the only support they'd be receiving from the Kaiser, as he had already cancelled the rest.

Fitzhugh was aware Germany had begun their grand scheme by interviewing Allied prisoners of Irish descent and offering them a position in a special counter-unit they were forming. What he had not known was that the Irish Brigade was the idea of Sir Roger Casement, a former British civil servant and knight of the realm.

Casement had first made a name for himself in Africa, where he helped survey part of the Congo. Later he built a railroad through the region for the African International Association and its leader, the explorer Henry Morton Stanley.

Fitzhugh recalled he knew about Casement's love of Africa and the local tribes he encountered; during his work he shared a cabin with Joseph Conrad, another adventurer who was sailing up the Congo on the steamer *Le Roi des Belges*. Conrad was hoping to find a lost European in the dark heart of the continent, but what both men found was unthinkable horror.

Murder, maiming, rape, slavery—brutalities forced on the natives by a heartless European power, hidden from view by the tyranny of distance and the fact that this was happening to Africans.

Both men were disturbed by what they saw, and each channelled these horrors by writing about the experience in totally different ways. Conrad penned his most famous novel, *Heart of Darkness*, based almost entirely on his journey along the African river. Casement wrote a report on the horrid condition the locals were being kept under by their European masters, and through this experience he became interested in the subjugation of one group by another.

Accepting a position in the Colonial Service, Casement was instructed to travel into Africa and research human rights violations against the natives on the continent. What he found disturbed many—especially when he described the horrors inflicted by the Belgians on the natives working their national rubber plantations. This nightmarish world of torture, mutilations, and murder, inflicted on the Africans to ensure the extraction of rubber from the local rubber trees, fuelled Casement's growing frustration against all imperial rule.

When Casement returned home, he went on a crusade against such tyranny, in part driven by the realisation his railway and the work completed by Stanley had laid the foundations for King Leopold III's reign of terror in the Congo.

In 1907, Casement was ordered to follow up similar reports of abuses on native Indians by the Peruvian Amazon Company. What he found in South America mirrored the horror of Africa, again all in the name of rubber, and he returned to England a now devoted champion of universal freedom for all the world's people.

All of this was public knowledge, but what Fitzhugh's team had just uncovered from their prisoner was the darker side of this tale. Casement's known love of freeing the oppressed also included his homeland of Ireland, and at the start of the war he travelled to New York to discuss the possible intervention of Germany in Ireland with the Kaiser's agents there. If Germany could supply weapons and men to train an Irish army, this battle for Ireland would soon divert Allied troops away from the Western Front, so it was clearly an advantageous relationship for both.

The Germans loved the idea, and even took the plan further by asking Casement to visit the country's vast POW camps and recruit captured, disillusioned Irish volunteers. However, instead of a brigade of thousands of determined fighting Irishmen, Casement could only sign up fifty or so prisoners. In the face of this lacklustre response, the German command secretly cancelled many of the efforts it had planned to support the Irish, only following through with those schemes that helped their own efforts. This included the recent failed attack on the Canadian lines.

This betrayal meant the rebels in Ireland—including one of its greatest supporters, the Countess Markievicz—were about to take on the might of England's Royal Irish Constabulary, itself far more an army than a governing police force. Count Markievicz was spilling all in hopes they could save the countess before things went too far and his wife ended up hanging from the end of a British rope.

After waiting an hour, the doors to Birdell's office finally swung open and both men were ushered in to meet the chief secretary. On the large table before them lay their report, a map, and a few opened files.

'Come in, gentlemen, and please sit,' said one of the numerous officers standing about the table.

Walking over to one of the two offered chairs, Fitzhugh couldn't hold his temper in check any longer. 'Sir, I really must insist ...' But any further outburst was stopped when the chief secretary waved him away.

'Yes, I know, I know. I have read your report, Captain. It is Captain, isn't it?'

In that one sentence, Fitzhugh knew things were about to go very badly.

'Yes, old boy, we've looked over your report and find it disturbing.' This comment came from Nathan Matthews, Birdell's undersecretary, the man who had invited them to sit.

'As did I!' Chamberlain added, not yet picking up the difference in tone those already in the room were using.

'As you can see,' Birdell asserted, 'we have read your report and tapped into our own information service. We do have resources in the field you may not be aware of, and though you seem to have a few valid arguments, I must say we have heard nothing about even the possibility of an Irish uprising.'

'That, sir, is complete rubbish. I personally have warned you about a possible uprising several times over the past month,' Chamberlain argued.

'Indeed,' Birdell said, giving his subordinate a look that told him how much he valued those warnings. 'The island is whole-heartedly behind the war effort, and many leading Irishmen are working hard, positioning themselves in a strong position for when the conflict ends. We believe they intend to continue playing their part to earn some sympathy, so that later they can get back to the foolish "self-governing" issue once Germany is defeated.'

'Foolish?' Fitzhugh asked, dumbfounded.

'Oh certainly, behind closed doors it's possible to see the Irish probably have every right to ask for their freedom. If we were in a similar position, I'd argue for the same. But let's face it, they're incapable of controlling and policing their own popu-lation. If we were to pull out of Ireland, and I mean right now, the country would become a bloodbath. Neighbour would attack neighbour, county versus county, Catholic versus Protes-tant, and all that rubbish. The Irish may want self-rule, but do you honestly think they could succeed? It's our belief Parlia-ment has already come to the same conclusion, that offering any sort of freedom guarantee would be a mistake. At this time, and for the foreseeable future, we will not be leaving Ireland. Indeed, if what you say is even remotely true, it would be the height of insanity to have a German ally just miles from our shore—one it would be almost impossible to police.'

'Wait,' Fitzhugh stammered, taking everything in and latching onto something the man before him had said, 'did you say "if" what is in our report is true?'

'Ah, to the crux of the matter. I thank you for your work, and applaud you for your tenacity following up this matter, taking one for king and country and all that,' Birdell said, gesturing to Fitzhugh's bandaged hand and foot. 'I want to assure you, we will be making our own enquiries. For now, it's the belief of this office that the likelihood of an Irish rebellion is infinitesimal at best. We won't be asking the Home Office for any forces to suppress something that, let's face it, even if it did happen, would be on such a small scale that our own troops stationed in Ireland would be more than capable of suppressing it.'

'Suppressing? Army?' Fitzhugh said in disbelief. 'Did you not read my conclusion? This isn't about crushing a revolution. It's about stopping the damn thing before it starts. People are going to get hurt! People are going to be killed, and right now we have a chance to fucking stop it. But instead of even taking this simple step, you're sitting here with your fingers in your ears and hoping it will all go away.'

'Now hang on, old man,' Matthews said, stepping in like a shield between the chief secretary and the enraged soldier, 'there's no need for that sort of language in here. We understand you're close to this thing, you're in pain, you're tired and a little upset, but we won't have you speaking like that to your betters.'

'Betters?' Fitzhugh bit, pushing past Matthews. 'You're fucking kidding me! I've flushed better shits than you idiots in the last few days. At least the Irish are trying to do something noble. You … you're sitting here trying to save face in case I'm wrong.' In frustration Fitzhugh slammed his fist onto the table between them. 'But I'm not wrong. The Irish are going to rise, and if you don't do something about it, and I mean right now, I'll make damn sure you're the first in front of the firing squad when the dust has settled, and the baying and the lit torches come out. You're going to massacre your own people, and you will pay for it.'

The tone in the room had cooled considerably, and finally the chief secretary, his eyes as cold as ice, said, 'Well, according to the Irish they're not actually our own people, now are they?'

Fitzhugh, teeth clenched, head throbbing, and ready to punch the man before him, took a deep breath and said, 'Even if that was true, you still have a responsibility to them, as well as the English soldiers in your command who are also going to die for your inactions.'

CHAPTER FIFTY-ONE

WITH ALL THREE OF HIS PASSENGERS NOW TAKING THE U-BOAT, Spindler prepared the *Libau*, now under its third identity change. He made a final check that everything was safely stowed, including the suitcase the Irish had given him, and then set sail into the Atlantic. The Irish Revolution had formerly begun.

Hidden under its new name, the SS *Aud* sailed high into the polar North Atlantic. After about a week, Spindler turned the vessel south, intending to travel past the west coast of Ireland until he cleared the UK entirely; he would then turn north and arrive along the southern coast of the island. It was hoped any vessels the *Aud* encountered during the voyage would be fooled into thinking the transport was an Allied ship due to the direction it was coming from ... and it was a gambit that worked perfectly.

Looking like an innocent British vessel, the *Aud* sailed right past the Royal Navy's 10th Cruiser Squadron, only to head right into a brutal storm. This weather proved perfect for Spindler to begin his next task. The *Aud* was nearing the end of its journey, and the weapons would need to be unloaded as fast as possible.

With this in mind, the captain ordered for the provisions the ship was carrying to hide the weapons to be thrown overboard. All but invisible thanks to the weather, this suspicious activity could begin and would reduce the time the vessel would have to be docked during unloading. This meant he could head for home and lessen the risk of the *Aud* being discovered.

Two days later, the merchantship arrived at its rendezvous point along the Irish coast and weighed anchor at Tralee Bay. Spindler looked up and once again checked the pre-arranged signal flags fluttering high above the deck. He hoped to quickly make contact with the Irish rebels so he could get underway again. The plan was for local custom agents to meet the boat and ensure the vessel could be unloaded safely, without drawing any unwanted attention.

The entire day passed without notification from shore, so when night fell, the Germans prepared to meet with the U-boat that had brought Casement to Ireland. If there had been any change to the plan, this was the last chance for Spindler to find out. Either the U-boat would pass on this information, or the vessel would not appear, indicating it had been sunk and Casement was likely never delivered.

After a long night of staring into the dark Atlantic, waiting to be uncovered at any time and jumping at every perceived shape in the cold water about them, when the submarine failed to show, Spindler started to get a bad feeling. He ordered the men to retrieve their German naval uniforms from their hiding spot and wear them under their Norwegian clothes. If they were to be captured, it would be as German sailors. This would also ensure they would avoid being shot as spies if caught.

Afraid of failing his very first command, Spindler decided to wait instead of turning and running for home. He returned to Tralee Bay, ensured the flags above displayed the correct message, and once more watched the shoreline for any sort of response. Hours passed, and now thoughts ran through his head that the revolution had already been suppressed and everyone he was expecting to meet had been arrested. The German felt his ship was the cheese in a mousetrap, one about to snap shut over them. Yet still he stayed.

His stress was doubled when the U-boat again failed to appear that night. Something had most certainly gone wrong, and yet Spindler refused to sail home. If his commanders were correct, this one small action could have a real effect on the war, perhaps even help win the thing. What was the cost of a few more hours of boredom to achieve that?

Men continued to watch the coastline for any sign their contact had arrived to take possession of the shipment. As they were scanning the shore, a British vessel approached and signalled a demand to see the strangely acting *Aud's* papers.

With his hold empty except for the guns, there was little Spindler could do but prepare for visitors. The young captain stood on his bridge and readied himself to entertain the British boarding party. Everything now depended on him pulling off one of the all-time bluffs of the war.

CHAPTER FIFTY-TWO

As the British vessel approached, Captain Spindler gave thanks to all the preparations he had undertaken.

Perhaps it was because this was his first command, or perhaps it was because he was born a cautious man, he had taken several extraordinary steps to ensure his mission was a success. The first was to pretend he was Norwegian, and he even went as far as to carry photos and letters from a phantom girlfriend, written in his supposed native language. He also had his vessel outfitted with everything Scandinavian, including the bedsheets, plates, and stored food. He hoped these small details would be the icing on the supplied fake cake of papers the SS *Libau* was hiding beneath, explaining they were a neutral ship on the way to Genoa.

Spindler had also learned a few words of Norwegian, not enough to hold a conversation, but he hoped enough to fool the British Navy. Little did he know how important these preparations would prove to be.

On the morning of the third day, a steamer pulled from shore and approached the *Aud*. The Germans gave a cheer as the small vessel seem to be flying the recognition signal to their own prearranged message.

Any hopes the Germans had that their long-awaited Irish contacts had finally arrived were dashed when the steamer —Setter II—raised the British battle ensign. This was an enemy warship now bearing down on them, and somehow it just happened to be flying the recognition colours the Germans were waiting for.

With no way of getting up to speed in time to escape, Spindler prepared to play out his charade as the British ship pulled alongside. A voice below demanded to see their papers as the vessel had been acting weirdly, and Spindler realised returning three days in a row and never approaching the harbour had been a major mistake. Realising he needed to check his cabin to ensure everything important was hidden, he grabbed one of his sailors, a junior officer called Dusselman, and asked him to stall the enemy. He then disappeared into the depths of the vessel.

* * *

The Setter II proved to be no warship, but a tiny pilot vessel, and by the time it docked alongside the Aud, it was all but invisible to the Germans.

'Where are you from?' came a voice from below.

Dusselman stood in the doorway to the bridge listening in, but did not answer.

'Hallo! Where are you from?'

The men standing about looked at him nervously, but still he said nothing.

'Goddam! I asked you, where are you from?' the voice yelled angrily.

The sailor finally walked to the edge of the deck and called down pleasantly, 'Good morning.'

'Hell and damnation,' shouted the captain of the *Setter II.* 'I don't want your civilities. I want to know where you come from.'

'Then, first of all, would you mind telling me who you are?' asked Dusselman, trying to keep the mirth out of his voice.

'I'm the captain of this ship. Are you the captain of the *Aud*?'

'No, I am the second officer,' the German answered.

'Where's your captain?'

'Shh! He's asleep.' The men about him started to laugh, but a grinning Dusselman gestured them to be quiet.

'Well, wake him at once.'

'The devil I will,' Dusselman yelled back, leaning over the side and catching his first sight of the enemy captain. The man was overweight, almost bald, and angrier than any human being he'd ever seen before. 'The old man would half kill me if I called him for no good reason.'

'Very well then, I'll do it myself,' the English captain roared, going a shade redder in the face.

Dusselman thought there was a good chance the man was about to have a heart attack if he did not calm down. Right there and then he decided to see if he could make him suffer one.

'Do *you* want to get killed? He's an ogre of a man when awoken.'

'I don't care. I'm coming aboard to knock the sleep out of your captain,' the man below yelled. 'You'll see how the captain of a ship in the service of His Britannic Majesty deals with men like him.'

'I'd like to see that,' Dusselman answered with a taunting laugh. 'Let's see you do it.'

There was a long pause before the English captain yelled, 'How do I get up the damn side of the ship?'

The German sailors could no longer contain themselves and

fell about laughing, some holding their sides as if they were about to burst.

Everyone soon managed to calm down and Dusselman wiped the tears from his eyes. He then took a deep, cleansing breath and answered, 'I suppose the captain of a ship in the service of His Britannic Majesty will show us how it is done.'

There was now an even longer pause, and the Germans strained to listen in as the British far below discussed how to scale the steep side of the ship without the aid of the crew above.

Eventually the English captain asked in a far more polite voice, 'Please, could you let down a ladder?'

Dusselman waited a beat, allowing the tension to build. 'Certainly, with the greatest pleasure.' He then waited, and just as the English captain was going to thank him, he added, 'But I must first call the crew, they are all still asleep.'

Everyone around the bridge burst out in laughter again, and this time there was no controlling it. Things were not helped when Dusselman began stomping around the deck, cursing and yelling to supposedly rouse the crew into action. He eventually returned and, with a nod, ordered the men to begin lowering a ladder.

After a few minutes the English captain, blowing hard from the climb, arrived on deck with two armed guards.

'Now then, where's your captain?' he demanded.

'Don't shout so loud,' Dusselman whispered. 'If you wake the skipper, you will know about it. He is the most feared captain in all Norway.'

Taken aback by this, the Englishman stammered, 'But it is most urgent that I speak to him. So, come along with me.' He then gestured for the German sailor to enter the bulkhead first.

'All right,' answered Dusselman, deliberately standing to the side. 'But you will have to go first.'

'No, you go in front,' said the Englishman, clearly thinking there was something suspicious about this entire conversation.

'All right, but don't say I didn't warn you,' Dusselman said, and stepped inside.

* * *

Spindler came to his cabin door, cursing in a way he hoped would sound Norwegian. 'Damnation! What's the meaning of this confounded drumming?'

Dusselman saluted. 'Good morning, sir! I am very sorry to have to trouble you.'

The German captain looked past his subordinate at the Englishmen behind him. 'If you wish to speak to me, be good enough to wait until I have dressed.' He then slammed his door.

Astonished, the English captain turned to Dusselman and asked, 'Are all your Norwegian captains such bounders?'

'All I can tell you is that this one is a regular tartar,' the German answered.

Finally, Spindler reappeared, dressed and looking like he was ready to skin everyone in sight. He led the worried-looking English sailors back up to the bridge.

With a nervous gulp, the British officer got right to the point. 'Papers? And why have you been holding offshore for the last three days?'

In as harsh an accent as he could, Spindler explained, 'We got caught in a storm near Rockall. The waves hit us so hard they shifted the cargo. We have been here the last few days, where it's sheltered and a lot easier to redistribute and tie everything back down.'

From where he stood, the British officer could look across part of the ship's main deck. There he could see some of the goods the Germans had placed to get at the weapons they'd been hiding. This chaos did seem to indicate the crew were indeed in the middle of redistributing the cargo about the hold.

Spindler hoped the English didn't look too closely; some of the cases sitting on the deck for all to see were full of ammunition.

'Destination?' the English captain asked.

'First Cardiff, then on to Naples, and finally Genoa,' Spindler answered.

'Storm damage, huh? That must have been rough,' one of the British guards asked.

'Yes,' Spindler said shortly.

'We caught the edge of the storm a few days ago. I remember thinking I'd hate to be one of the poor fools caught in that.' The English captain laughed, swatting Spindler playfully on his back.

'More fool us,' Spindler replied with his own fake smile. 'I remember thinking I hope the whiskey we're carrying does not shatter. That is one thing the owners will not understand being "damaged" in a storm.'

Clearly, he had said the right thing; the officer and his men became intensely interested in his story.

'And was it?' one of the Englishmen asked.

'Was what?' Spindler said, letting his prey run a little with the line before he hooked them and reeled them in.

'The whiskey. Was the whiskey okay?'

'Oh that.' Spindler could swear the Englishmen were leaning toward him, desperate for an answer. 'One crate was damaged, and a few bottles were lost. I am thinking I should write off the entire case, then we can have a great voyage, don't you think?' He elbowed one of the soldiers playfully.

'That does sound like a great plan,' the British officer said. 'Whiskey is in short supply here.'

Was that an invitation to offer a bribe? Spindler saw no

danger in asking. 'Oh, that is a shame. Say, would you boys like a bottle? I'm not a big whiskey drinker, truth be told.'

The Englishmen could not say yes fast enough.

Hooked little fishy, Spindler thought. *Now to reel you in.*

Regulations stated there was a zero-alcohol policy on Royal Navy vessels during wartime, and the armed guards were happy to admit they had not had a drink since their last furlough, nearly a month ago. Spindler felt like he was now caught in a tricky predicament. He did not want the enemy to stay too long onboard and perhaps uncover their secret, yet he was keen to find out what had been happening in Ireland.

Spindler pulled a few glasses from a cabinet, cracked the seal on a bottle, and poured his new friends a healthy shot each. The British did not even pretend they should not drink it; they just downed the liquor in a single gulp and were lining up for more.

Within minutes the first bottle was gone and the sailors began powering through the next, and everyone was getting along famously. The men talked about what they had seen so far in the war, with the Germans being very careful to limit their drinking so they could keep a clear head and their stories straight.

As the English drank, Spindler signed the official log their officer carried as Niels Larsen, captain of the Norwegian steamer *Aud*, carrying pit-props. These were small pieces of scaffolding used to support tunnel walls and ceilings.

At the mention of pit-props, the enemy captain remarked cheerfully that this cargo was badly needed in England, and in confirmation of this statement he emptied his glass at a gulp and admitted they had to get moving. Referring to the Norwegian newspapers lying on the table, partly to ensure the English captain saw them and help strengthen the charade, Spindler asked if there were any English newspapers they could take to catch up on the news. The English proved happy to supply the

few papers they had, and immediately called down for someone
to send them up.

While the English drank and everyone waited for the newspapers, the chat around the table eventually turned to the war.
The Germans found themselves in the tough position of having
to bad mouth their own side to the enemy.

When the newspapers arrived, Spindler threw a cursory eye
over the pile, and right on the front page was a story explaining
several Sinn Fein leaders had been arrested in Fenit on suspicion of a conspiracy against the English government.

Desperate to read more, the German suggested to his
English counterpart that it might be time for them to move on,
but their guests were more interested in drinking. Some of the
Germans exchanged looks, hinting they should take the opportunity to kill the Englishmen and make a run for it. Instead, they
kept up the conversation, chatting about mindless things and
their hopes for a better job after the war.

Everything went smoothly, and finally the British, with only
a small amount of prompting, decided it was time for them to
head back to shore. As an afterthought, the English captain
warned them there were U-boats around, but not to worry, they
would guard the entrance until the Norwegians were ready to
leave.

Spindler thanked the British officer for the offer and the
newspapers. He also ensured the English left with an extra
bottle, and they each wished the other a safe war.

These last comments seemed to catch in the British officer's
craw, and he suddenly turned back to Spindler, his face serious.
Between hiccups, he said, 'I should warn you before you leave,
there is supposedly a German auxiliary cruiser sailing these
waters. It's apparently landing weapons to the Irish.'

The German officer tried to conceal the cold flash of horror
that washed over him.

'Look here, I will tell you how it is. You Norwegians are

good fellows, so there is no harm in my telling you, although it is really supposed to remain absolutely secret. Well, we, that is to say, the Naval Staff, have discovered that the damned German swine want to join the Irish in bringing about a revolution. They chose me to capture the auxiliary cruiser, which is due to come in here and bring arms for the Irish. Look at the harbour and the entire bay—the whole place is bristling with guns! What a fine reception those Germans will get from us. Of course, the beggars are clever—but we English are a jolly sight cleverer.'

Spindler and Dusselman laughed, partly in relief, as the enemy captain, believing they were laughing with him, repeated with a grin, 'Yes, they are terribly stupid, despite all their cunning!'

No sooner did the *Setter II* pull away than Spindler yelled at his men to prepare to sail. That evening, the *Aud* fired up her steam whistle and gave one long, loud blast. She then signalled the British ship, informing them they were underway and thanking them. The British signalled back that they would keep their promise of protecting the merchantmen safe from U-boat attack, and built up steam to follow.

Spindler became concerned when the *Setter II* suddenly increased speed and began to cross his bow.

Dusselman stepped up to his side. 'Sir, they're cutting us off. I think they are on to us.'

Watching the way the British ship moved, he could not help but agree. 'All right, bring us up to full speed. We're going to ram the little shit and send them to the bottom.'

Across the bridge, orders were issued and answered, and the atmosphere became far grimmer. Empty as she was, the ship answered her crew and sped up, closing on the *Setter II* quickly. The gap between the two vessels shrank, and that's when Spindler noticed the smaller ship's crew were waving at them in a friendly goodbye and signalling a safe voyage.

He yelled at the helmsman to pull away, and the *Aud* cut across the bow of the smaller ship and aimed for the harbour exit. Realising he had been holding his breath, Spindler exhaled, then called for their whistle to be blown as a sign of thanks. The *Setter II* then took up a position off her stern and followed closely as the Germans sailed into deeper waters. There the warship stayed for nearly five miles, ensuring the *Aud* was free and clear from attack before turning back to harbour.

The Germans watched the little steamer pull away and began cheering. They had escaped and were on their way home.

CHAPTER FIFTY-THREE

WOLK AND ANDREWS WAITED ALONG THE SIDE OF THE ROAD WITH the twenty marines Fitzhugh had managed to scrounge from the British naval units searching for the *Aud*. As there had been no help forthcoming from Birdell or the Irish constabulary after the heated meeting, they just had to make do with what troops Fitzhugh could find about town.

If their reports were accurate, the Irish brigade would be rushing down to the beach with trucks to help transport the weapons and ammunition the Germans were about to deliver. If the Royal Navy botched their side of the mission and missed the *Aud*, allowing it to reach the coastline, it was Wolk's job to make sure at least the trucks never arrived.

Wolk was bored and cold. They had been manning this outpost on top of the grassy hill overlooking the road to Keerys coastline without so much as a kid on a bicycle riding past. But orders were orders, and he was in command now that Fitzhugh's injuries had finally taken a toll on the man. For what felt like the thousandth time, the Mountie picked up his field glasses and began scanning the horizon for any movement.

Next to him, Andrews checked to make sure his rifle had a round chambered.

'Leave it, will you? You're bugging me,' the Canadian snarled. The sergeant just gave him a cool look and returned his attention to the weapon.

'Sir,' one of the marines called from a different section of the hill, which overlooked a small dirt road leading to the Irish countryside. 'Lights.'

Keeping his silhouette low so that he could not be seen with the lighter sky behind him, Wolk moved over to the marine and immediately saw the line of trucks bumping their way toward the coast. Four trucks meant they were facing maybe ten men to load the goods onto the vehicles.

Wolk checked down the hill and ensured the large tree they had cut down was still in place across the blind corner on the road. He then cursed himself for doing pretty much what he'd just bawled out Andrews for doing as well. He had checked that damn tree at least twenty times today and nothing had changed. They were as ready as they could be, and now it was just a matter of seeing their plan through to the end.

It took nearly twenty minutes for the first truck to rattle down the lane, its twin light beams illuminating the countryside and hedges on either side of the road, as well as the road itself. Here and there, small pinpoints of light flashed, and Wolk was about to call out a warning when he realised what he was seeing were the eyes of rabbits and foxes out on their nightly chores.

'Remember, wait until all the trucks have stopped,' he whispered above the distant din of the truck engines.

Leaning up on his elbows, he checked the far side of the blockade to make sure everyone on the hill opposite was ready, with their weapons all trained on the trucks. Even in the dark he could tell their faces were grim with determination and fear.

With a screech of ancient brakes, the first truck pulled up to a sudden halt before it hit a large tree laying across the road.

Immediately, two dark figures dropped from the truck's cabin and walked forward, while three more leaped from the back. From his position, Wolk could hear what the men below were saying, and when he heard key words like ship and guns, he knew he had his men. Despite this, he did not give the order to attack; instead, he watched with anticipation as another two men from the rear of the first truck got down and walked backward, waving at the following vehicles to slow down. If the first truck had at least five men, how many more where in the trucks following?

Inwardly, Wolk cursed himself. Of course, there were going to be a lot of men. Loading weapons and supplies would take time, and the more men they had, the faster the job would be done and the German ship could return home.

Raising a hand to protect his eyes from the glare of the truck lights, the MP tried to spot what weapons the Irish were carrying. He could see a few had shotguns, while one or two men carried what looked like hunting rifles. The Mountie knew exactly what damage a high-powered hunting rifle could do in the hands of an experienced shooter, but he still felt that if this was all these men had, the odds were still very much in favour of his marines. All were carrying modern military rifles, which they were trained to use. They had even procured a Lewis gun, which sat halfway along their lines.

Back down the hill, there were now four men trying to move the tree trunk Wolk had earlier ordered placed across the road. He watched warily as one of these men walked to the far end and noticed that the tree hadn't fallen—it had been cut down.

'Sergeant,' Wolk whispered.

Tracking the man, Andrews waited until he'd cleared the tree and looked like he was about to call out. The Mountie slowly squeezed his own rifle's trigger, and the weapon suddenly bucked once and, less than a second later, the man near the tree pitched backward. Immediately, the rest of the firing line opened up at the Irish men and the vehicles. The Lewis gun began chattering away; its mission was to first blow the truck tires, then turn on the Irish if they had not already surrendered. There was a hope the rebels would simply submit in the face of such overwhelming odds.

At the bottom of the hill, like an attacked ants' nest, men leaped out of the trucks, with most dropping into cover and returning fire. The men without rifles and shotguns carried pistols, which they fired and reloaded as quickly as they could.

Wolk could hear the occasional round sing over his head as he fired. Each time he fired he knocked down a figure, and he reloaded and ordered his men to keep up the pressure. When a few men below made a break for cover, leaping over the fallen tree and running for a gully that led toward the coast, the Canadian waved the flashlight he'd kept next to him. Answering this signal, the five-man squad Wolk had hidden on the other side moved out of their positions and intercepted these rebels after a short exchange of fire.

What Wolk and his men couldn't know was that the Irish had no intention of surrendering. They knew treason carried a death sentence and, if they survived, the vindictive British government would eventually find out what they knew and who else was involved. They also felt that if they could fight long enough, the Germans, who even now they believed to be waiting for them at the end of the road or on a distant beach, could use this distraction to escape and hopefully land the weapons elsewhere. The guns they were delivering were the only real hope the rebellion had for winning their long-sought freedom, and so this was a sacrifice well worth making for the cause.

As the battle raged about the convoy, one by one the Irishman fell. Their shotguns were mostly out of range, and though the few men with rifles had managed to gun down one marine and wound three others, the outgunned rebels never really had a chance.

As the few remaining Irishmen fought on, wherever their muzzle flash was spotted, the Lewis gun soon swung into action and silenced them forever.

Less than twenty minutes after Andrews' first shot, the fight was over. The marines moved down the hill and searched the bodies for any information that could lead to more rebels. They also found two survivors, one a woman. Their wounds were so severe they were expected to pass before the night was through.

Wolk walked back up the hill and over to a nearby farmhouse with a phone he had organised earlier in the day to call in his report. Fitzhugh was waiting for his call at the local police chief's office, and he ordered the Mountie to load all the bodies onto a single truck and bring them to their temporary HQ.

Here the captain and the police completed another thorough search of the bodies for information. When they were done, Fitzhugh ordered the truck to drive to a rarely used wharf along the coastline. At the top of the small hill leading down to the wharf, the British rigged the truck's acceleration pedal and let it go. The truck rolled down the hill, across the wharf, and broke through the small railing at the far end, plunging into the ocean beyond.

The marines waited to see if any of the bodies inside floated to the surface, and when none did, they returned to their barracks, allowing the local police to take charge of the 'accident' and begin writing up their reports on the apparent tragedy.

CHAPTER FIFTY-FOUR

ROGER CASEMENT FELT SICK, BUT HELD ONTO THE VEGETABLE soup he had for lunch as he made his way along the rolling hull of the submarine. This was the first thing he'd managed to keep down since climbing onboard the U-19.

The U-boat, large for a submarine, had been tossed around like a cork in the violent, choppy English Channel, and things only got worse when the vessel entered the open Atlantic. Her captain had been successful at sneaking past the swarms of destroyers and corvettes protecting England from such an attack by heading north, and then moving down the western coast of Scotland and on to county Kerry. Once the Irishmen were off the warship, it was then to move on and rendezvous with Spindler's *Aud*.

Stepping onto the small rubber dinghy floating alongside the hull of the U-boat, which already contained the newly minted Major Monteith and Sergeant Beverley, Casement settled himself in the flimsy vehicle's bow. The three men picked up small oars and began rowing toward the beach, barely visible in the dark night. As the little craft bobbed up and down and from side to side, a victim of the ocean swell, Casement was sure they were about to capsize at any moment and he would soon lose the vegetable soup.

Beverley explained that he was a fisherman before the war, and promised him they would be fine. The waves were actually small, and not the monolithic pulses of death Casement was proclaiming. He assured everyone they would be on shore in just a few minutes.

While both soldiers rowed, Casement looked back and noticed the submarine's captain standing on the conning tower, watching them move away. He tried to remind himself that the carefully crafted swashbuckling look Captain Raimund Weisbach maintained was all too real. During their time onboard, Casement had learned that it was Weisbach who'd been a serving officer onboard U-20 when it attacked and sunk the ocean liner RMS *Lusitania*. The man was a wolf in a snappy uniform.

The submariner noticed the Irishman watching and fired off a crisp salute, before turning and disappearing within the tower. Shortly after the U-boat dived, hungry to begin her search for more victims, and the three men were alone.

As the Sergeant had promised, after a few minutes Ballyheigue Bay grew larger and larger as the men paddled closer to shore. Though Beverley continued to shout instructions, his words were lost over the crashing of the nearby surf, so Casement decided to just sit and ride it out. Though he believed the small rubber craft was possibly the flimsiest boat humanity had ever created, and so all but useless for such a journey, it in fact proved itself to be a hardy vessel. Its inflated tubes rode easily over the churning surf, and all three men were soon deposited safely ashore.

Pulling the vessel onto the beach, the revolutionaries immediately slashed the sides of the dinghy, deflating it. Casement next took out his map and compass from a waterproof bag and took a bearing for their first meeting place: an old fort clearly marked on the map, which happened to lay miles from the nearest town and farmhouse. Once he was orientated, the map was wrapped with their rifles, papers, and life preservers inside the ruined rubber boat, and the entire package was buried in the sand for later retrieval.

All three men then headed into the Irish countryside, leaving the Atlantic behind.

* * *

Only hours after the spies had landed, a British home guard patrolman walking the beach with his two dogs spotted footprints running from the waterline to the far edge of the sand. Flicking the flashlight on, he noticed the footprints only headed in one direction, toward a large section of churned up sand that was not as smooth as the sand surrounding the area.

Correctly believing something had been buried there, the guardsman only had to dig up a few handfuls of sand before he found the ruined dinghy. Once the vessel was cleared off, he unwrapped the contents it contained, and if the German-style weapons were not enough to warn him the enemy had recently landed on the beach, the map of Ireland, printed in German, certainly was.

Deducing that a lone man with a single bolt-action sparrow gun was no match for trained Boche invaders, the guardsman hurried back to the local HQ and made his report.

* * *

The report that someone had landed at a nearby beach was enough to entice Fitzhugh to limp back out into the field. By first sunlight the following day, he was hot on the trail of whomever had climbed off the U-boat. Radiating out from the beach, teams of men with dogs headed inland searching for any sign of the spies. At the same time, a line of men, like beaters on a pheasant hunt, left the village of Ardfert and walked through the landscape toward the coast. The hope was this would push the spies back toward the soldiers searching for them from the beach.

Dogs barked and pulled at leashes once they had the scent, and the soldiers followed them, weapons ready, believing they were about to stop a full-scale invasion. Like terriers after a fox, the pursuers closed in slowly on an ancient Celtic walled settlement called McKenna's Fort. This proved to be no fort at all, but little more than an earth hillock surrounded by thick hedges.

By the time Fitzhugh and the home guard caught up with the Irishmen, the three men were sheltering under a small tree. Roger Casement was shivering, suffering from another bout of malaria, a disease that had plagued him since those horrific days sailing along the Congo.

Cold, hungry, and confused about what to do next, the three men were huddled around a small fire trying to keep warm. The men were taken to the local police station, where Casement urgently began to recount his story in exchange for Fitzhugh's help in alerting the revolutionaries about Germany's betrayal, and so help avoid a massacre. The man was sick, distressed, and praying for a miracle.

The captain immediately sent messages to the offices of Nathan and Birrell. He then contacted the Royal Navy and warned them about the imminent arrival of a German merchantship carrying the weapons Casement had been hoping to meet.

CHAPTER FIFTY-FIVE

FITZHUGH NEVER HEARD BACK FROM EITHER BIRDELL OR NATHAN. His was not the only report to arrive on their desks, warning them of the imminent uprisings of the Irish, yet neither man acted on this intel. Perhaps it was because Casement had been captured, Germany was clearly no longer interested in backing the Irish, or that the *Aud* had not delivered the weapons, but the men in charge of Ireland's defence apparently believed the revolution was over.

They were wrong.

The military council of Shinn Fein met Easter morning to decide what their next step would be. One leader, a man called Eion MacNeill, understood that the combined disasters of the failed attack on the Canadian trenches, the lost *Aud* shipment, and Casement's capture meant there was no longer any international support for their cause, and he pleaded with the council to cancel their plans.

With over 200,000 members, many at the meeting still felt this was their one and only chance to win their freedom. There were also rumours that the British, after capturing Casement, were about to commence a series of raids throughout Ireland

and arrest many of the movement's leaders. There was no longer any time for debate, the rebellion had to start now. They next elected a president of the Irish Republic, and all members returned home with orders to attack.

On 24 April 1916, the Irish revolution commenced. Forever known as the Easter Rising, across the island free Irish volunteers appeared on the streets in their thousands. Most just wore their everyday work clothes, though many proudly identified themselves by sporting yellow armbands.

There were few weapons, just those they had managed to collect themselves, and the German weapons that had arrived earlier. The civilian army charged into the centre of Dublin and seized a number of key buildings, such as City Hall and the general post office, and then with a great cheer raised the Irish flag. These positions were then fortified as best as possible, trenches were dug, barricades created, and food brought in to help the defenders hold off the coming siege. Phone and railway lines were cut out of the city, and roads blocked to create a safe zone around the rebellion. Police and British military stores were captured, their men arrested, and their weapons distributed. A large store of ammunition was detonated with the hope the explosion would herald to all that the revolution had begun.

For a short time, there was quiet, and the revolutionaries took stock of what they had so far achieved. They were disappointed when a rough headcount revealed their numbers were far less than anticipated. Later this was put down in part to Casement's warning, but mostly due to MacNeill ordering his supporters to stand down. Because of the contradictions in these orders, although other counties and cities in Ireland answered the call, the numbers were never great and most disbanded after only a few hours, though not before scoring several minor victories against British units. One of these was around the government's official wireless station, where the rebels broadcasted to everyone that the revolution had begun and they had taken the capital.

Fitzhugh had arrived at Dublin Castle to personally kick Birdell's arse when he heard the explosion from the distant armoury. He stepped into the courtyard and began climbing the stairs along the fortress wall to get a better view, when someone yelling caught his attention. He gave up on the wall and hobbled toward the large arched front gate where a single police guard was calling out to an approaching group of men. As they drew closer, one of these men pulled a pistol and shot the policeman dead. The rest then charged into the nearby guard room, and a fight broke out.

Fitzhugh managed to limp back into the rear of the courtyard and met with the castle garrison as they began to file out of their barracks.

'What's going on?' one of the policemen asked.

'It's the Irish. They've just taken the front gate,' Fitzhugh answered. 'Now pull your damn pistols and follow me.'

One of the men pulled out his gun, checked it, then ducked back inside, only to return and exclaim, 'We have no bullets. Our ammunition is in the guard house.'

'What do we do?' another policeman asked, moving to the edge of the building and covering the courtyard with his own empty gun.

A third guard doing similar yelled out, 'It's all clear.'

'He's got a point. What are we going to do?' Sir Matthew Nathan said. Fitzhugh looked around and recognised the Under-Secretary for Ireland, who was wearing a soldier's helmet and carrying a pistol.

'What are we going to do?' Fitzhugh said, pulling his own loaded pistol. 'We're going to take that gate back.'

* * *

Inside the guardroom, the Irish tied up the few policemen that had surrendered, then started searching the room. There was a locked cupboard, which they were about to break open when a gunshot brought their attention back to the courtyard. Outside, several policemen were gathering at the far end of the space, and they began charging forward. All were brandishing pistols.

'Jeysus, we need to get out of here,' one of the Irishmen yelled. Though the numbers were pretty equal, only a few of the rebels were armed, and to stop a bloodletting, the man who had shot the guard at the front gate called for everyone to escape while they could.

* * *

Fitzhugh aimed and fired, knocking down one of the rebels by the gate. Next, he stepped behind a stone column, cracked his pistol, and discharged its empty shells. He then clumsily reloaded it with fresh cartridges from his belt, cursed his bandaged hand as pain shot up his arm, snapped the gun closed, leaned back into the courtyard, and fired another round.

'They're running,' one of the policemen said.

'Let's make sure of it,' Fitzhugh yelled, and stumbled toward the gate like an enraged Egyptian mummy, firing as he went and trailing unravelling bandages about him. Somehow their attack proved enough, and the police managed to push the Irish out of the castle altogether and take control of the front gate. Sir Nathan ran forward, grabbed the large armoured door, and shoved it closed. He then snapped the lock in place, checked that the enormous gate next to the door was also locked, holstered his pistol, and vomited all over the entry's ancient cobblestones.

* * *

Caught totally unprepared thanks to no warning from the men in charge of Ireland, the British forces stationed around the city moved in, unsure what was occurring, and started taking fire. Civilians were killed, and when the police joined the army in cordoning off the area, this triggered a wave of looting and pillaging.

Martial Law was declared and strongpoints created. From here attacks were initiated, underneath the cover of machine-gun fire, and in certain regions the army managed to push the rebels out, though they did not get it all their own way. When a squad of soldiers tried to repair a section of destroyed railway tracks, they were attacked by the Irish and forced to retreat.

Days passed, and the British reinforced their lines. They brought forward more men and heavier guns, including artillery and armoured trucks, and even small warships began sailing up the rivers into the city. These opened fire at the strongest points in the Irish defences and, without really trying, Germany had opened up a new front in the war.

Forces from both sides began pushing forward, the Irish to take the railway stations and the British to occupy buildings that dominated the city. Both had successes and failures, but without the ports, rivers, or any mass transit system under its control, the Irish had no way of being resupplied and one by one their strongholds fell.

Both sides began tunnelling through buildings in an attempt to break the stalemate or breach a stronghold. Hundreds were being killed, with thousands injured on both sides—and this brought its own horrors. Enraged British soldiers, their mates dying at the hands of supposed countrymen, killed several unarmed citizens, revolutionary prisoners, and wounded in revenge.

After nearly a week of almost unending bloodshed, the Irish commanders sent forward a surrender document.

In order to prevent the further slaughter of Dublin citizens, and in the hope of saving the lives of our followers now surrounded and hopelessly outnumbered, the members of the Provisional Government present at headquarters have agreed to an unconditional surrender, and the commandants of the various districts in the City and County will order their commands to lay down arms.

The Irish revolution was over, though it did not go quietly. When the British attempted to inform many of the distant rebels that their command had laid down weapons, many simply did not believe them. In an attempt to avoid further bloodshed, the British allowed the Irish to send representatives to their prisons, where the Irish heard about the surrender first-hand from their arrested countrymen.

CHAPTER FIFTY-SIX

OVER FOUR HUNDRED DIED DURING THE REVOLUTION, WITH THE majority either British or civilians. Some eighty Irish rebels were killed, and taking into account the number of battles and skirmishes fought, this number could be considered light. Fitzhugh could not help but contemplate how much worse things could have been if the *Aud* had delivered her guns, yet also fumed at the number, which could very easily have been zero.

With the capture of Roger Casement and the end of the siege at Fort Dublin, Fitzhugh's involvement in the revolution came to an end. He'd been proud to note that when the relieving British forces arrived at the fort, a concerned Sergeant Andrews was with them. Though the fight for Dublin would last several more days, the two men had then made their way to the temporary British headquarters outside the city. Here Fitzhugh was thanked for his efforts in saving the fort, and was shown the reports on what had happened across the city.

When he read that a single Canadian had died fighting alongside the British, Fitzhugh became concerned for Wolk. He immediately found Andrews, and together they began searching for the missing MP. After visiting the morgue and all the hospitals, including the makeshift ones that were busy with the hundreds of wounded from the rebellion, they eventually found the Canadian in a pub, with a fair Irish maiden on his arm.

The Mountie claimed he'd become separated from the British units when the rebellion began and was forced to go into hiding as he'd somehow got himself trapped within the zone occupied by the Irish. The MP recounted how he'd taken shelter in the flat of the young lady sitting next to him and, unsure what was happening, had ridden out that first day with her. They had only escaped a few hours ago, after he noticed a small blind spot in the Irish defences.

Fitzhugh could see that the stress of being stuck in a young girl's bedroom with little to do had taken a toll on the man. In fact, he felt so sorry for Wolk that he could not help but kick him in the arse of his chair and walk away. Of course, he was so angry that he briefly forgot about his wounds and kicked the chair with his ruined foot.

He was really starting to hate this war.

* * *

It took all three a few more days to return to France and make their way back to Fitzhugh's office. Here they caught up with the other members of the team, and everyone shook each other's hands warmly after a job well done. Ash even produced a few beers and handed them around. Fitzhugh thought it wise not to ask exactly where a man who'd been stuck in the trenches for the last few months had managed to find the beer, especially as it seemed to be Haig's favourite brand.

The only person missing was Jean Danjou, who, McGavin explained, had returned to the French lines to report what had happened and how the MPs had just saved France. This last line induced a warm cheer amongst the men in the office, and another round of beers.

Yes, Fitzhugh thought, it was a very good idea not to ask how the Australian had procured the alcohol, though it did give him an idea. The captain moved through the cramped room and painfully inched behind his desk and took a seat. He then fumbled open his order book to a blank page and began to write with his good hand.

'Well, that broke the monotony,' Ash said as he took a long pull from his beer.

'I applaud your sense of humour,' the captain said dryly, now thumbing through the pile of messages awaiting him. When most proved to be from his own team, and the rest did not seem of immediate concern, he turned his focus back to his motley crew of MPs.

'Well, gentlemen, I think the case is closed.'

'Not this case of beer,' Ash laughed, taking more bottles from a partially hidden crate and handing them around. 'Not yet anyway.'

'We got our man,' Wolk said, and the others groaned at the terrible joke. 'What did I say?' the Canadian asked innocently.

'Any idea what's going to happen to Casement and that arse-hole O'Connell?' McGavin asked, planting himself on the captain's luggage.

'Nothing good for them, I can assure you. Casement has very powerful friends in the government, but they have been so embarrassed by this episode, I don't think they are capable of saving him.'

'Could not happen to a nicer guy,' Ash said, putting his nearly empty bottle down and sliding the MP band off his arm. He then placed it on the desk before Fitzhugh in such a fashion that no one missed the symbolic meaning of the gesture. The other two sergeants followed suit.

'So, what about us?' Wolk asked.

'Well, as I said, the case is closed. My own commander has taken the entire affair out of my hands, so I am thinking that might be it. We don't even have to write a report as no one wants to read it. I believe they hope it will be all swept under the carpet.'

'Back to our units?' McGavin asked.

'Back to the stockade for me.' Ash grinned. 'A nice bit of peace and quiet sounds good right about now. Saving the bloody empire can wear a fella out.'

The entrance to the room opened and Andrews shouldered his way into the tight space. He then placed a telegram in the hands of Fitzhugh. McGavin handed a beer to the sergeant, who nodded thanks and downed the entire bottle while his captain read his message.

Fitzhugh turned ashen and all the humour left his face. The others in the tent picked up on his growing distress and waited patiently until he was done.

After reading the telegram twice, Fitzhugh put the sheet down on the table and began trying to push it flat with his hand, as though he could wipe away any wrinkle in the paper.

Wolk was the first to break. 'All okay?'

'No,' Fitzhugh said, passing the message to McGavin.

Though there were few words, the message said a lot.

To all senior officers,

Between 24 to 28 April, rebellious Irish forces fought an insurrection against crown forces in Dublin. Military response ended the revolution, with the loss of hundreds of lives. Despite the limited action of the Irish, news of this must be suppressed, especially to Irish troops in the face of recent events along the front. Please take steps to isolate any Irish forces under your command from this news, and immediately report any incidences with these men.

'Well, that doesn't sound too bad,' Ash said, scratching his head in confusion over the captain's reaction.

'It's not what the report says, it's what it doesn't say,' McGavin explained, having lived with official whitewashing jargon on reports most of his career. 'What this report is saying is that we failed. The Irish revolted, there are likely hundreds, if not thousands dead, and Headquarters is afraid that not if but when the information reaches the front lines, our valued and necessary Irish troops may decide they have more in common with those standing on the opposite side of the battlefield than those standing next to them.'

'Jesus,' Wolk said, shaking his head. 'We were there, fellas. The locals are not happy at all on that little island of theirs ...'

'Of England's, you mean,' Ash reminded him. 'That's the whole point after all.'

Fitzhugh stood, retrieved the armbands from his table, and tossed them back to the three men before him. 'Looks like our job isn't done after all. We may well have another revolution on our hands right here and I need to know about it before the blood rebels themselves do.'

Ash held the cloth for a minute, looking at it intently as he rubbed it between his fingers. He then slid it on. 'Okay, where do we start?'

Fitzhugh put the telegram in a desk draw for safety. 'First, we investigate those pricks Matthews and Birdell. They caused this tragedy, and if they think they can sweep their contemptible inaction under the carpet, they have another thing coming. This was not part of the war, this was a crime, and I intend to crucify them, so to speak, for their part in the deaths of the Irish.'

'And the British,' Andrews reminded him. Fitzhugh gave him a nod of recognition.

'Sounds good to me,' Ash agreed, patting the MP band on his

arm fondly. 'This will help bring down a toff or two, something I could grow to enjoy, I must say.'

'So I've heard.' McGavin laughed, giving the Australian a slap on the back.

'Actually, Sergeant Ash, for now I have a different job for you,' Fitzhugh said, tearing the completed order sheet from its pad and handing it to the Digger.

Ash read the paper, then looked up at his commander. 'This has to be a joke.'

'No joke at all, Sergeant. I want you to return to your unit, go undercover, and start ferreting out this Barney Hound chap. There's the unresolved issue of a bank robbery, after all. And if you happen to come across Tommy Kirkland, the trench mafia, or the whereabouts of the Great King Rat, well, let's just say their time is up too.'

'But they know I'm an MP.'

'No, they know you were on a short-term assignment for a specific purpose, and now they can see that purpose is over.'

'Hey buddy,' McGavin said, putting his hand on his friend's shoulder. 'This is the job. You're a copper now.'

'We do the shit job no one wants to do. But it needs doing,' Wolk agreed.

Ash looked at the men who had both served their lives as professional policemen before signing up. With a grimace, he gave them a firm nod of agreement and understanding.

'The added bonus is, you get to kick arse and have everyone hate you.' Fitzhugh laughed and took his first sip of beer.

'Jesus, Simon, you really know how to kick a man when he's down,' Ash said, using the officer's Christian name for the first time. Fitzhugh had been around long enough to understand that was actually a sign of respect from an antipodean.

'And where the hell is Pozières anyway?' Ash continued to read, before folding his orders and placing them in his tunic pocket. He then looked at the MP band on his arm as though it were a live snake, removed it, and slipped it in the same pocket for safekeeping.

'Oh, I think you'll find it all right, Sergeant,' Fitzhugh said. 'Just follow the sound of the guns.'

EPILOGUE

22 APRIL 1916

LIEUTENANT SPINDLER GOT HIS VESSEL UP TO FULL SPEED, leaving the *Setter II* behind, which turned back to its own port once it saw the *Aud* was safely underway. There was no way their presence could remain hidden now, and any chance of getting the weapon to the Irish was gone. If the *dummkopf* English captain was correct, they had been extraordinarily lucky not to have been uncovered so far.

What the German could not know was that the Royal Navy had indeed been keeping an eye on the *Aud* since her arrival, and were waiting for the local Irish rebels to make contact with the vessel so that they could capture everyone in a sting operation. When the vessel met with the pilot ship, and immediately after powered up to exit the harbour, the Royal Navy warships watching the Germans knew the trap had been blown. Radio messages were sent to the British admiral and the fleet that had been shadowing the *Aud*.

Calling an end to the surveillance operation, the admiral ordered his fleet to power up and catch the *Aud* before it slipped away.

As his vessel chugged its way into the Atlantic, from the

bridge Spindler could see the danger approaching, yet could do little about it. His mostly empty ship was fast, but not fast enough to outrun a frigate at full speed, such as the British warship approaching them. When they were signalled by the HMS *Bluebell*, he ordered his men to pretend they were having communication problems.

This time there was no bluffing, and the frigate soon imposed its impressive bulk on the *Aud* by sailing closer and closer, forcing it to slow. Understanding the end was near, Spindler called out to his men to begin removing the Norwegian uniforms they still wore, showing themselves to once again be German sailors. He then asked the men to prepare two lifeboats and had them lowered to the ocean.

The British frigate was shepherding them toward nearby Queenstown, and as they passed the entrance to the harbour, Spindler ordered the explosives that had been placed along the hull of the vessel for just such an occasion to be detonated. At the same time the Norwegian flag was lowered, and in its place soon flew the battle ensign of the German Imperial navy.

To Spindler's horror, the explosives failed to detonate, and the crew tried the trigger again and again with no luck. There was no time to check the ignition cables as they were only minutes from being boarded. Grabbing the suitcase bomb the Irish had left with him, Spindler went below to the front bulkhead, set the timer, and then ran for his life.

He reached the deck just as the bomb detonated, and he could feel the *Aud* was already taking on water and slowing. He ordered everyone to abandon ship, then joined his crew in the lifeboats below. As the few men with oars began to pull their little boats away from the scuttled and now sinking *Aud*, Spindler could not help but look back and watch as his first command slipped under the waves.

It had been just over one month since he was first made her captain.

Inside the lifeboats, the men began waving white flags, surrendering themselves to the Royal Navy. This was a move sanctioned by Spindler, who expressly called on his men to surrender if they got caught. If the *Bluebell* fired on them now, it would be in violation of international law.

The rest of the British fleet tasked with their capture sailed about them, with sailors on their decks sporting rifles and tracking every move the Germans made. Spindler was astonished to see that the men without rifles seemed to be brandishing cutlasses, like pirates in a movie. The Germans waited for the order to be given and the British to open up on them, a not impossible thought after the Baralong incident. It had only been a year earlier that British sailors had executed a number of Germans in the water after sinking their U-boat, a belated act of revenge for the sinking of the RMS *Lusitania*.

It was finally the *Bluebell* that sailed in and collected the Germans. Once everyone had clambered up the side of the destroyer, an English sailor approached and asked if any of the prisoners had any weapons. A large German called Bruhns said he did.

'Where?' the sailor demanded.

Bruhns looked down at his boots.

When the Englishman began patting him down, he stopped when he felt something thick and heavy. Another sailor immediately trained a gun on the German as the first sailor reached in and pulled out a sausage, or as the laughing Bruhns called it, his 'emergency rations'.

The *Bluebell* proved too small to hold so many men, so the *Aud*'s crew were transferred to a larger cruiser, the HMS *Adventure*. After a short trip, they docked at an Irish port, where the Germans heard the rebellion had begun, but its leader, Roger Casement, had been captured.

The warship then sped the Germans to England, where they were unloaded, sent to Chatham, and then on by train to

London. Everywhere they went they were interrogated, and Spindler began to believe the English were all working from a set sheet as the questions were always the same.

Deposited in Scotland Yard, Spindler was again set on and asked the same questions, though this time they were interpreted for him by a man called Captain French. When the captain not only translated poorly, but to the German's mind was deliberately altering his answers, Spindler bamboozled them all by suddenly replying in perfect English. The detectives of the Yard, however, began to ask new questions, precise questions, and not for the first time Spindler realised the English had known all about his voyage and had just been playing with them.

One day, a new officer walked into his cell and explained that he was terribly sorry, but they were going to have to shoot him. The man's reasoning was simple: as Spindler had sunk his ship while under arrest, that no longer allowed him to claim status as a prisoner of war—instead it made him nothing less than a pirate. The German sat there, dumbfounded, and let the man talk until he left the room. Hours ticked by and he could not help but notice he was not shot, so figured this was yet another plot to somehow get him to talk.

And then one day, it was over. Guards arrived and escorted the captain of the *Aud* to a truck, and he was driven to the Donington Hall Camp, near Derby. Here he was able to catch up with the news of the day. Casement was arrested and eventually executed for his crime. Word came that he had been betrayed by one of his fellow travellers, the Irish sergeant called Bailey.

Spindler also met the captain of the U-boat who had been carrying the Irishmen to the island before being sunk. Weisbach admitted he had arrived that night to meet the *Aud*, and had even seen the ship in the dark, but he had thought the *Aud* was an English destroyer and so had remained hidden.

If the British believed this war was now over, they had

underestimated the cunning of Lieutenant Spindler. During his exercise time, the German studied carefully every feature of the prison, searching for a way to escape. He investigated several plans, some of which led nowhere, others proved unfeasible. This included making a vaulting pole out of broom handles to leap over the barbed wire, but this snapped in two during a trial run.

At one stage he learned that his crew, held elsewhere, had attempted their own escape in an effort to rescue him, but all were recaptured. He then noticed that a small car visited the prison every day, and after striking up a conversation with the driver, eventually bribed the man to help him escape for £500, half now and half after the war.

On the planned day, the car pulled up, the driver called him over, and then claimed he needed more money or else the deal was off. Spindler admitted he could get no more, and so the driver shooed him away.

Understanding there was almost no chance of escape by land or sea once he got out of the prison, the sailor came up with a brand new notion: he would escape by air. Never having even sat in an airplane in his life, Spindler began combing his fellow prisoners until he located Flight Lieutenant Winkelmann, a man who'd been shot down over the Western Front. The pilot quickly agreed to help them both escape.

Speaking English very well, the sailor befriended enough British soldiers to uncover the news there was a military airport at Donington, and even managed to build a rudimentary map of the region thanks to an old encyclopaedia. Figuring it was around six hours march away, he then began to plan.

First was to create new ground works for the camp, such as a tennis court, but in reality these plans were building blind spots to hide in when they began their escape. That was when it struck him there was a serious issue with the plan.

Spindler realised he was the famous 'Casement Captain', and

he had personally befriended many of the guards during his planning. His absence, even for a short time, would be noted. The German was not going to let something as annoying as celebrity stop him though, and he came up with a simple idea. Spindler searched the camp for a man who was roughly his size, dressed him in his clothes, and organised for the doppelganger to sleep in his bed on the night of the breakout. This ruse would give him enough time to get away.

On 12 July 1917, they were ready to go. The naval captain and the fighter pilot snuck through the wire, but this was far harder than they had anticipated and the effort tired them greatly. The run across country also proved far more strenuous than expected, for they had not accounted for the numerous hedges, ditches, fences, and especially the canals in this part of the country.

Yet the Germans struggled on and eventually reached their objective. Unfortunately, they arrived two weeks too late. After spending a day searching for the airfield, they could see no sign of it, so with no food and being very thirsty, they risked everything by asking a local boy walking along the road where the airfield was. The boy happily explained the air force had moved a few miles away just a few weeks earlier.

Sick, cold, hungry, and down on energy, the two men walked to where the airfield was now located. Meantime, their escape had been discovered and descriptions of the two men were circulated throughout the region.

Despite everything seemingly going wrong, over the next three days the escapees moved closer to the next airfield, and they found their destination in the easiest way possible—they followed the planes flying overhead.

One morning, they arrived at a bridge guarded by the police. Not wanting to stand out, they waited until later in the day to cross when traffic would increase. This gave the two men the opportunity to rest along one side of the river, so they sat under the shade of a tree to wait. After a while, a policeman walked into view, leading four prisoners in chains. As they neared, the prisoners dropped their shackles and all the men surrounded the Germans, forcing their surrender.

When their prisoners asked the police what had given them away, one of the coppers admitted that when they were first spotted, no one had actually recognised them. It was only when one of them stumbled and both hurried to walk in lock-step again that the police realised they must be German military men. Weakened from his escape, Spindler meekly went back to prison, never to attempt a breakout again.

But if Lieutenant Spindler believed his part in the war was over, he had underestimated how popular he was in Berlin. He became part of a prisoner exchange and shipped to the Netherlands, where he was then supposed to head back to Germany.

Rather than return home, the German who had pretended to be Norwegian and now found himself in the hands of the Dutch made one final national change: he turned his back on Germany to move to the United States.

In this new country, his luck refused to change. After many decades, the Second World War began, and the former German Imperial Naval officer was detained in an internment camp as an enemy alien. Tragically his health suffered during this time and, upon release after the war, Spindler moved to North Dakota, where he died.

A HISTORICAL CONCLUSION

This is a book of fiction, yet many of the events it contained are indeed true—though some liberties were taken with some timelines, real characters, etc. Though there's little evidence there was ever a crucified solider, the reaction to the myth was most certainly real. On 10 May 1915, *The Times* printed:

> *Last week a large number of Canadian soldiers wounded in the fighting round Ypres arrived at the base hospital at Versailles. They all told the story of how one of their officers had been crucified by the Germans. He had been pinned to a wall by bayonets thrust through his hands and feet, another bayonet had then been driven through his throat, and, finally, he was riddled with bullets. The wounded Canadians said that the Dublin Fusiliers had seen this done with their own eyes, and that they had heard the officers of the Dublin Fusiliers talking about it.*

Many historians doubt the veracity of the rumour and a number of inquiries, both during and after the war, came up with little evidence the story was true. The strongest point made when refuting the rumour is that there is not a single credible witness account of those who supposedly found the body. British politicians even brought the matter up in Parliament several times, yet always their enquiries were met with the explanation that there was no evidence of the episode. Eyewitnesses were presented but their stories were one by one debunked when further inquiries showed the area in which they claimed this all happened had never been occupied by the Germans, or those making the claim had not been along the front during the right time period. The official stance was this had been some form of wartime propaganda that had got out of hand.

For years, the myths of the crucified soldier became just that, a mythological tale of Allied propaganda that was used to garnish hatred of the Germans. The demonised enemy also weighed into the argument, refuting at all times that they had ever been involved with any such atrocities. Yet such stories rarely die easily, and the belief the Germans had taken a captured soldier and nailed him to a barn door with bayonets continued to circulate.

It turns out there was a single report with some validity as it actually named the soldier killed. Sergeant Thomas Elliott was believed to be the one who died on the cross, and this was only refuted when Elliott himself came forward to explain he had actually survived the war.

A 2002 British documentary investigated the story of the crucified soldier and came to the same conclusions—that many of the myths were simply that, stories and propaganda swirling around a particularly nasty moment in history.

The story doesn't end there though. Tapping into previously unknown sources, not only did the show's producers find there was indeed an eyewitness of some merit to the story, they even found the crucified soldier's name.

Sergeant Harry Band of the Central Ontario Regiment was

reported missing on 24 April 1915, the very date of most of the crucified soldier stories. He was also fighting along the front near Ypres, right where most of the accounts claim the crime occurred. Evidence to the fate of Sergeant Band came years later in the form of letters from men in his unit who wrote to Harry's sister.

Elizabeth had never given up on her brother and made numerous enquiries into exactly what happened to him. The standard MIA telegram was never going to be enough, and she continued to seek information as to her brother's fate. This led men in his unit to feel sympathy for the woman, and many wrote that her suspicion that the rumoured crucified soldier was her brother was indeed true.

Harry's sister later wrote to another sibling:

Dear Martin: I have got another letter admitting the crucifixion of Harry ... I have got it at last, the horrible details. Don't tell Bertha them all. I told her he was crucified, but they took him down alive. He was all hacked to bits and spat on and his eyes out. Oh, Martin, think of it, and yet the War Office has never notified me ...
    Elizabeth Petrie, 20 June 1916

Further proof was found in reports from a British nurse, Miss Ursula Violet Chaloner, who was told by a wounded soldier called Lance Corporal C M Brown that Sergeant Band was 'crucified after a battle of Ypres on one of the doors of a barn with five bayonets in him.' The letter she wrote this in wasn't found until her death years later, when her family began searching through her papers.

As for a 'credible' witness, recently a report was uncovered written by a Corporal William Metcalfe.

On or about April 23rd, 1915 ... My platoon was proceeding along St. Jean road when I noticed a soldier pinned to a barn door with bayonets ... There was a bayonet through each wrist and his head hung forward on his breast as though he were dead. I could not see any bullet wound but did notice Maple Leaf badges on his collar.
    27 February 1919

Corporal William Metcalfe was born in Maine, USA, but joined the Canadian forces at the start of the war, like so many young men of the time, to join the adventure. Running away from home, he signed on with the Canadian army, telling recruiters he was twenty-eight years old, when his true age was nineteen.

Harry's mother discovered the ruse, and she contacted the Canadian government, who in turn contacted the American ambassador in England. When the ship carrying William to the war docked in England, the ambassador himself was standing at the wharf and pulled young William aside. He asked the soldier if he was the William Metcalf from Maine whose mother was crying for his return. William replied, *'I'm not the man, I'm from St David Ridge, a little farming town outside St Stephen, New Brunswick.'* When William's own colonel backed up his story, the matter was dropped, and William marched off to war.

There is a great photo of William in his Canadian uniform and a kilt, because the Canadian unit he joined was the 16th Canadian Scottish ... not even I could make that bit up.

Metcalfe would become one of a handful of Americans to win the Victoria Cross when he:

rushed forward under intense machine-gun fire to a passing Tank on the left. With his signal flag he walked in front of the Tank, directing it along the trench in a perfect hail of bullets and bombs. The machine-gun strong points were overcome,

very heavy casualties were inflicted on the enemy, and a very
critical situation was relieved. Later, although wounded, he
continued to advance until ordered to get into a shell hole and
have his wounds dressed.

Whether you agree that winning a Victoria Cross makes you a better witness to a crime than anyone else, the fact is that such a prominent soldier did indeed put his name to a report stating he'd personally seen a crucified soldier. Metcalfe's placement and timing is all but exact to other witness reports, and these all point toward the fact there had indeed been a Canadian soldier crucified on the field of Ypres.

After Gallipoli, the Australians were sent to a remote section of the Western Front called Armentières, which was indeed supposed to be quiet and relatively safe. Here they were expected to learn how to survive this unusual style of warfare—but the experienced ANZACs quickly adapted to the European conditions and were soon harassing the Germans the way they had the Turks.

In this section, the Germans indeed were sweeping no man's land with a searchlight, which caused several casualties within the Allied ranks. The Germans would soon grow to respect the Diggers' fighting abilities along the trenches, as can be seen in this captured letter one German soldier wrote to his mother.

We are here near ALBERT, I am in the foremost line, about
200 metres opposite the British. We have Australians in front
of us here, they are very quick and cunning. They creep up in
the night like cats to our trenches so that we don't notice them.
Last night they were in our trench and killed two men and
dragged one away with them.

The attack on Pinchgut is entirely based on the Battle of Pozières, a brutal affair where a small group of Australians held off an overwhelmingly numerically superior German assault. The only differences are that they had been sent to Pozières, and that the Diggers never retreated. Indeed, their efforts at this battle helped create the idea in the Allied HQ that these men were something special and could be used as shock troops against the Germans.

The ill-discipline of the Australian troops at the Western Front was legendary, but it was not always despised. General Haig liked the Diggers and often commented favourably on them, though in 1918 he did note in a letter to his wife:

> *We have had to separate the Australians into Convalescent Camps of their own, because they were giving so much trouble when along with our men and put such revolutionary ideas into their heads.*

The reasons for the misunderstanding that the Australians were undisciplined was best summed up by Lieutenant General Sir John Monash, who said:

> *Very much and very stupid comment has been made upon the discipline of the Australian soldier. That was because the very conception and purpose of discipline have been misunderstood. It is, after all, only a means to an end, and that end is the power to secure co-ordinated action among a large number of individuals for the achievement of a definite purpose. It does not mean lip service, nor obsequious homage to superiors, nor servile observance of forms and customs, nor a suppression of individuality ... the Australian Army is a proof that individualism is the best and not the worst foundation upon which to build up collective discipline.*

The Bush Orchestra was a true event. In Belgium, the

Australians were camped near the 10th Royal Fusiliers, when Private C Miles later recalled:

The Colonel decided that he would have a full dress parade of the guard mounting. Well, the Aussies looked over at us amazed. The band was playing, we were all smartened up, spit and polish, on parade, and that happened every morning. We marched up and down, up and down.

The Aussies couldn't get over it, and when we were off duty we naturally used to talk to them, go over and have a smoke with them, or meet them when we were hanging about the road or having a stroll. They kept asking us: 'Do you like this sort of thing? All these parades, do you want to do it?' Of course we said, 'No, of course we don't. We're supposed to be on rest, and all the time we've got goes to posh up and turn out on parade.' So they looked at us a bit strangely and said, 'OK, cobbers, we'll soon alter that for you'.

The Australians didn't approve of it because they never polished or did anything. They had a band, but their brass instruments were all filthy. Still, they knew how to play them.

The next evening, our Sergeant-Major was taking the parade. Sergeant-Major Rowbotham, a nice man, but a stickler for discipline. He was just getting ready to bawl us all out when the Australians started with their band. They marched up and down the road outside the field, playing any old thing. There was no tune you could recognise, they were just blowing as loud as they could on their instruments. It sounded like a million cat-calls.

And poor old Sergeant Rowbotham, he couldn't make his voice heard. It was an absolute fiasco. They never tried to mount another parade, because they could see the Aussies watching us from across the road, just ready to step in and sabotage the whole thing. So they decided that parades for mounting the guards should be washed out, and after that they just posted the guards in the ordinary way as if we were in the line.

Barney Hound was based partly on John 'Barney' Hines, an Irish immigrant who travelled to Australia, where he joined the AIF. He was considered the 'King of Souvenirs', and a photo taken of the man seated around one of his enormous hauls from the Battle of Polygon Wood in 1917 would become famous.

There is a rumour that the Kaiser saw this image and became so outraged that he put a price on Barney's head— though there is no evidence this ever actually happened. Barney was an effective soldier who survived the war, despite being disciplined several times. There is also a rumour he robbed a bank in Amiens, and that he returned to his unit with suitcases full of French francs.

The Canadian Mounties have been in existence in some form or another since the 1870s. They were originally held back from entering the Great War as Canada feared its own population with European ancestry—especially German. Many were eventually sent to Europe, though a number also were concentrated in Alaska to help with the Russian Civil War.

Though many of the characters in this book are based on real individuals, most of them are not. Hank Ash and his fellow MPs are fictional, yet some of Ash's war record was based on real soldiers. There was indeed an Australian soldier, Gunner William Vandertak, who was arrested for striking an officer when he found the man toasting the health of the Kaiser.

In 1916, Irishmen in Berlin were trying to organise a German invasion of Ireland to help support their own rebellion there. Though the Germans were warm to the idea and indeed sent shipments of arms, it was clear they cared little for the Irish cause and were more interested in simply trying to disrupt England's involvement in the Great War.

Everything about the SMS *Libau* and her captain, Lieutenant

Karl Spindler is true ... or so he says. We have a firsthand account of the German naval officer's voyage and subsequent arrest. This was partly written after the war, and partly based on letters he claimed to have mailed while in captivity. I hope you found the story of the *Libau/Aud* amusing, as this was almost verbatim, right down to the Monty Pythonesque conversation between a German sailor called Dusselman and the captain of the *Setter II*.

Spindler took his first command in the 10th Cruiser Squadron of the Royal Navy, and the true identity of the ship, her captain, and crew were hidden under fake papers claiming she was a Norwegian ship called the *Aud*. This included letters from phantom families and girlfriends, all written in Norwegian.

If the British captain of the *Setter II* had been more seasoned, there was every chance he could have recognised the *Libua/Aud's* lines as those of a British merchant ship, which the *Aud* had originally been before her capture at the start of the war.

What Spindler did not know was the British ships had been ordered, if they encountered the *Aud*, to follow the normal routine and inspect the ship, but not to try to stop it by themselves. They wanted to watch and see where it was going and who they were meeting.

The *Aud* reached her rendezvous point along the Irish coast and weighed anchor. Men stood watch on her decks, scanning the coastline for any sign the Irish had arrived to take hold of their shipment. When no one did, they sailed to meet with the U-boat bringing Casement. What Spindler would discover later (because he would be imprisoned with the captain of U-19), was that the submarine had seen the *Aud* through her periscope and believed her to be a British destroyer.

Having no luck finding the U-boat, the *Aud* returned to her rendezvous point with the Irish, only to meet and be boarded by the captain of the *Setter II*, who barely looked at the fake papers before allowing them to pass.

This encounter had been nerve-wracking for the German crew and, when a second trawler appeared off the port bow a few hours later, Spindler ordered the transport up to full speed. He did not escape though, as the Royal Navy had been watching the Germans and sent two warships, the armed sloop *Bluebell* and the smaller armed cutter *Zinnia*, to capture her. These Royal Navy vessels signalled the *Aud* to stop and follow them into port.

Spindler tried to play for time, and after a lot of ignored messages and warning shots, the crew lowered the Norwegian flag, raised the German ensign, put lifeboats in the water, and detonated bombs placed along the hull, sending the *Aud* to the bottom of the sea.

Weeks later, divers were sent into the wreck and they discovered the *Aud* had a secret hold under her shipment of pots and pans, containing 20,000 rifles, a number of machine guns, and an estimated one million rounds of ammunition. Not enough to win a war, but certainly enough weaponry to win a few battles during a revolution.

The weapons were of Russian design, captured at the battle of Tannenberg, and years later there were claims the weapons were inferior and that's why the Germans handed them over to the Irish. In reality, the Mosin—Nagants were of a fine quality, the equal of most weapons on the Western Front—indeed they can still be found in use today. The Germans simply passed the Russian weapons on as they were uniformly of a different calibre to their own weapons and would cause logistical problems to soldiers in the field needing resupply.

As for Spindler, he was captured and sent to a POW camp after a lengthy interrogation to find out what he knew to help with the Roger Casement investigation. He eventually escaped the camp with the brilliant idea of stealing a plane with a newly arrived officer of the German air force. They spent a week or so trying to find the airport, which had moved just weeks before, and they were finally caught, cold and hungry, by the clever ruse of a policeman escorting shackled prisoners along the river —only for those prisoners to turn out to be policemen themselves ...

As I mentioned previously, you could not make this stuff up!

I encourage you to read Spindler's book on the entire affair, *Gun Running For Casement in the Easter Rebellion*—it's a great read.

When the SS *Libau* arrived at Tralee Bay, it was to be met by a number of Irish revolutionaries. Tragically one of the cars coming to meet Lieutenant Spindler crashed into the River Laune, and everyone was killed. Because the ship had no radio, it was impossible to let Spindler know what had happened, so when no one arrived, he sailed for home.

The biography of Roger Casement was also accurate. He was a famous British politician and served time in the Congo, travelling with writer Joseph Conrad. This affected him greatly and he spent the rest of his life fighting for individual freedoms. He was hung in 1916 for his part in the Easter Uprising, though for a while this sentence was in doubt as he officially had not broken any British law. For his execution to be legal, he had to have been planning this sedition on English soil, but he was in Germany at the time.

The Germans did try to recruit a division of Irish from within the ranks of the POWs; only a few dozen joined up and the idea was scrapped.

Onboard the U-19 with Casement were two Irish soldiers. Sergeant Daniel Beverley (or Bailey) had fought for England in India and Burma, where he was a very naughty soldier indeed. Discharged from the army, he travelled to Canada, was recalled to his original unit, and arrived back in England in time to join the British Expeditionary Force's trip to France, where he managed to get himself wounded and captured.

When Germany asked if any Irish prisoners wished to be separated from all other Allied prisoners and be placed in a new, far superior camp, Bailey was one of around nine hundred who agreed. He then volunteered once again when Casement showed up at the camp and asked the prisoners to join the new German Irish Brigade. Though Casement was booed out of the camp, he did leave with a number of troopers. Bailey went to train in Berlin, was made a sergeant, took the name Beverley, and sailed to Ireland with Casement on the U-19.

He rowed ashore with Casement, both were captured, charged with High Treason, and imprisoned in the Tower of London. To strengthen the case against their leader, the British asked the sergeant to turn 'King's Evidence', which he was happy to do. Casement was found guilty, executed, and when his own trial came before the court, Bailey was found not guilty.

Amazingly he re-joined the army and served in Africa and the Middle East. At the end of the war, he returned not to the UK, but Canada, where he died in 1968.

The other man on the U-boat was Robert Monteith, an Irish soldier who joined the Royal Horse Artillery as a lad and went off to England to do his training. He later served in India, where he helped patrol the Khyber Pass, before being sent to South Africa in 1900 to serve in the Boer War.

He cashiered out of the army in 1911, having served for well over a decade. He worked various jobs, became disillusioned with his former masters, and joined the Irish Volunteers.

When the war came, the British needed experienced men and offered Monteith a job training all of Ireland's forces, but he said no, so the government kicked him out of Dublin. He heard the Irish were thinking of sending people to Berlin for support, and pretended to immigrate to New York. Instead he arrived in the US, only to turn around and head to Berlin, where he would meet Roger Casement and take command of the Irish brigades.

There is a suggestion because he was of low rank (a mere captain) that the Germans never considered him the right man to lead this unit. Casement seemed to have had other ideas, and wrote to a friend (Count Wedel) in 1915:

> *Mr Monteith will do very well in most respects to keep the camp in order. I am appointing him pro-tem 'Commanding Officer' of the Irish Corps. That gets over the difficulty that he has no prior military rank.*

He eventually joined the sick Casement (who was suffering from malaria, which he caught in the Congo) and a sergeant called Beverly, on U-19, after Casement refused to sail with the weapons the Germans had supplied for their revolution on the *Aud*.

At Ireland, they rowed ashore, reached the ruins of McKenna's Fort, and the two Irish soldiers went for help. Monteith was noticed by two Irish police officers, and almost talked his way free of them until a young boy reported the man had thrown away a piece of paper when he first noticed them. The police found the paper, and it was covered in German codes. He somehow escaped their grasp, went on the run, and eventually made his way to America. Here Monteith was eventually questioned by authorities, and he supposedly admitted to everything he had done. They thanked him for his time, served him a cold drink, and basically said well done!

He took many jobs, including working for Ford, where he helped organise their union, and he remained there until retirement. In 1947, he decided to return to Ireland and caught a boat to England, where he was met with a Scotland Yard sting. It seems England had a long memory, but they did not arrest him; instead they immediately placed Monteith and his family on a boat to Ireland—noting the man would not sleep a single night on English soil. He arrived in Ireland a minor celebrity, and he lived there the rest of his life.

In one of those weird coincidences that often happens in history, Monteith died on 18 February 1956, the very same day that the judge who sentenced Roger Casement to hang, Sir T Humphreys, also died.

Francis Holstein was the German-born proprietor of the Peacock Hotel at Leith. He was contacted by F Reimers from Germany about the condition of England and its war readiness. Reimers was later discovered to be a German spymaster called Gustav Steinhauer.

Eoin MacNeill was a real Irish revolutionary who did indeed call off his part of the rebellion during the Easter Risings. This meant vast numbers of lives were saved on both sides as many of his poorly armed men did not fight.

Countess Constance Georgine Markievicz was an Irish revolutionary who not only fought in the Easter Rising (and apparently killed a police officer), but designed the uniform for the Citizen Army and even composed their anthem. She was arrested after the revolution, was found guilty, and spent a few years in jail before being released. Count Casimir Dunin Markievicz was a Polish playwright who may or may not have just started calling himself a count when he moved to Paris. Here he married Constance, then moved to modern Ukraine when his wife returned to Ireland. Though they kept in contact, they never lived together again—and he never joined the German Army.

There were many warnings and reports sent to the chief secretary for Ireland, Augustine Birrell, and his undersecretary, Sir Matthew Nathan—this included the report that German arms were about to be landed on this island by sea. Yet neither man ever acted on them, and reportedly doubted 'there was any foundation for the rumour' of an Irish uprising.

The proceeding Royal Commission laid no guilt on the men, though it was highly critical of their total inaction to end the Easter revolution before it began.

In the story, Hank Ash comes across a British soldier that had been crucified by his own commanders for a minor infraction. In a war where one of the worst crimes committed was the crucifixion of a soldier, a horror so great that it is still talked about today, the mechanism for such punishment was a very real one. The following is a summary of the actual rules for this sort of reprimand.

Rules for Summary Punishment make under S. 44 of the Army Act.

1.a court-martial, or a commanding officer, may award field punishment for any offence committed on active service ... to one of the following punishments, namely:

(a) Field punishment No. 1.

(b) Field punishment No. 2.

2. Where an offender is sentenced to field imprisonment No. 1, he may, during the continuance of his sentence, unless the court-martial or the commanding officer otherwise directs, be punished as follows:

(a) He may be kept in irons, i.e., in fetters or handcuffs, or both fetters and handcuffs; and may be secured so as to prevent his escape.

(b) When in irons he may lie attached for a period or periods not exceeding two hours in any one day to a fixed object, but he must not be so attached during more than three out of any four consecutive days, nor during more than twenty-one days in all.

(c) Straps or ropes may be used for the purpose of these rules in lieu of irons.

To end, I would like to explain that the plot point of the German attack on the Canadian section through a trench laid bare by traitorous Irish is simply that, a story plot point. There is no truth to it; it just happened to be the Canadian lines where the crucified soldier incident most likely occurred.

The Canadians were a formidable Allied force during the war, as were the Irish. Many would be surprised to learn that, even though their own country was suffering the turmoil of revolution, some 200,000 Irishmen served in the British army, with about 50,000 killed, making their service comparable to Australia. This number of course does not include the numerous Irish men who fought for other nations, such as Canada, the US, and, of course, Australia. I would never purposefully tarnish their sacrifice.

ABOUT THE AUTHOR

Born in 1969, Phil likes to point out he was one of the last children born before man walked on the moon. Working at Australia's National Dinosaur Museum since 2000 and as an educator at the Australian War Memorial since 2006, he has previously worked at Questacon Science centre and could be seen haunting the halls and specimen rooms of London's Natural History Museum and The Smithsonian's National Museum of Natural History. Here he even played famed palaeontologist O C Marsh during the Smithsonian's centenary celebrations, and when asked why the 19th century palaeontologist was speaking with an Australian accent, happily pointed out that everyone in the 19th century spoke with an Australian accent.

Published in newspapers and magazines across the globe, since 2007 Phil has been the paleo-author for the world's longest running dinosaur magazine, *The Prehistoric Times*. He has also been a comic shop manager, a cinema projectionist, a theatre technician and gutted chickens for a deli. All of these influences seem to make an appearance in his writing, especially the chicken guts bit.

facebook.com/phil.hore
twitter.com/Phil_Hore

ALSO BY PHIL HORE

The Brotherhood of the Dragon

Strange things are happening at Stamford House.

It was not that Mr Fortey was particularly loved, but that he died in such a horrible way, and in the presence of almost the entire household. We must have been only a few feet away, yet no one heard or saw anything. If it could happen to a strapping veteran like the footman, it could happen to any of us.

Phil Hore's debut novel crackles with thrills and chills as two unlikely allies join forces with two of history's greatest writers, Arthur Conan Doyle and Bram Stoker, to save England from the ancient Brotherhood of the Dragon and the horrible secret they protect.